THE BOOK OF STOLEN DREAMS

"Listen to me carefully... Take the Book to the corner of Heine and Hopkins Streets. A man called Solomon will be there reading a newspaper and wearing a white flower in his lapel. Give the Book ONLY to him. Until then, keep the Book safe. Tell no one you have taken it. Promise me!"

Rachel promised. Robert just looked horrified.

Felix lowered his voice to a quiet murmur, his eyes burning: "This Book contains more secrets than you know. Now go!"

This edition first published in the UK in 2022 by Usborne Publishing Ltd., Usborne House, 83-85 Saffron Hill, London EC1N 8RT, England. usborne.com

Usborne Verlag, Usborne Publishing Ltd., Prüfeninger Str. 20, 93049 Regensburg, Deutschland, VK Nr. 17560

First published 2021. Text copyright © David Farr, 2021

Illustrations by Kristina Kister © Usborne Publishing, 2021

Title type by Sarah J Coleman / inkymole.com © Usborne Publishing, 2021

Author photo © Susannah Baker-Smith

A CIP catalogue record for this book is available from the British Library.

ISBN 9781801315135   JFMAMJJASO D/22   07549/6

Printed and bound using 100% renewable electricity at CPI Group (UK) Ltd CR0 4YY.

THE
BOOK
OF
STOLEN
DREAMS

DAVID FARR

Illustrated by Kristina Kister

USBORNE

Let the true dreamer wake...

BOOK ONE

Introduction

If you are reading this book, or if someone is reading it to you, you will know we are living in strange times.

A shadow has passed over the land of Krasnia. And people are afraid.

The shadow has a name. It is President Charles Malstain.

He came from nowhere and now he is in control of everything.

You cannot fight him. Not if you value your life.

You cannot persuade him. Not if you value your tongue.

You can only stay and suffer – or flee.

Look up!

High in the night sky there is a great silver airship. The airship is heading west over the ocean. It is called the *Pegasus*. It is taking desperate fugitives away from Krasnia, from the cruel control of Charles Malstain to the welcoming arms of a foreign city – Port Clement.

Look closer, through the windows into the airship's first-class compartments. Those sad, lonely faces. They are leaving loved ones behind. Will they ever see them again?

Now move your gaze lower. Down through the shadows, past steel girders and ladders, to the second-class deck. It is open to the winds and bitterly cold. A single lantern at each corner barely produces a glow to ease the darkness. Thin grey blankets drape over thinner shoulders, hats are thrust down over ears.

Look closer still. Can you see a figure standing alone on the far corner, looking out into the night?

A girl!

She is twelve years old. She is skinny, she has dark hair and a freckled nose. She has fingerless gloves, carries a strangely elegant small travelling bag and she wears a worn woollen coat, under which is a red checked shirt, a grey jumper, and trousers that seem more likely to belong to a boy. Her black leather shoes are a size too big and could do with a clean.

And now look. There is another figure approaching her across the deck. Oh no! Is she in danger?

The man is slight, dressed in a shabby suit that no longer fits him. In his left hand he carries a battered violin case wrapped in a blanket.

And unless Rachel Klein is very much mistaken, he seems to have a penguin on his head.

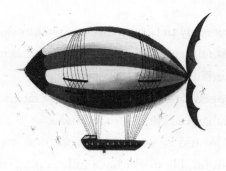

1
On the Lower Deck
of the Pegasus

"Excuse me. I couldn't help noticing you are alone. Please, my dear girl, you have no reason to fear."

Rachel said nothing. The scruffy man stood in the frozen darkness and smiled. His suit jacket was missing several buttons. His eyes twinkled but were sad at the same time. He looked the way a kind uncle would – if Rachel had a kind uncle. What age was he? Rachel wasn't sure.

He spoke again, words tumbling from his mouth like laughter.

"You will want to know my name. Quite right! Who am I? Why am I talking to you? Why am I here on this huge airship travelling across the night-sky to Port Clement? How did I get my ticket away from that miserable city of

Brava? Why is my ticket for this trip pink and yours blue? Is my moustache real? Why am I wearing a hat in the shape of a penguin?"

He stopped for breath. Rachel stayed silent and looked down at her shoes. They were so obviously too big. Would he notice? Would he see the little bulge in her sock? She must be careful. He might have followed her from Brava. From Meyer's House of Illustration. These days you could trust no one.

"And you, my dear? How old are you?"

"Twelve." Rachel could tell him that. That was safe.

"Good Lord! You don't look a year older than eleven! Your name?"

Rachel Klein thought fast. Remembered her false name.

"Isabella von Gurning."

"An utterly charming name. Do you live in Brava? Which side of the city are you from?"

Rachel took a deep breath and lied again.

"From the west? A charming area. Full of the best-dressed women." He studied her. "And yet I sense in you a different spirit."

Oh no. He had seen through her! How could he tell?

The man scrutinised her carefully. His breath was visible in the dim glow of the deck's lighting.

"No. I suspect you come from the poorer north of the city, from a family of artists. Your eyes are musical, and your nose gives me the strongest impression that you have a piano in your living room."

How did he know? How could he possibly know...?

"You do? Ha! I knew it!" He jumped in delight. "Where are your wonderful parents? Are they getting you a hot chocolate from the cafe? I'm afraid to say it isn't very good."

Why was she nearly crying? Was it lack of sleep? Was it the mention of the hot chocolate? Memories of muffins in the old family apartment?

"But, my dear – why do you look so sad? Is it the poor quality of the hot chocolate? No, I see now. Your parents aren't here with you. You are alone. Where are they?"

Rachel looked into his understanding eyes, and told him the truth: "My mother is dead."

The man's face fell.

"Oh, my poor girl. How tactless I am. I could beat myself with a stick! I should have thought that there might be a darker reason for you being on this journey. Oh, you're shaking! Please take my blanket. It smells slightly of salad cream due to an unfortunate accident with a baguette earlier today. You will find out in time why it is flea-bitten and why the design is of watermelons."

Rachel shivered and took the rather grubby piece of old rug that he had unwrapped from around the violin case.

"And your father? Where is he?"

"He's in prison. Soldiers took him."

"Oh, my dear Isabella! But it's an all-too-common story these days. Did he put up a fight? No? It was probably wise of him. You don't mess with Charles Malstain's state police. In the days of the Emperor, if soldiers came to arrest you, they offered a polite smile, a bunch of flowers or a box of chocolate hearts. But these days the police have neither reason nor manners. And there are no chocolate hearts."

Rachel looked up at him. His ragged suit. His funny facial hair. He spoke again.

"Why are you going to Port Clement, may I ask?"

"My brother is there. I have to find him."

"Is he doing well there?"

"I don't know."

"You haven't heard from him? Do you know where he lives? You don't even have a telephone number? Then how will you find him? Now don't cry, I was only asking a question. Of course you will find him, even though Port Clement is a city of seventeen million people and he has no idea you're coming. Why are you crying again? Here I am trying to cheer you up and I only make things worse! My problem, Isabella, is I speak before I think. My mother – a marvellous woman – was very critical of this flaw of mine. Forgive me."

Rachel wiped her eyes and said she would. She looked out across the darkness. It was endless and unknowable.

As if sensing what she was thinking, the little man stood beside her at the rail and spoke quietly.

"My dear, listen to me very carefully. Your brother will find you – or you will find him. I promise you."

"How do you know?"

"Because he will hear your heart beating."

For a moment their eyes met. Rachel felt a little spring of hope deep inside her.

And with that the little man slapped her on the back.

"Now how about a cup of dreadful cocoa?"

2

Josef Centurion

They walked together to the sad little kiosk at the opposite corner of the *Pegasus*'s deck. A woman with long earrings dispensed thin dark liquid into plastic cups. The little man paid for two. He handed Rachel hers.

"I'm afraid it tastes of dead moths," he whispered. He was right. But it was warm, and that was something.

Together they sat in the bowels of the airship's huge lower deck. The little man wound the watermelon blanket tightly around her. It did indeed smell of salad cream – with a hint of gherkin. Rachel's hands clasped the warm cup like a friend.

It was a long flight over the ocean to Port Clement. She didn't want to be alone. Yes, the man was odd, he dressed like a shabby clown, he smelled of something unpleasant – was it vinegar or soil? – but he had such a kind smile. And she did want to know about the weird hat.

So long as she didn't tell him her real name, nor the secret she was keeping – the REAL reason why she was travelling to Port Clement to find her brother Robert. Meyer's House of Illustration. The piece of paper that was hidden in her left sock. That was a secret she would not tell to any stranger, no matter how kind. That was a matter of life and death.

"What is your name?" she asked.

The man smiled. "Ah, well done! There I was squeezing information from you like a lemon and told you nothing of myself! My name is Josef Centurion. You pronounce the Josef with a 'y', like yoghurt. You pronounce the Centurion quietly, in case someone overhears you – a tax collector or a shampoo salesman. One should never tell a shampoo salesman anything!"

Rachel laughed. It felt like her first laugh in years.

He went on: "I was brought up in the East of the country. Ah, my childhood. Wonderful! All potato fields and folk music. Let me straightaway tell you about my sister Lotte, an angel whom I loved with all my heart. You remind me of her in so many ways, even though you are completely different."

So Josef Centurion chattered on about his childhood, his wonderful sister Lotte with her bright blue eyes and little mole on her left cheek, his kindly mother and funny father.

"My first memory in life was of a country doctor with ginger hair crying as he looked at me. This was apparently a reaction to my extremely ugly face."

And as he talked and laughed and twinkled, Rachel started to feel safe. Maybe she could let herself catch a little sleep. She'd been awake for so long and she would need all her energy for Port Clement and the search for Robert.

She felt her hand loosen on the cup of chocolate, then saw, through half-closed eyelids, Josef rescue it from going all over her and place it carefully on the deck beside them.

"My father was a terrible farmer but rather a good small-time thief…"

Rachel's eyes dimmed. She could hear the deep hum of the airship's engines. She felt the fires from the ship's cylinders blow gusts of warmth across her face. And the heat of the fires and Josef's lilting words warmed Rachel's frozen bones and slowly sent her into a kind of dream.

"Josef?" She spoke his name perfectly, saying Josef with a "y" like in yak's milk.

"Yes, my dear."

"Will you wake me when we get close to Port Clement?"

"Of course. You sleep now."

And so Josef started on a story about a brown cow that he and his sister Lotte had chased until it fell into a river.

And as the cow entered the river, with Josef running after it and Lotte in tears of laughter, Rachel Klein's eyes closed. And she slept for the first time in days.

Josef Centurion heard the gentle breathing of the sleeping child, felt her head resting against his shoulder. Her little mouth was nibbling something invisible as she dreamed, like a hamster checking a nut. Josef stopped talking and smiled to himself. His chatter had done its job. The little girl, so lonely on the deck, was now sleeping warm and safe beside him.

Which was exactly what he wanted.

For when, earlier that day, a tall, elegant woman had approached Josef Centurion at Brava airfield while he was playing his violin, she had tasked him with a simple mission.

To board the airship *Pegasus*. To get to know a young girl who was travelling under the name Isabella von Gurning, but whose real name was Rachel Klein. To appear kind and harmless. To ensure Rachel reached Port Clement safe and sound. To offer to pay for her to stay in a hotel for her first night in the strange new city. To take her to the legendary Hotel Excelsior. To leave her there alone in Room 341.

Where she would easily be found.

And then to return home to Brava using his pink return ticket. To earn himself two hundred groschen.

To ask no questions why.

And then to forget he had ever met Rachel Klein.

3

All About Rachel Klein

My dear friend and reader, as you quietly read this book, hidden beneath the covers of your bed, do be careful. This book is banned by President Charles Malstain's censorship committee, and to read it is in itself an act of great bravery. Perhaps place a false cover on the book, just in case. If you are in public, in a park or a pizza parlour, wear an unusual hat and answer to a false name such as Maurizio. (Unless your name is Maurizio. Then use Deborah.)

Or are you not reading the story but listening to it? On a secret radio station? Oh, cherished but secret listener, there is truly nothing better than hearing a story told well out loud! But be careful what other curious ears are listening in. Maybe wear headphones. And if someone asks what you are doing, pretend you are learning a language such as Finnish. (No one knows Finnish. Not even the Finns.)

There are enemies and informers everywhere.

And now, my dear, brave friend, it is time to find out all about our intrepid young traveller – our heroine, if we can call her that – Rachel Klein. And the secret of her socks. Or more importantly – what she is hiding in them.

In her left sock is a piece of paper. And on that piece of paper it says:

CG gone. TG dead.
KRF broken.
Only RK.
He has hidden the BSD.
IDLAMIRG 342. 3rd.

Let me tell you why.

Rachel Klein was born twelve years, two weeks and one day ago in a quiet northern suburb of the great city of Brava, capital of our fair country of Krasnia.

Ah, what a city it was back then! A riot of sunny avenues, palm trees and outdoor restaurants, all gently kissed by the blue ocean that surrounded the city on three sides. And populated by the happiest, cheekiest, most devil-may-care people on earth. You know the saying: God created the world. And when he got really good at it, he created Brava.

Rachel's birthdate (April 8th, to be precise) was sadly not remembered for her arrival alone. For on the very same day that Rachel Anne-Marie Klein slipped, mewling and tight-eyed, into this world, the rebel army of Charles Malstain entered the city of Brava from the east.

Two arrivals: one a newborn child that brought untold joy to a family of pianists and writers; the other an army that introduced untold misery to an entire city.

Such is life, my friend. There is no joy without accompanying sorrow. There is no despair so dark that a sliver of light cannot abate it. Our sliver of light weighed seven pounds two ounces, and for a whole day after her difficult birth Rachel was cuddled and held tight in her mother Judith's arms.

Never one for dramatic shows of emotion, Judith Klein sang a quiet little song she had learned as a child, and kissed Rachel's pink, shiny cheeks.

Rachel's brother Robert, nearly two years old and already full of freckles, couldn't wait to rush in to see his new sister, to tickle her and gently throttle her in the way that affectionate brothers do.

And her father? Her father Felix stood by the top of the bed and, for the first time in his life, said absolutely nothing.

Felix Klein was a librarian. In his spare time he was a writer of articles, funny jokes, plays, gardening tips, recipes, one good novel, thirteen bad novels, hundreds of letters to his family, even more letters to the government, love songs to his wife, and a small Latin dictionary.

Felix loved words. He wrote words about words. He sang about words. He was pretty much a walking word himself.

He worked in a temple of words. Its official name was the North Brava Public Lending Library. But to Felix it was much more than that. It was another family, a family of thousands of precious leather-bound children, each to be cared for and loved and nurtured through its strange and difficult life.

As well as reading and writing words, Felix also loved to say them. He was quite simply the best talker on earth. And since his job at the library required almost complete silence, he saved up most of his talking for home. Judith was used to it and had long ago given up on ever having a quiet night in.

And yet as Felix Klein stared down at his baby daughter, his words caught in his throat and a little gulp of joy came out. But nothing else. He was, miraculous to say, speechless.

For days Felix wandered around their sunny apartment, holding baby Rachel and saying nothing. Tears filled his eyes, dripped on to his typewriter, splashed on to kitchen surfaces as he made tea for Judith, or a hot crumpet for himself which he then forgot to eat.

Such was Judith and Felix's joy that it was five days before either left the apartment, five days before Felix went to get milk and a newspaper, five days before he lit his pipe and read in the *Bravan Daily News* that the east of the city was convulsed by fighting between the Emperor's defence guard and the invading rebel army of Charles Malstain.

Felix's eyes lowered to hide his feelings. He knew all about Charles Malstain, the military colonel who had gained popularity in the East of the country with his boasts of creating a greater, newer, shinier Krasnia. Malstain was a small man, with a love of brass bands and a loathing for children.

Felix rolled up his newspaper and said nothing to Judith about the fighting. It would only cloud his wife's happiness. That evening he quietly used the *Bravan Daily News* to kindle a fire.

For a month the family did not buy another newspaper nor listen to the radio. They therefore did not know that the soldiers of Charles Malstain had reached the old centre of Brava, laying waste to its sandy beaches, flower stalls, museums and gardens. One criticism of Brava's centre – that perhaps it had one too many statues of military horsemen – was swiftly corrected as Malstain's men toppled each and every one.

As Rachel celebrated her twentieth day on earth, the family drank tea, entirely ignorant of the fact that Malstain's soldiers had entered the royal palace, arrested the Emperor in his bed, executed his royal guard, imprisoned his wife and children, and set fire to the royal galleries.

But as Rachel approached thirty days old, the truth could be avoided no longer. For Charles Malstain's men had reached the north of the city. And the very streets where the Klein family lived.

One morning little Robert Klein peered out of his window from the third-floor apartment, to see black helmets below. When Felix anxiously went to the shop to buy bread, he was asked to show identity papers, and to hurry home once he had bought his "essential provisions". He asked why he was not free to go to the park and feed bread to the ducks, as was his habit (he would often return with less than half a loaf left, much to Judith's annoyance). But he was simply slapped on the cheek and told to stop asking irrelevant questions.

Felix Klein's life was based on asking irrelevant questions. He loved to ask "Why is the sky blue when you look at it but black when you're in it?" or "Why does a violin sound terrible until the moment it sounds wonderful?" or "What is the opposite of an opposite?" or "If there is nothing better than this, then what is better than nothing?" and all sorts of other utterly meaningless questions that would take up hours of his and his family's life. These were the questions that would, under the regime of Charles Malstain, become signs of a dangerous mind and a rebellious spirit. Felix would have to learn to keep his chatty mouth shut if he was to last long in the New World Order.

Two weeks later, on a fine spring morning as the cherry blossom hung heavy on the trees, the deposed Emperor of Krasnia was marched out into the square where so often he addressed his mostly adoring citizens. And in that square, as the sparrows hunted for crumbs and the blackbirds chirruped their morning song, his crimes were read out, and he was shot.

Rachel Klein grew up in strange times. She never knew a world where neighbours came out of their doors and chatted to each other about the weather, the price of bread and the terrible smell of the city sewer. No one dared gossip about anything, for fear of who might be listening.

Worse than that, Rachel never heard laughter of children in the street, never played hoopla or football with her brother in the city parks. For within months of taking over, Charles Malstain had banned children from playing in public. *Keep them in!* was the cry on information posters. *A seen child is a bad child!* Forests and parks were designated "adults only" and the beaches had wooden signs with a child's face crossed out in red.

For years Rachel and her brother Robert left the house only to go to the state school, for their learning and exercise. Rachel studied the same book as all the other children (all the textbooks had been reissued after Charles Malstain's instatement as President of the New World Order). She played the piano for seven minutes, did physical exercise for twelve minutes. She had lunch for fourteen minutes, always the same sandwich of cheese without butter, and a pale fizzy drink called Happy Hour that made no one happy at all.

Then she came home.

Robert, two years older and of a scientific bent, was determined not to get disheartened. Unable to explore parks or forests, Robert focused his energy on the natural kingdom within the apartment. God help any creature that came into his bedroom. Dead flies were dissected and studied, beetles had their wings examined. Judith Klein's gorgeous array of pot plants on the balcony were experimented on in groundbreaking ways. Gravy was applied to a rose bush. Hanging begonias reacted very well to a daily dose of cough medicine. Robert observed that when his mother played the piano, the wasps gathered. They seemed to love Schubert in particular.

So Robert got by, busying himself with his experiments. But Rachel Klein was different. She was a dreamer. And how can one dream if one is allowed to see so little of life? Felix's heart broke to see such a beautiful, joyous daughter take so little pleasure in her education. And so, to make up for the grey dull sameness of every school day, he determined that evenings at home would be different. Life at home would be an adventure!

One evening, on Rachel's return from school, Felix was dressed as a pirate and informed her, quite calmly, that she should quickly put on her sea-clothes for they were going on an ocean voyage to do some pillaging.

And that's what they did, without once leaving their living room. The old leather couch that had been in the family for years became the good ship *Sofa So-good*, the ceiling above them became the infinite sky, Rachel's mother became Good Seawoman McDuff, Robert (who had got bored of his wasp studies) became second mate Kurtz, and Rachel was allowed to mount the crow's nest (the bookcase in the corner helpfully had a little ladder attached), and to cry out "Land ahoy!" just before supper.

Together they did some very good pillaging and drank strong rum (water with a sugar cube in it). And when Good Seawoman McDuff tried to mutiny and became Bad Seawoman McDuff, they made her walk the plank off the *Sofa So-good* into the shark-infested ocean (which looked a bit like the family rug). And when she went to bed that night, Rachel was sure she could hear the gentle crash of the waves and taste the sea salt on her tongue.

On another day they were all polar explorers and spent an hour with their feet in a bucket of ice cubes (which really hurt and should not be attempted). On another they were the Bravan fire brigade, putting out fires caused by foolish firework manufacturers. They were butterfly collectors in Java (Robert's favourite) and gold-hunters in Peru. They even went to England, a land where no one smiles, and told jokes to cheer the people up.

And then one day something different happened.

4

The North Brava Public Lending Library

It was when Rachel was turning eleven. It was April 8th – her birthday. Her mother made her a special breakfast of orange and chocolate muffins – Rachel's favourite. How Judith had sourced the oranges Rachel would never know – no one had fresh fruit any more – but Judith had methods that only mothers know. And as they ate the muffins, Rachel's father promised her a special adventure when she got back from school. What would it be this time?

At school no one celebrated Rachel's birthday, except for a brief statistical mention at assembly which received no reaction. No sweets were handed out. No song was sung.

When Rachel got home, Robert was busy with some aphids in his room. Judith was resting from the chest illness that had got worse with every year of Charles

Malstain's reign. But Rachel's father was waiting at the door. And his eyes were bright.

"No need to take your coat off, Rachel my dear. For this adventure we need to go outside."

Rachel felt a tingle in her stomach, a mixture of excitement and fear. Outside? None of their adventures had ever involved going beyond the living room. Children were not allowed outside, except for school. Was this one of her father's schemes? Was it wise?

"Does Mum know?" she asked.

Her father turned a little pink and mumbled: "Of course, of course. But she's in bed with that terrible cough. Now do those laces up and bring a pair of gloves with you. And Robert will come too; ask him to get ready. We will need his help."

Rachel wondered why they needed Robert's help but said nothing.

They left the house as the sun was low in the sky. Robert, by now a seriously botanical twelve-and-a-half-year-old, joined them. "Where are we going?" Rachel whispered, but Robert just shook his head.

They passed a small group of state police, who loitered unpleasantly on the street, smoking and talking into their radios. Felix looked suddenly nervous.

"Where are you heading?" The question was barked.

"Just going to the doctor. The boy has earache," said Felix as casually as he could.

"Be back before dark!"

They nodded and walked on. When they reached the end of their road, they joined the main boulevard and took the first tram. Rachel wanted to be excited. She wanted to tell the owners of the sad faces in the seats opposite all about her birthday, about the present of a small chess set that she had received from her parents, or the box of chocolates that Robert had given her (with one chocolate missing, as usual). She thought maybe if she could catch someone's eyes, it would cheer them up. But no one looked up. Their eyes stayed firmly fixed on the floor of the tram.

They got off at Brava North Station and her father took her hand. His palm was hot and moist. *He's nervous about something*, she thought to herself. *He's holding my hand to keep himself calm.*

They approached a large and beautiful building overlooking the river. Three tall towers reached hopefully towards the sky. Statues of angels surrounded a main arched doorway. Some of the angels were playing instruments, others were holding their chins and looking wise. The largest two angels held aloft a huge stone ribbon on which was carved the name of the building.

THE NORTH BRAVA PUBLIC LENDING LIBRARY

"This is where you work," Rachel whispered.

She was excited now. She had never been to her father's workplace but had imagined it a hundred times.

"It's shut." Robert was being helpful. And he was right. The large iron gates leading to the steps that rose to the main doorway were closed and padlocked. The library's opening hours had recently been reduced by Charles Malstain's Committee of the New World Order to 10 a.m.–3 p.m. Felix's pay packet had been reduced accordingly and Rachel knew he was angry about it.

"Fortunately, someone has a key to the side door," her father said quietly. He opened his hand a little and showed them a small bunch of four keys. Two iron, one brass and one tiny and gold. Rachel noticed that her father's hand was trembling just a little.

Rachel felt a tightening in her stomach. She felt a thrill at the prospect of entering a secret entrance to an empty library, mixed with a growing fear – that her wonderful, slightly reckless father might be about to take her on an adventure they would all regret.

They waited a little longer, until dark had almost fallen.

"Let's go." Her father grabbed her hand tight and they walked towards a small arched gate at the side with a sign that said *Administrative personnel only. Please do not ring this bell.*

As Rachel wondered why there was a bell if no one should ring it, Felix quietly opened the gate with the first iron key, then pulled her and Robert inside.

They found themselves in a stone courtyard with a small cluster of apple trees and reading benches. The library rose above them, silent and impressive in the dusk.

They swiftly climbed narrow steps to a wooden door that led into the building itself. Felix's hand was now visibly shaking. Robert had noticed too. He looked worried. Felix took the second iron key from the bunch, dropped it, picked it up again, then dropped it again.

"It's slippery," he said.

Robert bent down, took the key from the ground and with small, swift fingers placed it into the lock and opened the door.

Felix smiled but Rachel saw fear in his eyes. Beads of sweat glimmered on his forehead.

"Well done, Freckles. This way."

They walked through passageways, dark and musty. The smell of books and glue played in Rachel's nostrils. Robert often claimed that the smell of books made him want to go to the loo but today he showed no sign. All of them were too gripped by the excitement of the mission. If only Rachel knew what the mission was!

She glanced at her older brother, hoping he would know more than she did. But he seemed equally puzzled. Their father increased the walking pace. Was he anxious someone was following them? Rachel glanced back down the dark tiled corridors but could see nothing. She felt her breath in her chest, her heart skipping, a strange high noise in her ears that she concluded must be her brain signalling a kind of discomfort.

Yes, that was it. She was scared.

They passed by several sections. All had little wooden signs. Ancient History, Greek, Egyptian and Roman. Then Modern History, European and American. Sociology. Anthropology. Ornithology. Zoology. (Robert glanced in with curiosity but was pulled quickly onward.) Human Biology. Bacteriology. Other ologies. Physics.

Then the languages section. Aramaic. Babylonian. Basque and Sami. Hungarian. Onward past Russian and German, great tomes of mysticism and philosophy, past French love poets and Italian post-structuralist novels.

Deeper and deeper they ventured into the bowels of the library. Into areas so quiet and obscure it felt like no one could have been here for years. Down corridors of deep shadow, round silent corners, and finally up a small flight of stairs. To another door.

The door was small, made of old oak, and carved with pictures of grapes, harps and more angels. Red velvet curtains hung either side of the door, making it look like a tiny theatre.

There was a copper plaque, at Rachel's head-height. It read:

RARE BOOKS ROOM.
BY INVITATION ONLY.

Felix smiled.

"You are invited."

He took out the brass key, no longer so nervous now, as if the thrill of the mission outweighed any fear.

"This key I am not supposed to have," he whispered. "But I stole it from Mrs Schrödinger as she slept this afternoon."

The key turned in the lock. The door creaked a little and Rachel jumped.

"Is there no alarm, Dad?" It was Robert who asked the question, his face staring up at the tall figure of his father.

"I turned it off as I left."

"And what about the nightwatchmen?"

"They don't begin their rounds until seven." Felix opened the door.

The room was almost completely dark. One solitary window high on the left-hand wall allowed in the glimmer of the dying day. The other three walls were lined with glass cabinets. And in the cabinets were the most beautiful, shabby and silent books Rachel had ever seen.

They rested under glass like sleeping ghosts waiting to be woken.

Rachel glanced at the old clock on the far wall. It was half past six. They had half an hour to do whatever they were doing and leave before the nightwatchmen arrived.

"Why are we here, Dad?" she asked, her breath making small jets of steam in the cool air.

He smiled and by way of answer he took her hand. Together they approached a cabinet at the far end of the right-hand wall.

In it was only one book. It was lying down, a slight slope to the cabinet. The book was faded, dark red, leather-bound, with a gold-leaf design on the cover showing a figure, horizontal, lying sleeping on thin air, with wispy lines around them like clouds.

And above the little drawing were five words also in gold leaf, in a kind of italic that was hard to read at first. But then Rachel understood.

The Book of Stolen Dreams

Rachel's breath stopped in her chest.

Her father had often told her about The Book of Stolen Dreams. It was hundreds of years old and the strangest and most beautiful book in the whole library. It contained forty-nine dreams, one on every page. The dreams were set in a garden and someone was sleeping. Felix had recited several of the dreams to Rachel and Robert by heart, as they lay in bed in their North Brava apartment. It didn't have a story like normal books do, but Rachel loved to imagine herself in the garden as she lay in her little bed and started to feel sleepy.

One night her father had told her a secret as he tucked

her in. He'd said that according to legend the dreams were capable of great magic. But no one knew how to make the magic work. It had long been forgotten. If it ever existed.

Rachel had never seen the Book. Until now.

"Oh, Dad, it's beautiful."

"You wait."

Felix took the fourth and final key from the key ring. Small and gold. He closed his eyes for a second. Then he opened the cabinet.

Rachel felt a shot of terror as if sirens would blare out, soldiers would come, lights flash and the world generally shatter. But nothing happened at all.

Felix lifted the glass door and rested it on its hinges. Then he took the Book in his hands, blew a sizeable portion of dust off its front cover, and held it out to Rachel.

"Happy birthday, my dear." He smiled.

Rachel took it, felt it in her hands. It was not a huge book, and not particularly heavy, but she felt herself go dizzy. The Book felt warm. As if it had a life that she as yet did not fully understand.

She sat on a convenient reading stool and opened the Book. The front page was blank. There was no author, no attributed publisher. No date.

Just an inscription at the very bottom.

Let the true dreamer wake...

Rachel held the Book and looked up at her father, smiling.

"This is the most special birthday ever," she said quietly.

He gleamed with pleasure.

"Do we have time," she continued, "for you to read me one dream before we put it back?"

"My dear, I can do better than that."

He quietly closed the cabinet.

"We are not putting it back. We are taking it with us."

Rachel stared at him, thunderstruck.

"But, Father, this is the Rare Books Room," Robert said. "No one is allowed to take books out of here."

Rachel nodded in agreement. "And this is *such* a rare book."

"It's not just rare." Felix smiled. "It's unique, Rachel my love. And there's something else. Shall I let you into a secret?"

His eyes glistened in the half-light.

"Tomorrow, I have it on good authority, four government soldiers will come to the library. And on the orders of President Charles Malstain, they will remove the Book and take it to the Presidential Palace. Where it will be declared an abomination against the New World Order and it will be burned."

"Why?"

"Because dreams are powerful things, Rachel. As of

38

tomorrow, The Book of Stolen Dreams will cease to exist. Unless someone takes it first."

There was a moment's silence. And Rachel remembered that strange feeling as she put on her gloves in the living room of her family apartment, that tonight would be both wonderful and very dangerous.

"Dad." Robert looked up at the clock. It was nine minutes to seven.

"My goodness! Well done, Freckles. No time to waste. Come on, Rachel. Let's go!"

Rachel gripped the Book tight in her hands as they walked back out of the reading room. Felix locked the door with the brass key, then they retraced their steps, down the stairs, through the hallway and then back past the languages and the sciences and the social sciences and all the realms of human history.

Until they reached the side door.

That's when they saw the soldiers through the window.

They were just outside, right by the side door. And Rachel saw to her horror that the soldiers had picked something up – Felix's tram ticket. He must have dropped it with the second iron key when he was trying to open the door.

Felix turned very pale. Robert froze. Rachel didn't dare breathe.

Felix silently gestured for them to follow him, back away from the side door. They returned into the main hall and then cut down a long corridor. It was almost completely dark. Robert took Rachel by one hand as she held tight to The Book of Stolen Dreams with the other.

Felix quickly ushered them past more rooms, past Ancient Civilisations and Greek Myths towards another exit. But when he tried it, it was locked. He desperately tried all the keys, but none worked. As Felix tried to force the last key into the inappropriate lock, he dropped the whole bunch and they rang out on the stone floor.

They heard soldiers cry out. "This way!" "I heard a ringing!" "They're inside!"

Felix grabbed his children and they ran, down another, narrower corridor. Felix knew the building by heart, and amidst her panic and terror, Rachel felt a surge of hope that this one fact, that her father had worked in this building and loved this building for so many years, must mean something. Must count for something.

This building was his friend.

Now Felix was leading them down steps into a basement area, full of forgotten storage space. Old books – ruined and beyond any reading – lay in strange abandoned rooms. They ran past empty trolleys that needed fixing, glass cabinets that were no longer fit for purpose. Felix dragged his children with him; the soldiers' footsteps could be heard above, amid cries of "Separate! Reach every floor. Man all the doors!"

Felix suddenly stopped. Rachel looked around her.

They had reached a dead end. He was trying another door, but it was no use. Locked. All locked. Her father cursed as she had never heard him curse.

"Dad. Look." It was Robert and he was looking up to the top of the basement wall. At a small ventilation grate. Daylight trickled weakly through.

"Yes! Yes! The ventilation shaft! Why didn't I think of it?!" Her father's eyes darted around the room. In seconds he had found a rickety old wooden ladder used to reach high shelves and had placed it under the grate. He climbed up, pulled the grate off, and leaped down.

"You first, Robert!"

Robert climbed the fragile ladder and lifted himself up and through the grate. His feet disappeared through the narrow gap.

"Now you, Rachel! Take the Book!" Rachel felt her feet move without her brain being involved. She felt her father lift her; she clutched The Book of Stolen Dreams tight with one hand, as with the other she grabbed and felt Robert's hand pull her through into the dusty and cramped ventilation shaft. It led diagonally up and away above the basement ceiling to a glimmer of light far ahead.

"Go, children!" Felix whispered, urging them onwards.

"But, Dad. You can make it too!" Robert pleaded.

But their father just looked at them with a strange ferocity.

"Listen to me carefully. Tomorrow morning at nine

o'clock precisely take the Book to the corner of Heine and Hopkins Streets. A man called Solomon will be there reading a newspaper and wearing a white flower in his lapel. Give the Book ONLY to him. Until then, keep the Book safe. Tell no one you have taken it. Not even your mother, for she will try to hand it over to the police to get me back. And that MUST NOT HAPPEN! Promise me!"

There was a seriousness in his eyes, a look Rachel had never seen before.

Rachel promised. Robert just looked horrified.

Felix lowered his voice to a quiet murmur, his eyes burning: "This Book contains more secrets than you know. Now go!"

And without further discussion, Felix grabbed the grate, replaced it in the ceiling, jumped down, and kicked the ladder far away from where it might indicate any escape.

Just as soldiers rushed into the room.

Rachel remembered what happened next with great vividness.

Through the grate she watched as Felix raised his hands in the air. The soldiers trained their guns on him, shouting, "Down on the ground!" Felix kneeled, explained that he worked here, he came back for something he forgot, he used a key he had kept by mistake, it was just a book he needed for some personal research about the lesser-known flora of the Amazonian River Basin, but he couldn't find it in the Geography section so he was looking down here...

But then another soldier came flying into the room and cried out, "The Book of Stolen Dreams is missing!" And the soldiers looked at Rachel's father and they screamed at him, "Where is it?" And Rachel wanted to shout: "It's here! It's here! Don't hurt him!" But Felix, on the ground, even as he was being punched and kicked by the soldiers, managed a quick look up and a small shake of the head as if to say: *No. Just go.*

And before Rachel could say a word, Robert grabbed her arm and pulled her along the small narrow shaft, towards the light, towards freedom – but away from her father, away from the man she loved most in the world, away from the man she felt certain she would never see again.

DREAM 1

The Garden

I sleep to find myself waking
I am in a walled garden of a thousand flowers
The birds are singing silently
Their perfect songs
The roses smell sweetly of nothing
I turn to see
The gate to the Hinterland is open
Yes I say to myself
This is the day
My loved one will come

5
Sorrow

Rachel and Robert made it home from the library without anyone seeing them. They told their mother they had been playing in the fields out by the old sawmill. She gave them a stern telling-off. Didn't they know they could have been arrested? She asked them if they had seen their father. They said no, isn't he still at work? She reminded them that Felix's hours had been reduced and he should have been home long ago. She looked worried.

They slipped into the back room while their mother cooked their supper. Robert hid the Book under his pillow, ready to take to Solomon the next day. And then they all waited "for father to come home".

But he never did.

The next morning was crisp and cold. Judith's anxiety

had turned to fear. It wasn't like her husband to spend a night away from home. She looked pale; she clearly hadn't slept. Rachel hated lying to her, but her father's instructions had been crystal clear: say nothing and give the Book ONLY to the man called Solomon with the white flower.

Robert and Rachel quietly got ready for school. In the night they had made a plan for how to get the Book out of the apartment and meet Solomon on the corner of Heine and Hopkins Streets. It was about a mile from their school. They would leave early, take a bus, complete the handover and then walk the rest of the way to school. Robert would place the Book in his school bag, which was just big enough for the task.

All the time Rachel could only think about her father. Where was he? What had happened to him?

At a quarter past eight, Robert and Rachel sneaked into their bedroom. "We're just getting our things," Rachel called out. Robert ran to his bed, lifted the pillow. He was just about to put the Book into his school bag when there came a firm knock on the apartment front door. Rachel looked through the gap between the bedroom door and the frame. She saw Judith answer the front door and three uniformed men enter the apartment.

"State police!" Rachel turned with a whisper.

Instantly Robert grabbed the Book from under the pillow, leaped up on to his bed, levered a panel from the ceiling, and hid The Book of Stolen Dreams in a tiny alcove that he had discovered six months before, during one particularly excellent game of Sardines. It fitted perfectly behind the plasterboard and insulation. Robert quickly replaced the panel and jumped down into a "relaxed" lying position, just as a very unpleasant policeman stormed through the door and ordered them both to come into the living room.

Their mother was looking paler than ever. She tried to steady herself on the arm of a chair. She told them that their father had been arrested the previous evening. Rachel tried to look surprised.

The tallest of the three policemen announced that there would be no school today. Rachel glanced at Robert – how would they ever meet Solomon now? The policeman closed the front door and one man stayed outside. Then the other two started to search the apartment. Rachel's heart was pounding. They ripped open cupboards, tore down books and music manuscripts from shelves.

But they did not find the tiny alcove above Robert's bed.

Then the children were sat down and questioned about the day before. They told the police that they hadn't seen their father after school, he hadn't come back from work. Judith nodded her agreement. She had been in bed with the recurrence of her chest infection, but she had also not seen him.

The police wrote everything down, then gave Judith a summons to attend court at three o'clock that afternoon and left. At which point Judith burst into floods of tears. And Rachel felt as bad as she had ever felt in her short life.

By the time all this was done it was nearly lunchtime. They had missed the nine o'clock deadline. There would be no meeting Solomon today.

At three o'clock that afternoon, Judith Klein and her two children arrived at the city courts. Only Judith was allowed into the balcony seats. "No children!" barked the tall court official. Robert and Rachel had to sit outside in the plain stone corridor while their mother was ushered in. The seats were cold, the corridor empty. The chocolate machine had not been refilled for years.

Then, over the crackly sound system, Rachel and Robert heard a solemn voice. "Felix Bartholomew Klein, thirty-six years old, you are formally charged with and found guilty of breaking and entering a government building, attempted theft of a publicly-owned item, and of high treason, for harbouring a book that is outlawed by the Committee of the New World Order."

Then they heard Felix's voice, as he once again refused to say where he had hidden the Book. Finally they heard the judge sentence their father "to life imprisonment and hard labour in a prison camp in the East of the country.

The family will not be granted permission to visit him".

Rachel heard her mother's voice cry out, "Where are you taking him? Which camp? I want to write to him!" Then came sounds of a struggle, then a door burst open and Rachel saw her mother tear out of the courtroom. She grabbed both children by the hand. "Come! Quickly!"

Together they rushed to the rear of the building just in time to see their father being bundled into a police van by two uniformed men. For a moment Rachel glimpsed her father's thin silhouette in the tiny, barred rear window of the vehicle as it disappeared around the corner. Judith screamed at the tall court official, begging him to stop the van and allow Felix one last moment with his family. But the man just told her to go home and stop causing trouble. And by then the van had gone.

It was all over in less than twenty minutes.

That night as Rachel lay in bed, she could hear her mother crying. Later when she slept, Rachel dreamed of her father and the library and the soldiers' fists and boots. She woke sweating. Robert came over and did his best to give her a hug, but it only made her miss her father more. She imagined him in a van or a train travelling to some remote prison camp in the frozen mountains of the East, far away from her and Robert and their mother and the warm apartment he loved so much.

The next morning their exhausted mother was badly sick and in bed. The clock in the hall said half past eight.

"Come on," whispered Robert, "let's try meeting Solomon again." The children sneaked from the apartment with Robert's school bag bulging. Rachel had barely slept but wanted to be brave to impress her brother. Robert was silent as they walked. She had never seen him so pale.

They arrived at the corner of Heine and Hopkins Streets in good time. At nine o'clock no one came. They waited anxiously for half an hour but there was no man reading a newspaper or wearing a white flower. Desperate and afraid, they bought a cough linctus for Judith, returned to the apartment and hid the Book in the small alcove before sprinting to school.

For three days they did the same, but the man with the white flower never came. If Solomon had been waiting for them on that first day, he had either given up, or been arrested himself. Finally a policeman spotted them on the street and they had to run to avoid him. Dejected and confused, they returned to the apartment.

"Let's tell Mother," Rachel urged suddenly.

"No!" Robert turned fast. "Father swore us not to. It's too dangerous, for him and for Mother."

Robert's eyes were fierce. He put the Book deep in the alcove. "We must keep it hidden and forget about it," he said. And though Rachel wasn't sure, she said nothing.

Two weeks later the North Brava Public Lending

Library was closed permanently. Soldiers were seen entering the building with hammers, drills and axes. It was rumoured that inside the library they were tearing off every piece of wooden panelling and ripping up floorboards in a desperate search for something. By the time they had finished, the place was apparently almost completely destroyed, books lay in tatters, but they had not found what they were looking for.

Only Rachel and Robert Klein knew why. They knew that what the soldiers were looking for wasn't in the library. It was in the north of the city, hidden two metres above Robert's head. And still the children hadn't told their mother anything, not even that they had gone with their father to the library that night. They didn't even talk about it to each other, for fear of being overheard and causing more pain and worry.

But when she was alone, Rachel remembered her father's final words.

"This Book contains more secrets than you know."

But what secrets? Rachel wondered. *And how can they help save him?*

In July, Robert had his thirteenth birthday, but they struggled to celebrate it. Summer turned to autumn. There was no news of Felix. No one would tell them what prison camp he had been sent to. Worse than that, from the moment he was arrested neither Rachel nor her family received one letter from him. Her father had written pages and pages for fun every day. And now not one letter. It was as if he had completely disappeared from the earth.

Despite her chronic cough, every week Judith went with Rachel and Robert to the state records office and demanded they tell her "WHERE MY HUSBAND IS!" But the officials laughed in her face and told her that if all the wives with missing husbands were to come here and make such a fuss, "Well, madam, we'd be deaf from the screaming." White with rage, Judith was dragged from the records office by security. Outside she sat in the rain and beat her thin fists against the pavement. Robert and Rachel pulled her to her feet, and together they got her home.

Winter set in cold. Brava suffered several power cuts. Judith's lungs, always fragile, started to give way, but despite Robert calling every surgery and hospital, no doctor would come to visit the wife of a convicted political criminal.

The neighbours in their block also did nothing. Everyone knew what had happened, the shame that Felix Klein had inflicted on his family through his "terrible crime". They smiled at Rachel politely on the stairs but, apparently deaf to the coughing and wheezing coming from the apartment, they never asked how her mother was. Rachel hated them all. Their polite faces, their half-smiles.

And as much as Rachel and Robert looked after her and administered hot honey and ginger-lemon drinks, Judith's condition grew worse.

"Why does no one care?" Rachel asked her brother as they made another hot compress for their mother's chest. "How can they be so heartless?"

"They're not heartless," said Robert. "They're afraid."

Then, one late-February Sunday morning, Rachel woke early in the unheated apartment to find her mother in bed, pale and wheezing. Robert was still sleeping. The air was sharp with cold. Rachel could see her mother's breath.

"Rachel, come to me."

Rachel did.

"I don't feel well, my love."

"Nonsense, Mother, you look better."

Judith smiled. "You've never been a good liar." She coughed. Then held Rachel's hand.

"Rachel, listen to me. Promise me one thing. Whatever people tell you, always remember your father was a good man. *Is* a good man."

Rachel nodded. "I will. Always."

"And remember, I will always be there with you. In your heart."

Rachel's eyes filled with tears. "Don't say that, Mum. You're going to get better."

"If you ever see your father again, tell him I love him."

Rachel shook her head. Her heart, she felt, might break. Suddenly she couldn't hide it any longer. She spoke quietly, in a hushed voice so Robert wouldn't wake.

"Oh, Mother, I lied to you and so did Robert. We were there at the library with Father the night he was arrested."

Judith's eyes went very clear and still. There was an unearthly silence in the apartment.

"Go on."

"We stole The Book of Stolen Dreams together. And we have had it hidden ever since in the small alcove above our room and we promised not to tell you because of the danger it might put you in and now I feel terrible that I lied to you."

Rachel told her mother the whole story in a whisper. Judith's eyes rested on her daughter. "You did right," she said. She leaned forward. "If your father told you to keep the Book secret, he had his reasons. And if I'd known you had the Book, I would without question have tried to barter his freedom with it."

Judith coughed again. She spoke slowly, her voice barely audible.

"Rachel. My darling daughter. You and Robert will be alone now. I have always taught you to have a strong moral compass. You must use it now to save your father. There is a reason he wanted to steal the Book. Find out why! Do whatever you can to help him. I know you, more than anyone, can do it."

She gripped Rachel's hand. Her eyes misted then became still. Her hand went limp. Rachel felt her mother's forehead, then cried out: "Robert, wake up! Come!!"

But by the time Robert dashed into the room to heed his sister's cries, their mother was dead.

6

Meyer and Sons

No local undertaker would agree to bury Judith Klein. They were too scared to allow the wife of a traitor to lie in holy ground. Rachel eventually found an old gardener with a kind heart and a large spade. Secretly, on a cold night, without the neighbours seeing, they dug a grave at the edge of the old churchyard. They cleared and then replaced the snow so no one would know. And though they dared not leave any headstone for the state police to find, Robert and Rachel did scatter flowers on the grave and water it with their tears.

The days after their mother's death were like a dark, muffled dream. Figures drifted through the frozen apartment. Valuers. Lawyers. Auctioneers. A government official. Decisions were made about the children's future without the children once being asked what kind of future they wanted.

Rachel was aware she ought to talk to Robert, about what to do, how to help their father as her mother had demanded. But they were rarely alone. And when they were, they were both so sad, that no sense of any future seemed possible.

Then one cold morning an orphanage director was with them in the living room. She was an elegant woman with a vicious smile. She sat them down on the *Sofa Sogood*. Outside, the lime trees bent in the wind.

"Children, let me be frank. You have no money left. Your family savings have been confiscated. You have no other remaining relatives. The apartment will have to be sold, and you will be sent to my orphanage for forgotten children. You, Robin," (she meant Robert) "will be sent to the boys' section. You, Rebecca," (she meant Rachel) "will be sent to the girls'."

Rachel looked at Robert in horror. They were to be separated! Worse than that, in being forced to leave the apartment, they would have to abandon The Book of Stolen Dreams. The apartment would be filled with another family, who would have no idea what was hiding in the small alcove above the second bedroom. And if they tried to take the Book with them, the state police would search them, arrest them, and destroy the Book and its secrets for ever. And with that, all hope of finding their father would be gone.

Then there was a sudden ring at their door.

"Who is it? Get rid of them!" snarled the orphanage director.

Rachel and Robert walked into the hallway. Rachel peeked through the coloured glass to see a tall, dark-haired man in a low-brimmed hat standing very straight at the door of the Kleins' apartment.

He was skeletal, as if he hadn't eaten for years. He had a dark coat, glasses perched on his nose, a briefcase at his side. He looked severe, like he might carry a ledger in the briefcase, and in that ledger might be written all the fates of man.

Rachel felt he must be from the government. She glanced at Robert. He nodded. Together they opened the door.

"I'm sorry. We're busy," Rachel said firmly.

"I won't take a moment of your time," said the man. He spoke very quietly, in a kind of hiss. "My name is Barrabus, Barrabus Clinch. I am an independent antiquarian and I have an enquiry to make."

Robert and Rachel had not a clue what an independent antiquarian might be.

"I wish to enquire about a book. A very particular book," he said. He said it in a whisper. "I am searching for it on behalf of a private buyer. A buyer who would pay very good money for the only edition. The Book of Stolen Dreams. Do you know it? Do you know where your father might have hidden it?"

Rachel's chest tightened. Robert shook his head. Rachel

clamped her lips tight. Robert said they hadn't seen their father since his arrest and tried to shut the door, but Barrabus Clinch put his foot in the door, and asked if he might trouble them with one more question. His lips were moist.

"Did your father say why the Book was so important?"

Robert's breath caught in his throat; he could hear his heart beating. Then suddenly Rachel stepped forward and spoke so loudly that everyone including the orphanage director could hear.

"We've never heard of a silly Book of Stolen Dreams. Our father was arrested because he hated Charles Malstain and everyone who serves under him!"

She saw Barrabus Clinch cower, as if even hearing such heretical words might cost him his life.

"As do I!" she called out loudly to him, the orphanage director and the whole world.

At this, the orphanage director came tearing into the hallway. "Who's there? What did you say, girl?!" she screamed. "YOU FILTHY CHILD!"

But when Rachel turned back to the apartment door, Barrabus Clinch had fled, his coat held tight against the late-winter wind.

That night, Robert and Rachel were alone, in the bedroom, packing the small number of things they were allowed for the orphanage. They were to leave in three days' time.

Rachel was putting a photograph of her mother into a small suitcase. She was quiet, with her thinking face on.

"I can't believe what you said to that man at the door," Robert said earnestly. "I didn't know you could be so brave."

"I just felt this strange feeling inside my tummy. I think he worked for Charles Malstain's secret intelligence division. Oh, he was a horrid, mean man. Father would have hated him!"

Rachel's face flushed with sudden angry tears. Robert held her tight. Then she let go. She looked serious.

"What is it?" Robert asked.

Rachel looked her brother in the eye.

"Robert. Before she died Mother said we must do whatever we can to help Father. Well, if we don't do it now, we never will. We'll be separated in some awful orphanage, the Book will be left here, and Father will be in prison for ever. I'm not letting that happen."

Robert looked at her with sudden admiration. It was as if both siblings had woken from their grief at the same time and realised the peril they were in.

Robert suddenly jumped up, climbed on the old wooden table they used for homework, opened the hidden panel in the ceiling, and did what he and Rachel had dared not do since the day their father was arrested.

He opened up The Book of Stolen Dreams.

Her stomach tightening with excitement, Rachel sat

beside her brother as first he looked at the outside cover, checked the binding, then opened the Book, looked at the frontispiece, the dedication –

Let the true dreamer wake...

Robert paused, perplexed.

"What are you doing?"

"Father said that the Book contains more secrets than we know. We need to find out those secrets. Then maybe we can find him and save his life."

The pages were soft and yellowed. Forty-nine dreams were written out in old Krasnian. Each dream had its own page, just as their father had said. And each page had beautiful illuminated illustrations. They were drawn in richly coloured inks – blue skies, gold light, bright red flowers and green grass. And birds. Birds everywhere.

But what did it all mean?

Rachel's eyes glowed with excitement. "Read it to me, Robert. Read all of it."

And so that night they read the dreams out loud to each other.

Each dream described a walled garden, filled with flowers. A man is in the garden, sometimes eating a meal, or gazing at the sky, or playing music. A gate opens and a woman comes through the gate. She is the woman the man loves most in the world. But she died. Now she is coming back from a place called the Hinterland. So they can be together again.

The old language was strange, not always easy to understand. But it seemed to Rachel that the dreams spoke to her.

As Robert read out loud, Rachel imagined herself in the walled garden – a place between life and death, waking and sleeping. Her mind started to drift to her mother. She looked at Robert and wondered if he was thinking the same thing. Could their mother possibly come to them from the Hinterland?

Robert finished the last poem.

They waited. The apartment was quiet.

Then suddenly Rachel felt a warmth in her chest, just like she did when her mother hugged her or kissed her goodnight. She turned to the door. Did she hear something, a figure walking?

And just for a moment – her mother was there.

She was in the apartment playing the piano. Father was reading out loud as he liked to do. Robert was eating a mint. And Rachel was sitting on the sofa in the rays of the sun as they angled through the high bay window. *This is happiness*, she thought. *It is a stillness, a moment in time, like a photograph, a moment that seems to last for ever and does not know it will be destroyed.*

"If only it was real." It was Robert who spoke. And with one line, he had snapped Rachel from her dream.

And slammed the Book shut.

"Maybe it could be," Rachel stammered. "Maybe the Hinterland exists, and if it does then maybe Mother—"

"It's just a story, Rachel. Mother is gone. We need to forget the past and focus on now. I think someone asked Father to steal this book before Charles Malstain could get his grubby fingers on it and destroy it. I'm going to find out who and why."

Rachel nodded sensibly, keen to impress on her newly energised teenage brother that she was someone who could be relied upon, however difficult and painful the circumstances.

"Hold on." Robert's eyes narrowed.

"What is it?"

"Look."

He showed her. After the forty-ninth dream, there seemed to be a page missing.

"That's strange," Robert said, fingering where the paper had been torn out by hand.

"And look here." It was Rachel's turn to notice something.

At the back of the Book, inside the cover, there was a small note in italics. Robert read out loud.

"All illustrations by Benjamin Meyer."

And then Rachel stopped dead. And her big eyes got bigger.

"Robert, do you remember? Over a year ago, when

there was no school one day, and Mother was teaching music, we went with Father to help him with some deliveries. He took a book with illustrations to a small shop in the old town because it needed some repairs."

Robert furrowed his brow in an attempt to remember. He was prone to doing things with great gusto and then forgetting all about them the next day, whereas Rachel remembered everything.

"Kind of."

"Oh, you must! It was down that passageway which was so narrow we had to go one at a time."

"Single-file alley!" Robert leaped up.

"And do you remember the name of the workshop we visited?"

"Yes! I mean no, not exactly…but if I try…oh, Rachel, stop torturing me with those cow eyes! What are you getting at?"

"The shop was called Meyer and Sons. House of Illustration." Rachel spelled the name out loud. Then she paused solemnly while Robert caught up. His eyes were dull for a moment then they lit up like a fire. "Meyer! I've seen that name!"

"You saw it just a few seconds ago."

A pause. Then he got there. "In the Book!"

He grabbed the Book and went to the back, past the forty-ninth dream, past the place of the torn-out page, and inside the back cover.

Robert and Rachel stared at each other.

"Rachel Klein, you have the memory of an elephant."

Robert was already reaching for the Brava City map.

The next morning they left early. Knowing that children were not allowed out except to go to school, they wore uniforms and coats and took school satchels with them for cover. Then they took the tram to the old town by the harbourside.

It was another cold, grey day. The sky was like a metal helmet. They reached the final stop; the tram driver rang his bell. They got out and, like fugitives, ducked down a side street. Robert consulted the map.

"This way," he said, leading.

They hurried along cobbled streets. This had once been the thriving old centre of Brava, but now it was broken and ghostly, a shadow of its former glory. Even the cherry trees had been cut to the root and never blossomed any more.

"Down here." Robert walked ahead, studying the map. Rachel followed, marvelling at her brother's sense of direction. Her father always talked about Robert's "internal navigation system". Robert could find his way through a forest blindfolded, whereas Rachel got lost going to the bathroom. She was too often thinking inner thoughts to know where she was in everyday life.

"There. Single-file alley!"

The street sign actually said *Paradise Lane*. It was the darkest, slimmest of passageways, with tall buildings towering over both sides. Robert went first. At times the buildings overhung them to such an extent that they had to sway back and forth as they walked to avoid hitting a wall. Rachel had a sudden feeling that the houses might move in on them and crush them from both sides. She shivered and accelerated.

The passageway grew dark and cold. Small dusty gold plaques announced what was going on inside each building. One was a lawyer's office, the next a military members' club, then a family of merchant venturers.

"The sun must only shine in here for five minutes each day." Robert looked up to the thin sliver of sky high above him. Rachel felt her hands go numb. It felt more like a coffin than a street.

Then she stopped. Her eyes narrowed.

A slim slate-grey house stood dusty and quiet before them.

"This is it. I remember it."

Its door was dark red, and it had a plaque.

MEYER AND SONS. ILLUSTRATING THE STRANGE AND THE FANCIFUL.

All the windows were boarded. A small sign had been placed behind the glass for all to read.

MEYER AND SONS REGRETFULLY ANNOUNCES THAT IT HAS CEASED TO OPERATE IN BRAVA.

And then a date, just a week ago.

Rachel pondered. A shop such as this going out of business was not exactly surprising. Everyone was so poor in Brava now, no one had any money to spend on food, let alone books with hand-painted illustrations. And books were seen by the Malstain administration as dangerous and undesirable. But still. That this particular House of Illustration should close one week ago, precisely the day their mother had died…

Robert rang the bell.

They waited, but there was no reply. He rang again.

Rachel was just about to pull him away when the door opened. A small old woman with a large nose looked at them.

"What do you want?" she asked.

Robert paused, suddenly unsure, but Rachel leaned forward and whispered, "Let the true dreamer wake."

The woman eyed both children. "Wait there." She disappeared. A distant crow cawed. Its cry echoed down the alley. The woman returned.

"Come in."

They followed her. The hallway was dark and it took a moment for Rachel's eyes to adjust. The boarded windows on either side of the door allowed in only the muddiest shards of half-light. Rachel expected a bat to come swooping across her face at any moment. A small mahogany side table stood on a rug by the right-hand wall. On it was a candelabra made for six candles, but only one was lit. Next to the candelabra was an old leather visitors' book, a black pen, and a jug of fresh white flowers. A flight of dark oak stairs led up to the other floors. A small door at the back of the hall offered the only other exit.

But what struck Rachel most were the paintings. Dozens of oak-framed portraits stared out from the dark green walls – old men with white beards, old women with hair covered. Their wrinkled eyes seemed to follow her as she crossed the dark floorboards. Each frame had a name on a small gold plaque beneath the picture. *Hieronymus Meyer. Florence Meyer. Rosica Meyer. Septimus and Aennie Meyer. Benjamin Meyer.*

The old woman had reached the door at the back.

"This way."

Robert followed briskly but Rachel paused to look up the stairs. There was a little sign on the wall. *Private. Artists Only.* Beyond the sign she could make out more framed pictures all the way up the staircase, disappearing into darkness. For a moment she thought she heard footsteps coming from the rooms above, like a scurrying of mice. There was a muttering.

A female voice whispered, "Family business. Family business." Male voices hushed the female voice. An anxious cough.

Rachel felt the cold and shivered. *We are not welcome here*, she thought.

"This way!"

The old woman spoke louder this time and Rachel nodded and followed her.

The woman led them into a panelled back study. It had one window with shutters closed. Another small door at its rear led who knew where. A solitary candle illuminated the walls, which were covered with more framed paintings from ceiling to floor, but these were illustrations – the most beautiful Rachel had ever seen. Unicorns and lions and forests. A ship on the sea. A woman playing some kind of guitar. All in the richest colours: golds and greens, corn yellows and deep reds.

"Sit down." The old woman seemed only to speak in single syllables. They did as she asked, on a dusty wine-red velvet sofa, its back curved. Rachel felt she was sitting in a large mouth that might eat her at any moment. The woman scratched her nose, walked back out and closed the door.

Rachel breathed deep and dragged her eyes from the illustrations to an old desk, with its black telephone, heaps of papers, a file for business cards, and a stuffed exotic bird on a perch that seemed to look at her with one eye.

"Woodworm," said Robert quietly. He nodded at the picture frames on the walls. And indeed they were dotted with holes.

Then a set of footsteps descended the stairs above them. Slow, unhurried. And Rachel suddenly thought how stupid they had been to come here, to a shop they barely knew, on a whim, without telling anyone. She gripped Robert's wrist hard, as if to say *Let's go*, but he just sat there, rested his hand on hers and said very quietly, "It's all right."

The footsteps approached along the hallway. Rachel's heart seemed to be beating outside her body like a clock in the room.

The door handle lowered as if of its own accord. Rachel jumped; the door creaked open. A thin old man entered the room. He was a shadow in the half-light. Rachel couldn't see his face. Just two eyes glinting from behind thick spectacles. But with no smile.

He studied them slowly. First Robert, then Rachel.

"You are the Klein children."

They nodded, surprised by his certainty, but eager to make any connection. He stayed in the doorway.

"I recognise you. Your father came here with you once. What do you want?"

"We are here about The Book of Stolen Dreams." Robert spoke boldly.

Did the man's eyes flicker for a second? "What do you know of it?" he said quietly.

"We know that you illustrated it."

The old man's eyes flared. Robert tensed. Rachel gripped his hand harder.

"Not me. I may be old but I'm not that old."

The man walked forward into the candlelight. His face was carved like a mask, his clear blue eyes framed by the pair of thick-glass spectacles, his skin slightly flaking, a dark stain across his forehead. His hair was silver at his temples, his head otherwise bald; he had a thin beard and unusually pointed ears. He looked like he might peck you.

"You've seen the Book?"

Robert nodded. "Yes. In the library. In the Rare Books Room."

The man's eyes held Rachel's in their pale stillness, not seeming to blink.

"But it isn't in the library any more. Your father hid it the night before the authorities were going to take it away."

"We know. They were going to destroy it."

"Do you know where your father hid it?"

"No." Robert's voice was clear. "But we want to know more about the Book. It may help us release him. Our mother has died and we are soon to be taken to the orphanage for lost children. We only have a few days. Can you help us?"

The old man surveyed them, as if deciding whether he trusted them.

"The Book of Stolen Dreams was written five hundred and sixteen years ago. It was commissioned by King Ludovic of Krasnia."

"Why did the King commission the Book?"

"His wife Queen Katarina died. Very young. A tragedy. The King was grief-stricken. Then someone told him that in dreams you could bring the dead back to life."

Rachel's heart tightened a little. She thought of her own mother, and the feelings the Book had given her.

"So Ludovic commissioned a Book of Dreams to bring his wife back to life for ever. Only one copy was made. The King hired my great ancestor Benjamin Meyer for the illustrations."

"And did it work?" Robert asked.

The old man paused. Rachel looked deep into his eyes. What secrets were they holding? Again she heard a scurrying in the building above them. The old man heard it too.

"No one knows. Now, I'm afraid that's all I can help you with." He gestured to the door.

"Why does your shop say you are closed?" Rachel spoke loudly, as if to speak quieter might admit the fear she felt.

"My son Walter closed it. Business reasons." The old man shuffled, uncomfortable. "I'm afraid I'm expecting a phone call. You need to leave."

He was awkward now, definitely hiding something.

"Please!" Rachel spoke even louder. "If you knew our father, you would know he is a good man. He is in prison because he protected the Book. All we want to do is help him."

The old man chewed his lip. He seemed to be struggling with an inner dilemma. "I liked your father. Very much. He came here many times. But this is not a matter for children. Go home. *Do not get involved in what you do not understand.*"

His voice cut through the air. The candle flickered. Then the black telephone rang loudly. Rachel jumped. The old man picked up the receiver.

"Lucius Meyer." His voice changed. "Wait. I will take this call upstairs."

The old man put the phone back on the hook. He rose quickly. His voice was deadly quiet in the half-dark.

"Leave now. And don't come back. Or you may face the same fate as your father." He walked out of the room, closing the door.

Rachel looked around the dark study. "Robert, it's no use. We should go."

But Robert was already heading to the phone and very quietly lifting the receiver.

"Robert!" she whispered, terrified.

Robert put his finger to his lips, then gestured her over. Together they heard Lucius Meyer's voice on the telephone, and a woman's on the other end.

The woman was speaking.

"Everything is arranged. Your son Walter is flying over with Charles Malstain. They will arrive in Port Clement, two weeks from today. Walter has been told that during their visit we are willing to sell them the missing Book. We are waiting for them."

"Constanza, listen to me. Try not to hurt my boy. Walter is foolish and angry. But he is not malicious."

"I can make no guarantees, Lucius. Walter is endangering all of us with his stupid act of revenge. It is insanity to give Charles Malstain the keys to the gate."

Rachel breathed in. Questions buzzed through her mind like flies. Why would Walter be angry? Why was he bringing Charles Malstain to Port Clement? And what keys had Malstain been given? To what gate? She tried to quieten her breaths but was too nervous, so she moved away from the receiver.

That's when she saw the business card on the desk.

Constanza and Theodore Glimpf.
BEHIND THE EYES BOOKSTORE.
Port Clement.

The voices on the phone continued.

"Constanza, I beg of you. Don't hurt my son."

"I can make no promises."

74

Rachel very quietly slipped the card into her pocket.

"Constanza, wait. I heard something. On the line."

"Malstain's spies?"

"Someone is listening."

Robert suddenly put the phone down. "I think he heard me breathing!"

For a second they didn't move. Then, both at once, they rushed out of the study and ran back across the dark hallway, towards the front door.

Suddenly, ahead of them, the candle on the small candelabra flickered. They stopped dead. Was it them making the flame dance? No, they were quite still now, but it continued to flicker. Was there a ghost in the room?

Robert understood better. He turned with a whisper.

"There's someone outside the front door. The movement in the alley caused the candle to flicker."

As if to confirm what Robert said, there was a slow knock at the front door. Robert peeped silently through the letter box.

"It's him!"

Rachel went to look through. Standing on the doorstep was none other than the dark-haired man who had come to the apartment door the day before – Barrabus Clinch. The same solemn face, the same starved body.

Now footsteps approached down the stairs. Lucius Meyer called out: "Who is it?"

And a sudden chorus of other voices from upstairs

seemed to echo him. "Who is it? Who is it, Lucius? Get them away, Lucius! They'll find us!"

Robert turned. "There must be a back way! Let's go."

They ran back into the study, past the strange bird and through the rear door into a kitchen area, where the old woman who had first greeted them was feeding a black cat milk. She turned, screamed and grabbed a large rusty kitchen knife.

"They're in here! They're IN HERE!"

There were shouts from within the house. "Intruders! Catch them! They heard us talking!"

The old woman lunged at them wildly with the knife. Rachel leaped back; Robert dived across the kitchen table, grabbed a bag of flour and threw it into the air; the room filled with a white cloud. They ran to a small back door, Rachel coughing and spluttering, the old woman screaming.

"Thieves! Murderers! Thieves!"

Robert struggled with the lock, turned the rusty key, opened the door and they ran outside into a street. He slammed the door shut; he had the key in his hand; he pushed it into the lock as the old woman tried to burst through after them. Rachel saw the key strain. The lock had a strange golden bird embossed on it; it seemed to be fighting them. The key struggled and turned. The rear door was locked.

And leaving the key in the lock, Robert grabbed Rachel's hand and they fled.

They walked back to the harbour, heads down, hands shaking. Their faces were white with fear and flour.

Rachel gripped the business card tight in her hand. She glanced behind her but could see no one following. The wind was coming off the sea, cold and biting.

"Let's sit here."

They found a faded wooden bench in the middle of the old city, close to the ocean. Rachel remembered her father saying how, when he was a child, grandfather Witold would buy him vanilla ice cream from a stall by the old medieval gates and they would sit eating them and looking at the sea. There was no ice cream stall now. Just a "government information booth" manned by two soldiers. They were grey-faced and indifferent, wearing large black gloves.

"We look like ghosts, and we're shaking like we saw one!" Robert said, trying to lighten the mood. He beat the flour off his coat.

But Rachel was already thinking. She handed Robert the business card she had taken from the desk.

Constanza and Theodore Glimpf.
BEHIND THE EYES BOOKSTORE.
Port Clement.

"Where did you get this?"

"I found it on Lucius's desk. Do you remember? Constanza was the name of the woman on the phone," Rachel said quietly.

"Yes, that's right!" said Robert.

"Lucius said Walter Meyer is his son. He is bringing Charles Malstain to Port Clement."

"But why?"

"And what did they mean by the keys to the gate? What gate? What keys?"

"And why mustn't Malstain have them?"

"Do you think it has anything to do with the Hinterland?"

Robert nodded, sensing his sister was having one of her brilliant days.

"Who were all those other people in the Meyer house?" Rachel continued. "Why has it closed so suddenly? And what has Barrabus Clinch got to do with it? Why was HE there?"

Robert looked back at the business card.

"And more than anything," he said quietly, "how can Walter Meyer think he is buying the missing Book in Port Clement, when we have it in our apartment?"

They looked at each other for a moment.

Then Robert's eyes drifted to the large bulkheads of the majestic steamships that waited by the harbourside, preparing for their long journeys across the ocean. Rachel followed his gaze. The steam belched out of the funnels into the winter air.

"What are you thinking, Robert Klein?"

He liked it when Rachel used his full name. It made him feel important. "I'm thinking that the answer to all our questions might be in Port Clement. And if that ship is the SS *Neptune*, as I am sure it is, then I happen to know it is sailing to Port Clement tonight."

"And so…?" Her big eyes searched his.

"So, I don't know." His lips pursed. Rachel looked at him.

"Yes you do, you big fat liar. You're thinking that one of us should go to Port Clement, find the Behind the Eyes Bookstore and get some answers. You'd love for us both to go but you know that we don't have the money even for one person let alone two. And you're thinking it's dangerous, so you should go and leave me here in the orphanage until you get back."

Robert turned to her. Was his sister a mind reader?

She stared at him. "Am I wrong?"

No. She was not. Robert breathed deep, turning the card in his hand. "I'm not going without you. We'll find a way to raise more money…"

"There's no time. In two days we'll be sent to the orphanage. We'll be separated for God knows how long and neither of us will be able to help Father. Father would want you to go. I am younger so they won't punish me for you leaving. I will simply pretend that you escaped alone and that I never liked you. And you must take the Book with you. It's not safe here, and you may need it."

She spoke quietly but there was a clarity in her that Robert recognised from their mother. When something had to be done, it should be done now, no matter what.

"It's our only chance of happiness, Robert." Rachel's eyes fixed on the harbour and the grey sky beyond. "We need to discover the secrets of the Book and why Malstain wants it so badly. Then perhaps we can clear Father's name…and maybe, just maybe, if he is still alive…"

She paused. She did not need to say it.

DREAM 9

The Return

The waiting is over
I have talked to the grass too long
And tried to get an answer from the trees
But now I hear the latch on the gate
The birds turn
And the tulips crane their necks
She is coming through the gate
With her dress trailing the stones
She sees me and smiles
"You have returned" I say
"No my dear" she says
"It is you who have returned
I was always here"

7

Behind the Eyes

Eight days later Robert Klein set eyes on the free soil of Port Clement.

He had heard so much about the city, and how different it was to the grey misery of Brava. How in Port Clement people could say what they thought, children could walk outside without fear of arrest, play whatever games they liked and read whatever books they fancied. But now, as the SS *Neptune* entered the harbour, he was seeing it for the first time. And it was astonishing.

A huge metropolis seemed to have sprung from the earth. Glass and metal shards pierced the clouds. The famous Skyline, a train-track high in the air, wound its way through the city like a ribbon on stilts. They said that a million people took the Skyline to work each day and that it never broke down. It was almost silent, the doors opening with a purr like a happy cat.

Everything here was light and magical and new.

Once the ship had made harbour, Robert joined a long queue through the immigration turnstiles, his grey suitcase with string for a handle tucked tightly under his arm. In the suitcase was a change of clothes, a small magnifying glass that had kept him company on the long trip across the ocean, his papers, the money that he and Rachel had saved – and a brown paper package, hidden under the cardboard base of the case, and only reachable by unfolding a secret flap at one end.

In the brown paper package was The Book of Stolen Dreams.

Robert had not dared once bring it out during the journey. Despite sensibly tying the case to his belt as he slept on deck, he was terrified that he would awake to find it cut loose and gone. But each time he awoke with a jolt and felt for the case, it was there.

Even this didn't fully reassure him. What if some clever cutpurse had forced open the case, and stolen the Book as he slept – replaced it with a different book, one about ballet or golf or some other tiresome subject?

Only when Robert was through immigration, had walked the mile and a half to his lodgings in the Lower East District (found through a helpful corkboard at the portside – *Cheap Stays for Runaways!*), and was safely stowed in his tiny third-floor room, did he dare unlock the case and open the paper package.

The Book was there, untouched. It seemed more beautiful than ever. Its embossed cover glimmered in the dawn light creeping through the tiny garret window.

Robert weighed the Book in his hand. He checked his money – enough for a week's lodgings and food, no more. In that time he had to find the Behind the Eyes Bookstore, discover why Charles Malstain wanted The Book of Stolen Dreams, and then return to Rachel.

For a second Robert thought of his brave sister, all alone in that dreadful orphanage. He wondered who was in the greater danger – him or her?

Then he got to work.

There was no address on the Behind the Eyes business card, and no mention of any such shop in the telephone directory in the hallway where he was staying.

Strange, Robert thought. *As if they don't want people to know it exists.*

So Robert did the only thing he could. He started to walk the city, on the lookout for any unusual bookshops. But all he could find were the standard glass-fronted emporia that boasted only the recent bestsellers. Robert knew he was after something different, something more obscure, a place with secrecy in its veins. He thought he would know it when he saw it. At least he very much hoped so.

Robert walked for miles. He passed one store that looked promising, but when he went inside, the young woman behind the counter swiftly revealed herself to be an aspiring actress, who proclaimed excitedly that the shop was going to be called Easy Reads and Coffee, but it wasn't ready yet because her boss had forgotten to order any books. Robert swiftly made his excuses.

That night he lay alone in his lodgings listening to a small radio that came with the room. On the radio he heard that President Charles Malstain was planning a journey from Krasnia to Port Clement for "political negotiations with the Port Clement government to ease recent tensions between the two great nations". Robert shivered with fear. It confirmed what he had heard on the telephone in the office of Meyer and Sons: Malstain was coming to Port Clement.

But what was the real reason for his visit?

The days passed. Robert's money was running out. He was down to eating soup and one bread roll for lunch a day, no breakfast, no dinner. Still every day he walked. But his morale was dipping with his blood-sugar level.

Then he saw another bookshop.

It was in a small and unremarkable area in the south of the city. He had barely noticed the cobbled square. A few gulls flew in off the sea in search of food; a dozing workman lay on an ugly brown bench; the sun peeked between buildings.

The shop was in one corner, shaded by tall tenements where poorer families lived. It had a wooden exterior in an appalling state of disrepair. The sign had half-fallen off and was now facing towards the shop, so that a visitor could only read the sign once already inside. Which slightly ruined the point, Robert thought.

Still, it felt promising.

Robert walked towards the door, which he knew before it opened would be rusty and have a creaking sound. It did.

Inside the shop, the first thing Robert noticed was the smell. It was the same smell as in the North Brava Public Lending Library. Musty, friendly, rarely cleaned.

At the counter was a plump old man looking down at a book on the counter. He appeared to be a sculpture, as if frozen in time. Robert's arrival had made no impression on him.

Robert breathed deep. And turned back around to read the fallen sign through the shop window. The letters were in red paint on wood, the paint chipped.

BEHIND THE EYES BOOKSTORE

Robert suppressed a very strong desire to leap up and down and punch the air. Instead he nodded quietly to himself and looked around studiously.

Robert had loved watching gangster films with his father. In the films, which Felix played on an old rickety machine in the family apartment as Charles Malstain had long ago banned all public cinema, gangsters in long coats were always "casing the joint". This involved acting normal while actually gathering enormous amounts of crucial information about a particular location. It was what all self-respecting gangsters did before a hold-up or a heist. It was what Robert decided to do now.

He wandered into an aisle and, with excellent acting skills developed through adventure games with Rachel and their father, pretended to look at the books. The section he happened upon was Russian poetry. This was not an interest of Robert's. If the aisle had been filled with books on reptiles there might have been a risk that Robert would have become distracted. But poetry? No.

He watched and waited, all the time wondering how this strange little shop connected to Charles Malstain and The Book of Stolen Dreams.

A few minutes passed without incident. Then the bell rang and a girl came in. She was a bit older than him, and rather pretty, Robert had to admit, with straight black hair and a heavy fringe. Maybe a student, serious in a way Robert liked, with a grey beret and a long woollen coat. She nodded at the old man, who nodded back without a smile.

The girl walked into the aisle next to Robert's. Robert

acted innocent, grabbed a book of poems by a certain Anna Akhmatova and then casually watched the girl over the top of the book as she drifted down the aisle.

One goes in straightforward ways,
One in a circle roams:
Waits for a girl of his gone days,
Or for returning home.

For a moment their eyes met across the books that lay between them. Hers were jet-black. Robert could have looked at them for ever. But the girl averted her gaze, walked to the back of the shop and, to Robert's surprise, seemed to disappear completely. Robert looked through the bookshelf but there was no sign of her.

Where had she gone?

The bell sounded once more. Robert's eyes narrowed. The shop door opened again and this time a loud female tourist with a leopard-skin handbag came in, asking directions to a very well-known monument. The shopkeeper pointed at his ears and shook his head as if to suggest he was completely deaf, and after some angry grumbling about "the locals", the tourist took her leave.

Silence in the shop. Robert took down another book of poems by a man called Rilke, just to be convincing. He started to read.

Everything is far
and long gone by.
I think that the star
glittering above me
has been dead for a million years.

Robert thought of Rachel, far away in an orphanage, cold and comfortless. *So this is what poetry does*, he thought to himself. *It makes us sad. But it does make us remember those we love.*

Another ring of the bell. The door opened a third time. A young man this time – long hair, glasses on his nose, a scarf carefully tossed round his neck to look careless. A kind-of beard. A student also?

"Is Marie here?" the young man asked the shopkeeper.

"Yes, she's here." The shopkeeper's deafness was miraculously cured, it seemed. "She's waiting for you. She has good news."

"Thank you, Herr Glimpf."

Robert's ears pricked. The name on the business card! *Theodore Glimpf*. Robert watched the young man walk down the same aisle the girl had minutes before. He also disappeared from sight.

Robert was desperate to know where they had gone. And what was the good news that the girl – Marie – had for this young man? Could it connect to Charles Malstain? To Walter Meyer? But to reach that aisle would involve

Robert walking around the bookshelf and being seen by Theodore Glimpf, who had quietly returned to being a sculpture with the book he was reading.

Then Robert saw a way.

On the lowest shelf, where the bigger books were kept, there was a gap big enough for a suitably gymnastic thirteen-year-old to squeeze through. Robert removed a couple of rather dusty tomes on Greek architecture, and quietly manipulated his body from one aisle to the next.

He looked up. Had he been seen? No, Herr Glimpf was unaware, his head buried in what he was reading.

Robert crept along the aisle to the back of the shop… and immediately understood why the two young students had disappeared. At the end of the aisle there was a small metal spiral staircase leading down. And from down below he could hear voices. First the girl's…

"He's already taken off from Brava airfield."

Robert quietly took off his shoes and listened.

"When is he arriving?" It was the young man who spoke now.

"They fly in at noon." Marie was clear, calm, efficient.

Robert, in only his socks, climbed the first few steps down the spiral staircase to see if he could spy on the strange young couple.

"And the hotel?"

"The Hotel Excelsior. Malstain always uses it when he visits here."

Robert's chest tightened. The young man spoke again. "He'll have security."

"Yes of course. He's bringing his own people. He'll be on the fifth floor. The Port Clement government has been asked to ensure the hotel is left entirely empty for him and his Bravan officials and bodyguards."

"Fifth floor? You're sure?"

"Yes."

"That's good. We'll need to get in there."

The girl's voice lowered. "What are you planning, Laszlo?"

Robert inched down another step, as if being physically dragged into the conversation.

The young man: "It's best you don't know."

The girl: "I want to help. I hate Charles Malstain with every inch of my body."

"Marie. What you've done is remarkable. But you're only seventeen. All I need to do now is get the hotel pass keys. To the service entrance and to the service elevators."

"Then let me help you!"

Suddenly Robert sensed something. The air seemed to get a little darker around him, as if a shadow had fallen on him.

Because it had.

He turned to see Theodore Glimpf on the top step, looking at him. With a gun in his hand. Pointed at Robert's head.

8

St Cecilia's

When Robert Klein left for Port Clement, Rachel did not see him on to the SS *Neptune* for fear of drawing attention. Instead they said their farewells at the apartment. Despite not knowing how long they would be apart, neither cried, which made Rachel very proud. Then Rachel spent two days alone in the family home. At night she dreamed of her mother and her father and she woke hoping they might still be there, playing music in the living room or baking bread in the kitchen. But the apartment was empty and silent.

Then the orphanage van appeared and the apartment bell rang. The elegant orphanage director was horrified to discover only one Klein inside. When questioned, Rachel said that she had woken one morning to find Robert gone, leaving a note saying he was taking a train south to make his fortune and that Rachel should not come looking for him. They had never been close as siblings, she said, and it was no surprise that he had left her. He was a rather selfish boy.

The orphanage director asked to see the note Robert left. Rachel had guessed she might do this, and produced a letter that she had written herself in Robert's handwriting a few hours earlier.

The director got on the phone to a man called Max and explained what had happened. Max was clearly furious, cursing and shouting down the phone line so loudly that in the end the director had to hang up for fear of damage to her ears.

Rachel had travelled in the van alone.

The orphanage was twenty miles outside the city of Brava amidst a barren and flat marshland that seemed to go on for ever. It was a horrid place. Once a hospital, it had been closed after a typhoid outbreak a hundred years ago and stayed empty. When Charles Malstain took over the country, his loathing for children resulted in many being left abandoned on the streets without home or parents. And so the building was reopened as an orphanage, and many unfortunate children ended up here. It was called St Cecilia's.

St Cecilia's comprised a series of stone and brick buildings, like army barracks. One half was boys, one half girls. And in each building children were grouped by age. Rachel was put in the ten–twelve years girls' section and assigned a metal bed and a wash jug. There was one tap in each building, and a disgusting outside loo. There were two meals a day.

There were no books on the walls, no lessons to educate them, no activities to entertain. There was a small outdoor concrete space surrounded by a high wire fence on all sides. The wire fence had spikes on top and was dug one metre into the ground to prevent prisoners escaping through tunnels. Rachel discovered this fact only when a rebellious girl called Katja tried to dig her way out and got caught. They never saw Katja again.

Rachel would have found all this perfectly unbearable but she knew she was doing it for Robert. She felt herself separate inside into two people. One was living this deadly dreary life, trying to avoid trouble, trying to make sure she ate enough protein and vitamins to stay clean and free of disease. But the other half was with Robert, on his adventure to uncover the secret behind The Book of Stolen Dreams. And that was where she sent her mind while her body continued on its daily toil.

For a week or so this worked fine. She spoke to no one. She had her twelfth birthday and no one even noticed. She fought off anyone trying to take her food. She knew by instinct that the one thing you must do in a place like St Cecilia's is make it crystal clear you are not to be messed with. She made no friends, attached herself to no one, allowed herself no loyalties. She felt nothing.

Then one day a new girl arrived and was instantly picked on by two of the tougher eleven-year-olds. Rachel found herself defending the girl and of course that meant the girl was deeply grateful, showered her with love and appreciation, and Rachel was forced to learn the girl's name, which was Laetitia. Laetitia was chatty and laughed a lot, even in painful situations. Pretty soon Rachel had decided she really liked Laetitia, and so her plan for survival was ruined. She could no longer send her mind over the ocean to Port Clement, to Robert and The Book of Stolen Dreams. She was here, with Laetitia, who needed her and wanted to be her friend.

Rachel and Laetitia became a gang of two. They looked out for each other, shared any lucky finds such as a dropped potato or apple core, and also shared sadnesses, such as Laetitia learning that her brother Gustav's illness had got worse (Gustav was in the boys' block just half a mile away). Rachel shared with Laetitia the loss of her mother but said nothing about Robert or her father. That was a secret too far.

Laetitia was tall and fair-haired. She was three months and two days older than Rachel. Laetitia had always lived in Brava too, but in the south of the city. Her father had been a doctor and the life they had lived had been much richer than Rachel's. Laetitia mentioned a big house, with dogs and a back garden, a country cottage that her family visited every summer, and holidays abroad – sometimes in warmer countries, sometimes skiing with her grandparents.

It all sounded wonderful to Rachel, but it occurred to her that it must have been hard to have had such luxuries taken away so suddenly. Rachel felt a strange gratitude that her family had never had too much. They'd had to invent all their holidays and adventures whilst never leaving the living room. She was used to making do and getting on with it.

One other thing occurred to Rachel. It seemed that prior to "the disaster", Laetitia's family had enjoyed levels of freedom very rare in the world led by President Charles Malstain. They were able to travel, they'd had money, their electricity didn't fail every other day, they'd had heating and clean water. Rachel wondered why. And why everything had changed so fast.

Then one day Laetitia said something that caused Rachel to gasp with surprise. It came after a conversation at lunch, when everyone had gleefully compared fathers – whose was meanest and the most angry, and so on. Rachel said nothing and nor did Laetitia. But that night as they were washing before bed, Laetitia whispered:

"I didn't know what to say. My father's not mean at all. He's a good man and an excellent doctor."

Rachel thought, then replied, very quietly:

"My father's a good man too."

There was a pause. Laetitia spoke first.

"My dad's in prison."

"Mine too." Rachel said it quietly and moved a little closer to her friend.

"Which prison?" Laetitia asked.

"I don't know," Rachel admitted sadly.

"Is he a doctor too?"

"No. He's a librarian and a great novelist."

"Mine is a cancer doctor. He looks after some of the most powerful people in all of Brava. He looked after Charles Malstain."

Rachel's bones froze. There was a silence in the room, as if just saying the name spelled danger.

"So what happened?"

Laetitia looked like she might cry but pulled herself together in a way that Rachel found very admirable.

"All he did wrong was to tell stupid Charles Malstain that he was ill with stomach cancer and that there was no cure. For that they put him in prison with no release date."

Rachel's breath shortened. "Is that true? Is Charles Malstain sick?"

"Yes. Very. Unless someone finds a miracle cure, Charles Malstain will die very soon. And I for one will not be sorry at all."

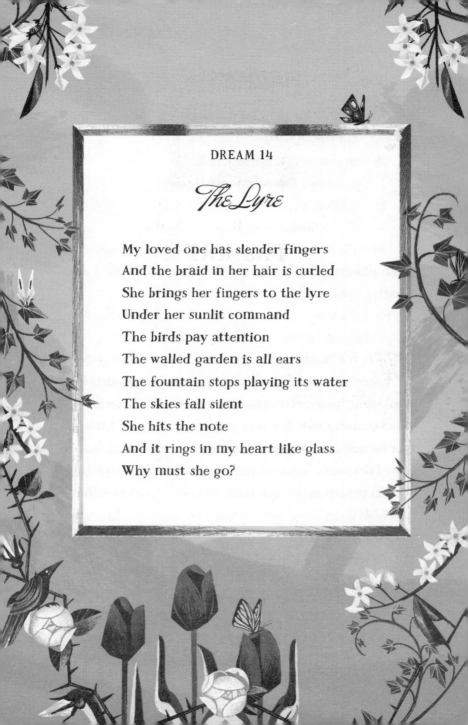

DREAM 14

The Lyre

My loved one has slender fingers
And the braid in her hair is curled
She brings her fingers to the lyre
Under her sunlit command
The birds pay attention
The walled garden is all ears
The fountain stops playing its water
The skies fall silent
She hits the note
And it rings in my heart like glass
Why must she go?

9

The KRF

When Theodore Glimpf found Robert halfway down the stairs at the back of the Behind the Eyes Bookstore, his eyes bulged and for a moment he seemed as shocked as Robert. The gun in his hand shook a little, his face turned a strange colour, he seemed to splutter. Robert feared the old man might shoot him by mistake.

Then with a sudden and surprising speed, Glimpf grabbed the young boy roughly by the shoulders and hurled Robert the rest of the way down the stairs. Robert landed with a crash on the cold hard stone of the cellar floor. A sharp pain shot through his shoulders, but before he could get to his shoeless feet, the young man with the scarf had rushed to Robert, pulled him up and pinned him against the wall, causing several dusty volumes of philosophy to tumble around him.

"Who are you, who sent you, what do you want?!"

Not sure which question to answer first, Robert paused. But this only resulted in him being pinned all the harder against the red brick of the cellar wall as the young student's eyes burned into his.

"No one sent me, I promise! I came on my own!" The words tumbled out of Robert's mouth as fast as he could utter them.

"You're lying!" snarled the young man. He went to slap Robert with the flat of his hand, but the girl with the jet-black eyes cried out.

"Wait, Laszlo! He's only a boy!" Marie approached Robert slowly. She had a calm, steady look that could not be refused. "Did no one send you?"

"No one. I promise," squeaked Robert. He was finding it slightly hard to breathe through the dust from the books and the young man's grip on his collar. "I'm here because my sister and I are looking for someone!"

"Where is your sister?"

"She is far away, in Brava. She is only eleven – I mean, twelve. She means no harm to anyone!"

"In Brava?" The young man's face changed in a moment. He let go of Robert's collar. "You have come from Brava?"

Robert nodded.

"Why?"

Robert thought quickly. What should he say? "I'm looking for a man called Walter Meyer. I need to ask him something. Do you know him?"

Did the shopkeeper's eyes rise suddenly at the sound of the name? It was dark in the basement and Robert couldn't tell for sure.

"Walter Meyer?" the young man said. "I've never heard of him. What do you want to ask him?"

Robert didn't dare mention the precious Book that he had left back in his lodgings, neatly concealed in a very well-chosen hiding place. "I just want to ask him about my father."

"You came on the boat?" It was the young woman who spoke. Her voice was reassuring.

"Yes. A week ago."

"With the rest of your family?"

"No, on my own. My mother died. My sister is in an orphanage."

The young woman frowned. "You left her there? Alone?"

Robert smarted. It sounded awful. Without telling them the whole truth, how could he explain that he was not a bad brother, that Rachel had begged him to go?

"I just want to help my father. He is in prison and I want to get him out."

"Why is he in prison?"

"Because Charles Malstain put him there!"

There was a silence in the cellar. The bookshop owner lowered his gun. The girl lowered her voice.

"If you feel about Charles Malstain the way I think you do, Laszlo and I are not to be feared. For we are the same as you."

"What do you mean?"

"We are from Brava too." The girl smiled. "We've all lost friends and family to Charles Malstain, some dead, some in prison."

The old bookseller stayed very quiet at the bottom of the stairs.

The young man called Laszlo breathed deep. "I'm sorry I hurt you. But Charles Malstain will stop at nothing to overhear what the Krasnian Resistance Front are planning. He might hire children. He just might."

Robert felt his freckles go hot with indignation. "First, I'm not a child, I'm thirteen years old! Second, I am not a spy of Charles Malstain! I hate him and I'd kill him if I could!"

This seemed to go down very well indeed. Laszlo laughed out loud and slapped Robert on the back, which hurt, but not enough for Robert to mind.

The girl smiled. "Well, you are brave. My name is Marie Lim. This is Laszlo. And this is Herr Glimpf. There are others coming. You will meet them soon."

Robert looked at Herr Glimpf, who stayed silent in the half-light.

"And what is your name?" It was Marie who spoke.

"My name is Robert Klein."

At the sound of the name, the shopkeeper's eyes glistened in the shadows.

Now the door upstairs opened and more voices, more steps, more young people entered, and climbed down the rickety spiral staircase into the cellar.

"Who's this?"

Soon Robert was meeting the small group that proudly called itself the Krasnian Resistance Front. There were five of them and they were all under twenty years old, but to Robert they seemed very adult and impressive.

In particular Robert took notice of one woman with red hair who kissed Laszlo on the lips and had a gun clearly visible in her coat pocket.

"I'm Rudi," she said in a husky voice as Robert was explained and introduced.

Not long after that, Robert was learning that the group had a plan. Charles Malstain was to arrive in the city of Port Clement at noon the very next day, on an official visit to improve relations between the two countries. But the KRF had learned of the visit from Theodore Glimpf. And they had decided to act.

The KRF were going to assassinate Charles Malstain in his Port Clement hotel the night before the negotiations took place.

And slightly to Robert's surprise, by the end of that evening, he had agreed to help them.

DREAM 20

The Promise

A bell is ringing from beyond the gate
"I will come again"
She says with the grass in her hair
"And one day if fate agrees
I will not leave"
We gather ourselves
She stands, her long dress strokes the stones
She walks the path to the gate
I cannot go after
"Promise you will come again" I say
She only smiles
She passes through
And the latch closes

10

The Toothbrush
of the Poetess

The KRF talked long into the night, making plans for the assassination and what would happen immediately afterwards. Robert had become an important part of the plan and he felt very proud.

Laszlo and his glamorous girlfriend Rudi were group leaders and would be the lead operatives. They would dress as a hotel bellboy and maid, and shoot Charles Malstain as he took a bath in his hotel suite. Malstain was legendary for his long baths, which he took, people said, to try to remove the terrible smell that came from every pore of his body.

After shooting Malstain, Laszlo and Rudi would immediately surrender. They would make no attempt to escape but would hand themselves over to the Port

Clement authorities. They would be tried for murder but their defence would be simple. Charles Malstain was destroying a whole country. Killing people every day. Imprisoning innocent civilians in cells under his own palace, locking up children. Whilst murder is almost always wrong, Laszlo said, rather too loudly as he stood on a wine box in Herr Glimpf's cellar, the killing of a dictator COULD be justified in the most extreme of cases.

Robert thought Laszlo was marvellous. He had long hair and a great scarf and meant every word he said. Rudi was a little scary. She said less than Laszlo but when she did speak it was electric. She talked about a new dawn for Krasnia, freedom for all. No more emperors and tyrants! Power to the people! There were two other members – a small but muscular man called Stanley and a young student whom they called "Two-Salads" because he was so thin. They were support and backup. Two-Salads knew how to drive a car.

Robert reserved special admiration for Marie, partly because of her jet-black eyes and partly because even though she was, at seventeen, the youngest of the KRF, she was always so calm and made him feel safe. She sat quietly in the dark cellar as the others gave long speeches about equality and the future, and occasionally she turned to smile at Robert. And when she did, everything was right with Robert's world.

At the end of the meeting Theodore Glimpf suggested

that Robert should not return to his lodgings but stay the night with him and his wife in their apartment above the bookshop. Robert wasn't sure. Should he leave the Book alone for one whole night? But he desperately needed to talk to Herr Glimpf about Lucius and Walter Meyer and how everything connected. And he sensed the bookseller wanted to talk to him too.

Herr Glimpf gave Robert a small garret room high in the apartment. There were books everywhere. Even the bed was erected on volumes of old encyclopaedias. It made Robert feel warm and cosy. He took off his coat, dozed for a little while and then went down for supper.

Sitting at the table of the first-floor kitchen was a remarkably glamorous woman in her fifties. She was dressed in clothes that were by no means new, but suited her perfectly. A trim dark suit, with an angular black cap. Careful make-up. She was stirring a bright orange drink with a tiny pink umbrella. Robert recognised her voice instantly.

"So you are the Klein boy. I am Constanza Glimpf. Theodore tells me you have joined the KRF."

Robert nodded. He remembered her name from the business card.

"Well, it's convenient. Theodore and I need to talk to you. About The Book of Stolen Dreams."

The room went quiet. Constanza stirred her cocktail.

"The first thing to say is that the KRF do not know why

Charles Malstain is really in the city. But seeing as you overheard my phone call to my brother Lucius, I suspect that you do."

Robert blushed a little. How much did she know about him? He nodded. "Yes. He's here because he's trying to find the Book."

"You listen well, my little eavesdropper. Would you like a drink?"

She offered him a small glass of the orange liquid. Robert sat down. He felt it would be polite at least to try a sip. When it hit his lips he almost fainted. It tasted like the mouthwash at Dr Klitzbanger's, but five times as strong. It went down the wrong way, came back up, then went down the right way, which turned out not to be any better than the wrong way. Robert did well not to spit it out.

"What do you think?"

"Very nice. Thank you."

Constanza continued, unaware that Robert was almost choking. "But Malstain won't be buying any Book. It's a trick created by myself and my brother Lucius. We have lured Malstain to Port Clement to kill him."

"Lucius Meyer is your brother?" Robert asked. It was all starting to make a strange kind of sense.

"Yes. Thanks to the idiocy of Lucius's son Walter, Charles Malstain nearly got his hands on the Book last year. Only your father's heroics prevented catastrophe. We can't take that risk again. So we have to kill him. It is impossible to get close to Malstain in his own city. But here in Port Clement, he has less protection."

She sipped more of the orange liquid. Robert took the plunge and asked what he was desperate to know.

"Why mustn't Malstain get his hands on the Book? Why is it so important?"

She looked up at Robert. "That you don't need to know."

But Robert was curious now. "I think it has something to do with the Hinterland," he said boldly.

She stiffened suddenly. Her voice was raised. "Who told you about the Hinterland?"

Robert lied. "Father told me. He said it was in the Book. He said it was the place beyond the gate, the land of the dead."

"He should have said nothing!"

Robert sat back in his chair. Constanza sipped her drink angrily. It occurred to Robert that it must at least be crossing her mind that maybe he knew too much. Maybe it would be safer for her to kill him now. He looked around the room, at the bread and meat knives, the chopping cleaver, the heavy stone pestle. There are so many ways to die in a normal kitchen.

But now Constanza put the little umbrella into her glass and turned to him. "Where is the Book, Robert? Do you know?"

It was the question she had wanted to ask all along,

Robert knew it. He decided to say nothing. Not about the Book, or the missing page. He wasn't sure who to trust any more. "No. I never saw my father after his arrest."

She nodded. But something about her look made him unsure. Did she believe him?

"Well, what matters now is to kill Charles Malstain. In doing so we will bring freedom to Krasnia. Freedom to men like your father."

She slammed her glass down and stood suddenly.

"Enough talk. Theodore has made you soup. Eat it – you won't find better in the whole of Krasnia. And then you must sleep."

"Won't you eat?"

"I never eat before an assassination."

She rose and walked to the door. Blew a kiss to her husband. And left the room.

Robert breathed. Theodore brought the soup. The bowl was sky-blue.

"How are you doing?" Theodore laid the soup in front of Robert.

"Oh, I'm fine, thank you."

"I'm sorry I hurt you when I found you. I had no idea who you were."

"It's quite all right." Robert stirred the soup. Promising smells came with the steam.

Theodore took away the cocktail and poured Robert a glass of milk. "Don't be frightened of my Constanza. She is a Meyer and Meyers are emotional people. But she has every right to be. She has lost her home and many friends to Charles Malstain."

"Is that why she wants to kill him?"

"One of many reasons."

Robert nodded, and thought of his father, in some frozen prison camp somewhere in the East of the country. He had his reasons too.

He tasted the soup. It was good, with just enough paprika. His mother had made it like this and it made him remember home, suppers with his parents and Rachel, music and games and poetry readings that went on far too long. Oh how he would happily listen to a thousand of his father's poems, just to have him back again!

"Bravan potato soup is like no other." Theodore smiled. "It takes you back into your memories. And the herbs are fresh from Krasnia. I had them smuggled in."

The old man brought a bowl for himself and they sat quietly for a while. Robert enjoyed the silence. The tick of the clock and the slight slurp of Theodore's spoon reassured him. The bookseller spoke again.

"Robert. Say nothing of the Hinterland or The Book of Stolen Dreams to Marie, Laszlo or the rest of them. They must know only that they are involved in a political assassination. It is better for them and for us."

"In case they get caught? And interrogated?"

"You are a clever boy."

His kind eyes studied Robert's. Robert nodded then returned to his soup and finished it.

"You want seconds?"

"No, thank you. But it was delicious."

"Then you should go to sleep now. Tomorrow you have an important job to do."

The important job was this.

The assassination involved Rudi and Laszlo getting into the Hotel Excelsior the day of Charles Malstain's arrival. But there was one problem: the government of Krasnia had completely taken over the Hotel Excelsior for the visit. Malstain and his cronies had booked every room, even to the point of kicking out a poetess who had lived on the twelfth floor for over twenty years. Olga von Stangis had been forcibly relocated to an apartment nearby until the presidential trip was complete.

So how would they get in? Anyone of student age trying to enter would be immediately stopped by Malstain's terrifying security team. It was well-known that the exiled Krasnian Resistance Front was led by students and young radicals. They would be detained at the door, arrested and interrogated.

Marie had once worked at the hotel. She knew of a basement entrance that was used mainly for the weekly linen delivery. It was locked and only the concierge had the key. He kept it in his office right next to the hotel lobby.

But how could they get the key? The KRF had no idea. Until Robert Klein arrived.

It was immediately clear to Marie that Robert would be hugely useful to the plan. If she and Robert were to walk up to the hotel together and pretend to be the niece and nephew of the poetess Olga von Stangis, the one who'd been moved out of the twelfth floor, and say that the poetess had forgotten her toothbrush in the bathroom, the guards just might believe them.

At worst they would be turned away as foolish and naive relatives of a minor artist. At best they might get inside. It was worth a try.

"But, Robert, you must only do this if you want to," said Marie. "An assassination is a serious business."

At that moment Robert would have done anything to please her. "I do want to!" he cried.

Marie looked terrifically proud. "Good. Then you and I will get into the hotel foyer and reach the concierge's office. While you distract Malstain's men with the fetching of the toothbrush from the twelfth floor, I will steal the key, open the basement door and let Rudi and Laszlo in from the yard."

Laszlo nodded. Rudi was cleaning her gun. Marie continued:

"Then we can leave and they will take over. Two-Salads

and Stanley will be waiting in a car to take us away as fast as possible."

"You mean we don't get involved in the killing?"

Marie smiled. "No, dear Robert. You are thirteen and I am a first-year art history student. We'd best leave that to those who are trained."

It was Stanley who raised one possible problem. "What if they call the poetess in her temporary apartment and ask for verification?"

For a moment it seemed the whole idea had collapsed in their faces. Then Robert had an idea.

"My father loves poetry and he always said poets were on the side of the underdog," he said. "Perhaps if we asked her, Olga von Stangis would take pity on us and would agree to tell a white lie on our behalf."

Marie smiled. "Your father is a wise man, Robert Klein. We will visit her and ask her."

Robert flushed with pride.

The morning of the assassination was bright and clear. The Port Clement radio announced that President Malstain had flown in from Brava "bang on time". As the tyres of the private aeroplane touched the earth, Marie and Robert were taking the elevator that led to the temporary apartment of poetess, model and recluse Olga von Stangis. They had read in a cultural magazine that the poetess rarely rose before twelve, so had chosen the time accordingly.

They rang at the door. No answer. Marie looked nervous.

Then the door opened and a pink fluffy dog appeared, as if it had opened the door by itself.

A voice – female, loud, light and airy: "Come in, come in! You can start the wallpapering straight away!"

Marie and Robert walked in.

A woman of enormous girth looked at them. Her hair was dyed a kind of orange. She was dressed in silks of several very bright colours, a pink feather boa round her neck, but with the latest fashionable white training-shoes on her feet. She had a terrific amount of make-up on, which might explain, Robert thought, why she was never available before noon.

"Well, interior decorators get younger all the time!" she boomed. "Come in, come in. Where are your rollers and paste? And the wallpaper? I chose the tropical scenes from the catalogue because I simply love jungles, though I have never seen one in the flesh. As you can see, the current decoration is utterly dreary and unpleasant. Of course I am only staying in this apartment for three days, but it is simply inconceivable that an artist of my sensibility should look at these walls for even an hour without wishing to throw herself from the balcony. Charles Malstain will pay for everything. And quite rightly so! Now begin in the living room while I eat my French toast in the bedroom. Chintzie darling, you come with Mummy."

The unfortunately named dog yapped brightly. Robert and Marie stopped and stared.

"Madam poetess. Miss von Stangis. We hate to disappoint you. But we are not interior decorators."

There was a pause as the poetess surveyed her visitors – an arty girl in a coat and beret, and a teenage boy with a lot of freckles and just a few spots. Robert wasn't sure if she might scream or call the police. But instead she merely hummed.

"Hmmm. Yes. No indeed you are not. Hmmm."

She paused again. "Don't tell me. Let me see. My poetic instincts will help me understand this situation. I have it! You are the downstairs neighbours and you wish to borrow a towel. Feel free, my friends!"

They shook their heads. Her eyes widened and then narrowed.

"Hmmm. Don't tell me. You are unemployed circus performers offering impromptu acrobatics in the customer's own living room."

They shook their heads again. Marie opened her mouth to speak.

"Don't tell me! You are animal welfare campaigners trying to save the mountain gorilla and you seek a donation. No? You are pickpockets returning a small wallet, but you have the wrong apartment. No. You are urchin children looking for work, you are the descendants of piano restorers, you are assassins seeking an alibi—"

"Yes!" Marie spoke fast to interrupt the poetic flow. "We are assassins seeking an alibi."

"Interesting." The poetess smiled. "Yes, on reflection, of course you are. Now what alibi do you seek? Don't tell me too much, certainly not whom you are to kill. I should know as little as possible in case they torture me for information. Oh, I'm a tough old bird, but you never know how an artist may crack under pressure."

Chintzie barked her agreement.

Marie drew breath. "All we need, great poetess, is for you to confirm – if your phone should ring this afternoon and someone enquire – that you did indeed leave your electric toothbrush in the bathroom of the Hotel Excelsior and that you have sent your nephew and niece around to fetch it."

There was a solemn pause as the poetess chewed her splendid mouth.

She nodded sagely.

"Assassins, you have my word."

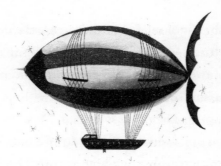

11

Dreams in the Orphanage

Rachel Klein had agreed the following plan with her brother: once his mission to Port Clement was completed, on landing back in Krasnia, Robert would send a coded letter addressed to *Miss Rachel Klein, St Cecilia's Home for Forgotten Children*. The letter would say: *Dear Niece Rachel, The weather is fine. I trust you are well in your lovely new children's home. Uncle Spinoza*. This would be Rachel's cue to escape the orphanage and make her way back to the city of Brava to meet her brother.

The plan was not without risk. Rachel knew all letters to the orphanage were opened and checked. If the officials realised that Felix Klein's missing son was sending his sister a secret message, it would never reach Rachel but would instead be confiscated and arrive on the desk of

Johannes Slick, Charles Malstain's terrifying Head of Secrecy and Communications. And that would be the end of everything. So Rachel watched with anxiety as every day the post arrived at the orphanage's mailing office to be sorted by three grey-looking women.

But whereas Laetitia received letters almost every day from her mother, some with very thin chocolate bars sneaked inside the paper, Rachel got nothing. And as the days passed, she began to feel worried. What might have happened to her brother?

It was a cold night in the orphanage. Rachel lay in her bed. She was in a room of sixteen girls. Laetitia slept loudly beside her. But Rachel didn't sleep. Every time she closed her eyes, she saw her mother back in the apartment – perhaps reading a book, perhaps making her special toffee sauce to go on Robert's breakfast cereal (Robert had a famously sweet tooth) – but when Rachel opened her eyes, her mother was gone. The disappointment was too much to bear.

So Rachel decided not to sleep at all. Instead she used the small torch she had brought with her from the apartment, and hid under the sheets reading the one book she had smuggled in with her – a book of adventure stories with pictures. But the endless nights without sleep were starting to take their toll. They made Rachel so tired she kept making mistakes in her orphanage chores and being punished. Tonight she could feel herself falling into slumber, and that would mean dreaming of the mother she no longer had.

Her eyes began to close…

And instantly her mother was there. She stood in the orphanage dormitory, right in front of Rachel. Judith was dressed in the same nightclothes she had been wearing the morning she died, and she seemed to drift across the floor, past Laetitia's bed, past a horrid girl called Clarinda, and towards Rachel.

"Oh, Mother," Rachel whispered. "You are stuck in the land of death and I in the land of the living. How lonely we both are."

But her mother just shook her head and smiled. "It does not have to be that way."

"What do you mean?"

"The Book of Dreams, my dear. Find the key. The key to the gate. Then maybe we can be together again."

And with that, her mother turned and began to drift away…

"No. Come back!"

Rachel tried with all her might not to call out too loud, but the hope was too much to bear and she shouted suddenly, "Mother, don't leave me, take me out of this dreadful place!"

But now her mother was reaching the door. And Rachel was crying out, "MOTHER! MOTHER!" and quite without meaning to, she was weeping.

The other girls woke; Clarinda smirked. Laetitia told her to shut up and be kind. Clarinda just laughed at that. Upon which, Rachel hurled herself on Clarinda. They rolled on the floor.

Rachel scratched and screamed with an anger that she did not know she possessed. An almighty fight began, with all girls taking one side or another. Pillows were torn open. Feathers flew.

The night watch heard the commotion and rushed in. Rachel was forced away from the moaning and bleeding Clarinda and given three days in a solitary cell without food as punishment.

But Rachel didn't mind. In that moment with her mother, she had suddenly understood something. The Book of Stolen Dreams *was* magical. It could bring back the dead. It *was* possible to feel her mother's arms around her again, to feel her mother's warmth. But she had to find out the right way to read the Book.

She had to find the key to the gate.

12
Foiled

At precisely a quarter to three in the afternoon, Robert and Marie walked calmly towards a crowd that was gathering outside an imposing building on the north side of Gravitas Square – the Hotel Excelsior. The square was leafy in the spring breeze. The crowd were expecting the imminent arrival of President Charles Malstain.

Robert had a strangely shaped object tucked in his left trouser pocket. It felt as unnerving to him as if he had a pistol with six bullets rubbing against his leg. In fact it was a rather delicate electronic toothbrush inlaid with mother-of-pearl.

On speaking to the poetess it had become clear the only flaw with their plan was that the poetess had of course NOT forgotten her toothbrush, so there was no toothbrush for Robert and Marie to pick up. Marie had brilliantly solved the problem. Robert would take the poetess's toothbrush with him in his pocket. He would walk into the bathroom, pretending to get the toothbrush, and simply take it out of his pocket. The poetess had loved the plan and was proud that her toothbrush was involved.

At five to three things started to happen. Hotel staff in brocade uniforms started to line up. Robert watched as the President's cavalcade approached. Sixteen black limousines in total. Charles Malstain insisted on always having dummy cars wherever he went, in case someone tried to shoot him through the tinted windows. That way they could not possibly know which car he was in.

Today it transpired that Malstain was in the fifth car. The doors opened and first out was Johannes Slick, his pencil-thin Head of Secrecy and Communications. As Slick gazed upon the crowds, the air seemed to drop a degree in temperature. Then the President climbed out. Bodyguards emerged from the cars in front and behind and formed a phalanx to usher the great leader towards the celebrated revolving doors of the Hotel Excelsior.

The crowds were large and divided. Some cheered, some booed. Those cheering booed at those booing. Those booing started to hurl insults at those who had cheered but were now booing at those who had booed.

Only Robert and Marie stayed silent. It was the first time Robert had seen Malstain in the flesh. He was shorter than Robert had expected. His dark hair was slicked back like oil. His face was pale, he seemed to have a constant sweat on his flat forehead and his tiny eyes darted constantly from one side to another, as if he felt surrounded by enemies. His suit was buttoned tight. His thighs were short – like stumpy carrots. His shoes were brightly polished. He smiled thinly, without opening his mouth, as if he feared catching some infectious disease. He waved briefly at the gathered assembly, though this was really for the cameras.

This man, thought Robert, *has buried people under his own palace. Has kept prisoners without trial, for years. Has sentenced my father to a life of hard labour for stealing a book.*

Malstain's bodyguards surveyed the crowds, hands quietly placed on pistols. Among them was the terrifying seven-foot giant Rufus O'Hare.

Robert recognised O'Hare immediately. His father had told him back in Brava that Charles Malstain had a prison and torture cell under his palace – so deep underground you could not hear people scream. Johannes Slick was in charge of the administration. Rufus O'Hare was in charge of the torture.

O'Hare's moustache alone was as big as Robert's head. His hands were like a digger's claw. He had a favourite restraint technique that involved taking his assailant in one arm, lifting him from the ground, turning him upside down and dropping him on to his head as many times as it took for him to fall unconscious or say what Johannes Slick wanted him to say.

Quietly Marie gripped Robert's hand. Robert tried to force a smile and look innocent, but it was difficult to look on such villains and lie.

Then he saw another figure get out of the car: slim, young, rather handsome, in a light grey two-piece suit and an elegant tie. His hair was beautifully combed. He reminded Robert of someone, but he couldn't work out who. Was it his eyes? The shape of his mouth? His ears maybe?

Robert suddenly froze. He knew exactly who the young man resembled. He resembled the old illustrator Lucius Meyer. He bore the same-shaped head. The same ears.

In a flash Robert knew he was looking at Walter Meyer.

Walter Meyer stood apart as photographers grabbed what photos of the President they could. Walter seemed aloof, almost uninterested. He smoked a thin cigarette and wore a playful smile on his lips, like he might be playing a game of croquet or gambling in a casino. Only his hands gave something away. They were clenched very slightly, half in his pockets, half out. He took care to be nowhere near any of the cameras.

The photographers asked for one more snap, then President Malstain was quickly ushered through the doors and inside the sanctuary of the hotel. The handsome Walter Meyer casually strolled after him.

That was it. The arrival was over.

The crowd, disappointed by the briefness of the glimpse of this notorious dictator, thinned out, returning to their jobs or their studies. A few protestors continued to wave banners saying *Where are our brothers? Release our sons!* and other similar demands, but soon the police arrived and, as they say in the newspapers, "dispersed the assembly".

By four o'clock there was almost no one left in the square.

But two figures remained. They had taken a seat on a bench in the grassy middle of the square, not far from a military statue. They were eating dumplings and pretending to chat idly. Robert looked up at the statue, a proud man in uniform with a sword pointing to the sky. Then he looked at Marie, who was quietly checking the side road where Stanley and Two-Salads were waiting in the getaway car.

"Marie," he asked. "Have *you* lost someone back in Krasnia?"

"Yes, I have, as a matter of fact," she replied quietly. "My boyfriend. He is in prison."

"What's his name?"

"Stefan. You would like him, Robert, and he would like you."

"I will like him. When we free him," Robert said proudly.

Marie smiled and put her handkerchief to her nose for a moment and then checked her watch. "Are you ready?"

He nodded, then paused for a moment.

"Are we sure?" he said under his breath. "That killing him is the right thing to do?"

"I asked myself the same question," Marie replied softly. "But letting him kill others is worse."

Robert felt suddenly confused and grown-up, in a world where nothing was easy and clear. Marie sensed it.

"I'm going to hold your hand so it looks like you're my brother. All right?"

He nodded again and finished the last dumpling. She smiled; he felt her hand take his. He stood up. They tidied their clothes and Marie put on a rather elegant red scarf. Without a word more, they walked towards the entrance of the hotel.

Four uniformed figures stopped them.

"No entrance. Hotel's closed. Private engagement."

"May I introduce myself?" Marie spoke clearly and loudly. Robert noticed a distinct change in her accent. She sounded like "part of the furniture", as his father would once have put it.

"My name is Countess Eugenie von Stangis, I am the niece of the poetess Olga von Stangis who lives permanently on the twelfth floor of the hotel and who has been much inconvenienced by having to move out for President Malstain. The poetess is a great supporter of the

President and would like it known that only for a man of such distinction would she have agreed to leave at all. But she has left her toothbrush in the bathroom of her suite and requires its immediate return."

"Can't she afford to buy another toothbrush?" muttered one of the guards and they all chuckled. Marie was quick on the uptake:

"Clearly, sir, you are not aware of the poetess's unique and serious dental condition. She has a rotting of the gums that if not controlled could lead to a complete collapse of teeth and face. The remedial electronic toothbrush she uses to avert such catastrophe was personally chiselled in mother-of-pearl by Cornelius Floss, dentition to royalty the world over. To use another kind of toothbrush would be dangerous to the poetess, not to say lethal. Court cases would ensue."

That shut them up. The guards looked one to another and every look spoke to the fact that they knew they would have to pass this request "up the line". And that was all that Marie and Robert wanted.

"Wait here."

It was Robert who spoke now. "We would prefer to wait inside the hotel foyer and to call Auntie Olga and reassure her that all is well. She is extremely agitated about the whole affair. She has a nervous condition."

The guards consulted.

"Come on then, but no further than the foyer. Clear?"

They were walked in by the heavier guard. Marie squeezed Robert's hand as if to say, *Good work*. Robert felt a glow of pride, but this was swiftly replaced by a queasy feeling in the stomach as he looked around the vast empty foyer, with its imposing chandelier, its huge sweeping staircase, and its famous stuffed leopard in a glass cabinet along one wall.

The entire place was empty but for two of Charles Malstain's bodyguards. One of them was Rufus O'Hare. Up close he seemed even bigger than outside, but Robert was astonished to see how small his eyes were – like black islands of hate set in the vast ocean of his face.

"What are they doing in here?" O'Hare snarled.

Marie explained the need for the toothbrush. O'Hare didn't even nod. He just looked at her with a withering gaze.

"Call the poetess. Check this nonsense."

They entered the concierge's office. Immediately Marie and Robert spotted the concierge's pass keys hanging on a yellow hook on the far wall. Each key had a written tag explaining what it was for. One was for the basement exit. They nodded quietly to each other. Everything was going to plan.

O'Hare's assistant, a sweaty little man who spoke with a weaselly sneer and hiccupped every time he reached the end of a phrase, got on the phone. "Yes. Hup. Is that the poetess? Hup? There are two…young people here, who claim to be your relations and are in search of—"

The man was stopped in his tracks by a torrent of words. Robert could just overhear down the phone line as a magnificently prepared speech gushed from the poetess's plentiful lips. It was an ode to dentistry, an elegy not just for her teeth but teeth everywhere, a homage to the pearly whiteness of the molar, the cutting brilliance of the incisor, the chomping efficiency of the canine. Several times the hiccupping man tried to staunch the flow but to no effect. Finally he gave up and handed the receiver to Rufus O'Hare, who held it at arm's length as the poetess reached her climax with the words, "But what, dear friends, is a mouth of perfection? Without a brush to stop and curb infection?!"

There was a pause and O'Hare sighed and asked, "So these are your nephew and niece?"

"Of course they are, you fool!" bellowed the poetess down the line. "Can you not SEE the resemblance to me?"

O'Hare looked at Robert then at Marie. He clearly could not.

"I swore to my sweet sister Vermicella on her deathbed that I would look after them..." Now they could hear the poetess sobbing down the phone line.

"All right, all right!" muttered O'Hare. "We'll get you your brush." And he slammed down the phone.

"You!" he said, pointing at Robert. "You come with me." And then to Marie: "You stay here with him."

He meant the hiccupping assistant. Robert glanced anxiously at Marie, but she just nodded as if to say: *Don't worry, I'll deal with him.*

The giant O'Hare and the somewhat smaller Robert Klein crossed the empty foyer together. As they reached the elevators, Robert glanced in a gilt mirror to one side. He saw Marie suddenly seem to faint to the floor in the concierge's office. The hiccupping assistant ran to her; she seemed to apologise, implying a need for water. And the assistant scurried out to fetch it.

The glass elevator's doors opened. O'Hare pushed Robert inside and pressed the gold button marked twelve. As the elevator ascended, Robert looked through the transparent floor down to the vast atrium below. The hotel was as quiet as a tomb. Robert could see no one – except, that is, for a young woman in a red scarf who, like an ant on a stone, very quietly crossed the lobby floor with a bunch of keys in her hand.

Robert's heart was pumping. The plan was working! Now all he had to do was walk into the poetess's bathroom and linger as long as possible. This would give Marie time to get down to the basement to let in Rudi and Laszlo, and then he could return to the concierge's office.

He secretly felt in his trouser pocket for the toothbrush. It was reassuringly present.

O'Hare glanced at him for a moment. "What are you fiddling with?"

Robert froze. "Just a sweet."

"No candy here, child!"

Robert nodded and took his hand away. The lift doors opened at the twelfth floor.

"Follow me."

O'Hare walked to the door marked *Suite of the Muses* and unlocked it.

"Go on! Get a move on!" O'Hare gestured him in.

Robert tiptoed in. The suite was vast, more of an apartment than a hotel room, and was decorated in quite the most extraordinary colours. Everything was lemon yellow and various shades of pink.

The floor was pure rose-pink tiles, with small yellow swans decorating each tile.

The walls were mustard and salmon, apparently at random. One wall switched colours halfway along as if the poetess had changed her mind in a moment of inspiration.

There was a large, open rosewood cabinet, decorated with lurid nymphs and naughty Greek gods who seemed to be up to no good. In the cabinet was a huge array of brightly coloured marshmallows, mostly pink and green and yellow, and a fine selection of flavoured vodkas, whiskies and brandy.

And along the main wall, opposite the huge bay windows, there was a painting.

Robert stood stunned for a moment.

It was a life-sized portrait of Olga von Stangis. The

poetess was well into her fifties and rather large, yet there she was, resplendent and magisterial, and naked but for a pink feather boa that carefully covered all essential areas. Robert couldn't help smiling, despite the enormous importance of his mission. He decided that he really rather liked this poetess. Something about the sheer madness of the portrait meant he felt he could trust her. Yes, that's what it was. She would bow to no one.

"Stop standing like an idiot! Where's the bathroom?" O'Hare spoke angrily. "I assume you've been here before."

"Yes," Robert stammered, suddenly unsure. "Yes, it's through here. I won't be a moment!" He walked quickly across the thick yellow rug. It shimmered like a violent field of wheat. In the rug his foot hit on something and he reached down into the shagpile to find a small gold cigarette lighter. *She'll have been missing that*, he thought and popped it into his pocket, then dashed through the door at the far end.

He was alone, in a vestibule with three doors. He had no idea where the bathroom was, but perhaps it didn't matter. By now Marie would be unlocking the door and soon they would be on their way back.

Robert took the toothbrush out of his pocket.

"Hurry!" The voice of O'Hare was rough and impatient. He was crossing the room. There was no time to waste.

Robert chose a door at random. It was actually the

poetess's workroom – it had a desk entirely decked in gold and emblazoned with pink flamingoes at every opportunity. More unexpected was a board of fluorescent pink Post-it notes that rested by a mirror with motivational mottos on each one.

You are the true voice of poetry. So sing! said one.

Talent speaks. Genius is silent, said another, possibly in contradiction to the first but Robert wasn't sure.

Remember to get milk, said a third.

Be still. The Muse will come in her time.

Talcum powder!

My heart is like a ripped flower. Oh, Bernard, forgive me…

"Where are you, boy?!" This was not a motto. It was the voice of O'Hare. He was about to enter!

In a flash, Robert grabbed the toothbrush from his pocket and walked out, slamming the door behind him.

He held the toothbrush high.

"Here it is!" he said. "Just where she said it would be."

"Then get a move on. You think I have time for this foolery?" O'Hare growled.

They started to walk back across the vast living room towards the door.

But then Rufus O'Hare's radio sounded. And a voice could be heard – low, calm, clear, and somehow very frightening:

"This is Johannes Slick. To all hotel security and to the President's personal entourage. We have intruders in the hotel.

They were caught entering the basement area and have been apprehended."

Robert's blood froze in his veins. What could possibly have gone so terribly wrong?

"By all accounts there was a boy with them. He must be brought immediately to the fifth floor where my interrogation will begin."

There was a silence in the room. O'Hare turned. Robert felt his breath catch in his chest. O'Hare was just two yards from Robert and barring the way out.

"Come here, boy."

Robert stayed still, assessing his options. There seemed to be none.

Then Robert the scientist had an idea. It revolved around the issue of flammability. And the chemical nature of ethanol.

Robert suddenly produced the cigarette lighter he had found in the poetess's rug; he moved in a flash to the bountiful collection of alcoholic spirits and, before O'Hare could stop him, he opened a bottle of lemongrass vodka that he poured on the rug.

And set fire to it.

Robert was correct in his assumption. The poetess, being of an artistic sensibility, had NOT had the rug correctly treated with fire-resistant chemicals. It went up like newspaper. Flames rose in the room, causing jets of water to spew forth from the sprinkler system in the ceiling. O'Hare rushed towards Robert. As fast as he could, Robert poured more bottles of whisky, rum and gin on to the flames.

Smoke filled the room. O'Hare coughed and spluttered as he chased Robert around the lurid yellow walls. The painting of the poetess was on fire now. It fell from the wall with a mighty crash on to O'Hare's back, the naked artist and flaming bodyguard tumbling as one on to the shagpile rug. O'Hare lay silent, knocked out by poetry.

Robert's brain worked faster than it had ever worked. He crossed the room in a flash, took the radio and pass keys from the unconscious torturer, and ran.

He reached the elevator and called it. It seemed to take a year to arrive. When it finally pinged open, Robert jumped in and hit the ground-floor button. The radio clicked on again. It was Slick.

"O'Hare. Is it true you're with the boy?"

Robert did the lowest possible grunt he could muster.

"Was that a yes?"

Another grunt. The lift was heading down. Now at the ninth floor, now the eighth. The seventh floor. And as it came closer to the lobby, Robert saw a terrible sight.

In the lobby of the ground floor Marie was being manhandled by two of Malstain's security. Rudi and Laszlo were tied with cords and were being punched and beaten. Slick was overseeing matters. Robert was caught between fury at seeing Marie being mistreated by such mindless brutes and the dawning realisation that he was heading to exactly where the danger lay.

He jabbed his finger at the buttons for other floors, but the elevator seemed to have made up its mind to take him right into the lion's den.

Then suddenly, as Robert reached the fourth floor, the radio came on again.

"O'Hare! We're going to the presidential suite on the fifth floor. Meet us there!"

Robert grunted over the transmission again. The lift continued to plummet, and in the lobby below, he saw Slick and his men push Marie, Laszlo and Rudi towards the other elevator. They entered, and the other elevator started to rise.

Robert became very still. It was now unavoidable that the two elevators were going to pass right opposite each other. And they were both made of glass.

How could they possibly not see him?

Robert suddenly lay down in his lift; he was just small enough that by curling up he could keep his entire body on the floor. His eyes peeked across the void as the other lift ascended towards him.

The lift was in chaos. Rudi was spitting at her guard. Laszlo was struggling and shouting, "Freedom to Krasnia!" Slick and the bodyguards were finding it a challenge to control them. They tussled and fought and shouted.

Which meant that only one person saw a small curled-up figure in the lift opposite, as it shot past and down to the ground floor of the Hotel Excelsior. Marie looked at Robert Klein in astonishment. And with those jet-black eyes she seemed for a second to give him one very clear instruction:

Tell the Glimpfs.

13

The Lice Inspector

There were no newspapers offered at St Cecilia's and no television sets. It was almost impossible for any of the children to learn anything of the outside world. Rachel Klein was desperate to hear from her brother. Still there was no letter. Had something gone wrong?

That evening, Rachel was on rota to wash up the sixty-five dishes after the orphanage supper. She noticed two kitchen orderlies listening to the staff radio and moved closer to overhear.

"We have breaking news of a failed assassination plot today in a hotel in the city-state of Port Clement. The intended target was President Charles Malstain."

Rachel's heart skipped a beat.

The news presenter continued, saying that four young

assassins had been arrested. Charles Malstain was demanding that the Port Clement government send the assassins back with him to Krasnia for questioning. The government of Port Clement were not prepared to do so as they doubted that the assassins would receive "a fair trial". In fury, Charles Malstain was flying back to Krasnia's capital city of Brava, closing all borders in three days' time, and cutting off all connections with Port Clement's government.

"And finally it is reported that an unnamed thirteen-year-old boy with an unusually freckly face, an accomplice in the assassination, is also being looked for."

When she heard the phrase "unusually freckly face", Rachel dropped seven of the sixty-five dishes she was washing. She was roundly reprimanded for being a useless good-for-nothing and told she would be on the rota again the next night as punishment for her lack of concentration.

But Rachel had no intention of being at St Cecilia's the next night. Robert was in trouble. He was somewhere in Port Clement. He was a wanted criminal, he was being hunted, and there was no way he would be able to get back to Brava. Worse still, Charles Malstain was closing the borders in three days!

Rachel knew she had to leave and find her brother.

It was after some very deep and tortured thinking that she decided to enlist Laetitia's help. Laetitia agreed immediately.

"Anything but staying in this beastly place," she said rather too loudly.

That night they came up with a plan that would allow both of them to escape the very next morning during exercise hour.

The escape attempts that had been made during Rachel's time at St Cecilia's had all failed and the children never seen again. They had all tried at night. Rachel decided that this was a mistake. At night was when the guards expected the children to flee. They were ready, primed. But Rachel planned to leave in the middle of the day, in broad daylight. And not by climbing a fence or digging a tunnel. No. She planned to drive out of the front gates in full view of absolutely everyone.

The key to her plan was the visit of the lice inspector. The lice inspector was a very unpleasant woman who came every Saturday to look angrily at the children's hair, make a loud tutting noise, lather their heads in the foulest most toxic-smelling chemical known to woman, and leave them for an hour to asphyxiate with the chemical burning their scalp. She then ordered them into the bathroom block to undress, doused them in a jet of freezing-cold water, and abandoned them to drip-dry without a towel. Finally she packed her things in her black medical bag, got back in her small box of a car and drove away, presumably to visit other victims elsewhere.

But Rachel had noticed one thing.

While the vile chemical was doing its murderous work on sixty-five young scalps, the lice inspector left the dorm and went to a small side room. There, for a reason that Rachel could not initially understand, she used a compact mirror and applied some ill-advised make-up to her face. She added a bright pink lipstick to her lips and an orange rouge to her cheeks. Then she added some terrible purple eyeshadow. All in all, it made her look rather like a dead clown.

Then she returned, marshalled her victims into the bathroom block, and did a triumphant bit of dousing. Only then, when the girls were frozen cold and the alleged lice brutally extinguished, did she get in her van and drive to the gates.

At the gates, the car stopped. The inspector got out and, for no obvious reason, talked to the same guard every week. The guard was entirely bald and had a moustache and a shrill voice. The lice inspector listened to him as he told her "funny stories", leaning on her car in a casual way, sticking out her lips like a frog, and laughing unnecessarily loudly at whatever joke he was making. Once the guard even touched the lice inspector on her arm and she giggled like a seven-year-old before sliding towards the car door and getting back in with a strange wiggle. Rachel saw her blow him a kiss as she left.

Rachel estimated that this little pantomime took about two minutes in all. And that if it was possible for her and Laetitia to get into the lice inspector's car during that time, they could hide under the back seat until the car was far away from St Cecilia's, at which point they would somehow make their final escape.

The problem was getting to the car. They would be wet still from the hose-down, they would have to dress very fast, and they would have somehow to get across thirty metres of open ground from the dormitory blocks to the lice inspector's car.

They would need a distraction.

It was Laetitia who had the idea of the spiders. There were dozens of spiders in St Cecilia's and several of the girls were terrified of them. Laetitia wasn't terrified at all, as her doctor-father had always been extremely keen that she see all creepy-crawlies for what they were – species trying to survive. The common spider – or *Tegenaria domestica* as Laetitia's father insisted she call it – was no different. It deserved our respect, not our fear and loathing. And so Laetitia had handled spiders all her life, with love and admiration.

Rachel didn't love spiders but felt it was a good challenge to overcome her fear. That night Laetitia and Rachel collected eight spiders, as the other girls in the dormitory slept. They hid the spiders in a box with air-holes and added a few dead flies to keep the spiders happy.

Then they hid the box inside the bathroom block, behind one of the basins.

The next morning the lice inspector arrived on time

and with even more cruel gusto than usual. She looked at them; she tutted.

"Line up!" she shrieked.

The girls obeyed sullenly. The lice inspector applied the toxic lotion and lathered, her blue plastic gloves rubbing each head with a terrible force, like she was forcing dirt out of a blanket.

"Stay here!"

Rachel watched her walk through the doorway and enter the small side room. She began to apply her make-up and her lipstick...

"No talking!"

Then she returned, and with two guards corralled them into the bathroom block.

"Clothes off."

The girls stripped. The lice inspector turned on the hoses and doused them all violently.

"Stay here until you are dry!" she barked.

Then she packed her things in her black medical bag and walked out.

Instantly Rachel and Laetitia looked at each other across the shivering bathroom. Through a narrow window Rachel could just see the lice inspector approach her car, put her bag on the back seat and drive the short distance to the gates. For a moment it seemed that she might drive straight through. But then she stopped. The same bald guard was there. The car door opened and the lice inspector got out.

Rachel nodded.

Quietly Laetitia, who had positioned herself near the basin, reached down and opened the box of spiders. Within seconds the spiders had started to come out from behind the basin, one, then another, then a third.

In the distance, Rachel could just about hear the lice inspector laughing at the guard's jokes.

It was a rather stupid girl called Wanda who saw the first spider. She screamed. She jammed herself against the wall of the bathroom. She cried out "Spider!" and did some pointing. Soon the other spiders were seen and the panic spread like wildfire. The girls started to make for the only exit from the bathroom, grabbing anything they could use to cover themselves. Then they dashed from the bathroom block, across the yard.

The guards stationed at the dormitory block stared in astonishment as sixty-three half-naked eleven- to twelve-year-olds fled across the fitness area away from the bathroom. They started to run after them.

What they did not see were two small figures running the other way, back around the bathroom towards the dormitory.

Rachel and Laetitia kept low. They ran into the dorm and dressed in seconds. They had their bags ready.

They left the dorm and glanced to the gate. The lice inspector was still chatting to the gate guard. Her laugh had become hysterical.

They stayed low and ran along the fence. They were yards from the car. The lice inspector was leaning on the other side of the car bonnet, looking away from them. She would not see them. But the guard might. He was looking right in their direction as he spoke to her. He was telling a story about a goat. Surely he would see them?

But then Rachel and Laetitia got that bit of good fortune that all escaping prisoners need. The guard's radio crackled, and he looked down. It was another guard telling him about the spider chaos. The gate guard cursed. He spoke into his radio then turned to the lice inspector, whom he called Barbara, and said that he had to go. "The vermin" were causing trouble again.

That was all the time Rachel and Laetitia needed to crawl across the stone ground and quietly open the rear-side car door.

The lice inspector laughed and said something about "treating the vermin for vermin!"

Then she turned to get into the car.

As she shut her front door, Rachel shut the rear door too. One noise covered another. They were inside.

The lice inspector turned to the guard, who was grabbing his gun and heading towards the tumult, and waved.

He waved back and the car drove through the orphanage gates and away.

14

The Gate

Arrested! Taken! What could have gone wrong?

Robert ran through the streets of Port Clement. His mind was a whirr of images. Marie's face in the elevator. Rudi spitting and struggling. Slick silent as a knife. The KRF in ruins!

Where was the getaway car he had expected? Where were Two-Salads and Stanley? Had they been taken too?

Robert's first priority was to put serious distance between himself and the Hotel Excelsior. He ran for what felt like miles. Finally he found his way through to a main street bustling with crowds, cars, horses and carts. It felt safer here. He walked, head low, heart pumping. Robert had no idea how to get from here to the Behind the Eyes Bookstore.

Then he spotted a street off to the left. He recognised it. The internal navigation system within him kicked in. He told himself to quieten his brain and feel the city, feel the direction of the sun, sense his place and the place he was trying to get to. He accelerated…he knew it was close to this area…he tried one square, then another. They all looked alike. The internal navigation system silently spoke again.

He looked to his left.

Something about the square through that alleyway. Something that said maybe. Just maybe. Something about the cobbles on the floor, the seagulls pecking, the ugly brown bench.

The sign that looked inward.

He ran to the door but it wouldn't open. A *Closed* sign hung on the window. Robert banged on the door.

"Herr Glimpf! Theodore! Constanza!"

The door opened just a touch and the face of Theodore Glimpf peeked through. When he saw Robert, he opened it a little more and Robert dashed in. Theodore closed the door fast behind him.

The old man was heartbroken. Constanza was packing. Coldness in her eyes.

"Betrayed! By Two-Salads! That skinny little creep! He told them everything!"

"Why?"

"Why do you think? For money! The coward! Just you

wait until I get my hands on him. Now Malstain's security will be five times what it was! We have no chance of getting close to him! He'll know the sale of the Book was a trap; he'll return to Brava and rip that library apart until he finds where your father hid it. Catastrophe! Catastrophe!"

Robert looked at the despairing old couple and made his decision.

"He won't find it." Robert spoke quietly.

"Quiet, boy! I'm thinking!"

"He won't find it, I tell you."

"Theodore, tell him to be quiet or I swear to God I cannot be held responsible…"

"Constanza, listen to the boy! He may have something to tell us."

Constanza turned, in a white rage. "This better be good, boy. This better be very damn good."

"I have the Book," said Robert.

Silence fell on the dusty bookshop.

"You what…?" Constanza stuttered. "Did you say…? You have the Book?"

"Yes. I should have told you before but I wasn't sure of you. My father told me to trust no one and you were so angry."

"You have it here? In Port Clement?"

"Yes."

Theodore and Constanza looked at each other. It was as if new hope had dawned on them.

"Oh, you brilliant boy." She rushed towards him and held him. "Oh, can you forgive me for being so mean to you when you are simply the most brilliant boy there has ever been?"

"Why do you have it, Robert?" Theodore said quietly.

"My sister and I helped our father steal it from the library," said Robert. "But then the soldiers came. My father was caught but we got away. He told us to give it to one person only. A man called Solomon."

"Solomon?"

"Yes. We were to meet him at nine o'clock the next day on the corner of Heine and Hopkins Streets. But we were late because of the police, and when we got there he was gone. So we kept it secret."

"You told no one?"

"No one at all."

Theodore turned.

"Then don't you see, Constanza? If we can get the Book, we can close the gate. Lock it for ever."

Constanza's eyes flamed. "My God, yes. Why didn't I think of it?"

"What gate? Everyone keeps talking about a gate and I want to know what it is!" Robert was firm. He was no longer a lost boy, but a young man demanding an answer.

Theodore looked to Constanza, who nodded.

"The Book of Stolen Dreams opens the gate to the land of the dead."

Robert stared, astonished. His brow furrowed. He remembered what Lucius said, about the King who'd commissioned the Book to bring his dead wife back.

"But it's only a book. How can it do that?"

"It's not just any book, Robert. It is a very special book, created for a special reason. To bring the dead back to life for ever. And it works."

"How do you know?"

"Because I have seen it with my own eyes!"

Robert looked at her in astonishment.

That was when they heard the car.

"What was that?"

They all listened. It was unmistakable. They looked out. Not one, not two, but seven black limousines were approaching the quiet square.

"Malstain."

"There's a back way."

They walked fast to the back of the shop and looked through a window.

Three more limousines were approaching up the alley. They were trapped.

"Robert. Go upstairs. Hide in the room you slept in."

"I want to stay with you! I want to protect you!"

"Robert! They don't know you're here. When we've gone with them, you must go to wherever you have the Book – don't tell us where it is. Get it, and return to Brava. If you need to, destroy it. Whatever you do, do not let

Walter Meyer get his hands on that book!"

Malstain's men were getting out of their cars now and approaching the shop.

"Go!"

Robert ran. He reached the stairs just as faces were peering in the shop window; he sprinted up the first flight as the glass of the shop door shattered. The door was forced open and in walked the giant figure of Rufus O'Hare.

After him came Johannes Slick.

And after him came Walter Meyer.

Robert stopped on the second flight of stairs. He turned and looked down though the staircase lined with books. He saw O'Hare grab Theodore Glimpf and push him hard into a broken old leather armchair. Slick had a gun in his hand, which he trained on Constanza. O'Hare had burn marks on his face and hands.

"Good afternoon, Aunt," said Walter calmly. "Good afternoon, Uncle. I did not know you were in the city. We could have had tea together."

Neither of them said a word.

"Search the place." It was Slick who took control now. Robert dived between piles of books under the second-floor staircase. He wriggled in, putting a few thrillers across the gap. He saw the boots of two Malstain bodyguards walk past. The sound of a brutal ransacking echoed through the apartment. Kitchen plates were hurled, tables upended, sofas cut into, cupboards opened, and clothes and crockery thrown about.

"That is our furniture, you pigs!" he heard Constanza cry out in rage.

There was a sharp noise and Constanza was quiet. The boots returned past Robert's hiding place. He held his breath as the last boot stopped for a second. A glove appeared, forced a gap in the books, someone seemed about to look in…

"Hurry! We don't have long." It was Slick's voice.

The glove disappeared. The boots descended back to the shop.

Robert stayed hidden but made a little opening to hear better. Slick was talking.

"A brutal attempt on the life of President Malstain was made earlier today at the Hotel Excelsior. What do you know about it?"

"Nothing." Theodore's reply was immediate.

"Liar." Slick's shoes walked smoothly across the floor. They had a different rhythm to the ordinary soldiers' – he almost glided.

Robert heard Constanza squeal in pain. "Don't hurt her!" Theodore cried out.

"Then tell me what I want to know. You sent a group from the Krasnian Resistance Front to the hotel to kill the President. That much is certain. What I want to know is your involvement in the sale of The Book of Stolen

Dreams that was supposed to happen this afternoon."

Silence in the bookshop.

"I would wager that the man who called Walter two weeks ago offering the Book at a discount price was you, Herr Glimpf. It was a trap, wasn't it? Designed to lure Walter and the President to Port Clement. Yes?"

Again a pause; again Constanza squealed in pain. Theodore could bear it no longer.

"Yes," he said.

"Tell them nothing, Theodore!" Constanza cried out.

"Why not tell them? They'll kill us anyway. Yes, we lured you here to kill the President. And I don't regret it. The man you work for is a monster. And a man who serves a monster, well, what is he?"

"Where is the Book?"

"I don't know."

"Where is it?"

"I don't know." Robert could almost hear Theodore smile.

"You'll come with us to the hotel. And we will encourage you to tell us what you know. Get them in the van."

Boots sounded on the floor. Through the gap, Robert saw the soldiers grab the old bookseller hard. But then Constanza spoke again. And this time it was to Walter Meyer, who was standing apart, smoking his customary cigarette.

"Walter, do you know what you have done? By telling Malstain about the Book, you have endangered a whole city, a country, maybe the world. And all for feelings of personal revenge. But it's not too late to change. Think again. Do not let Charles Malstain find the Book!"

"It is too late. I've made my choice." It was Walter who spoke. He seemed uninterested, bored almost.

"Then you're a fool!"

Walter turned away with just a hint of impatience. "Take them away. They're hurting my ears."

Constanza eyeballed him one last time as the black gloves grabbed her arms. "Beware the man who invites the devil into his house."

Walter's eyes flickered pale. "Get them out!"

Slick nodded. The soldiers went to push Constanza. And then something terrible happened.

Theodore Glimpf dived behind the counter and came up with a gun. The very same gun he had trained on Robert two days before. This time he fired it. O'Hare clutched his arm and howled in rage. Theodore made to shoot again but Robert only heard a barrage of bullets from the guns of Johannes Slick and his three guards.

Theodore fell, face up on the floor. And for a moment, as the blood trickled from his mouth, he looked above him and saw through a gap in the Joseph Conrad section, a boy's face staring at him.

And he smiled as the last breath came from him.

There was a stillness in the room. Constanza stared at her dead husband as if she had been shot herself. Walter shuffled. Slick gave orders.

"Get her in the car. Now!" He was furious. Like a man who hates a killing he hasn't carefully planned.

Constanza was grabbed and pushed out the door. She turned back and screamed at the top of her lungs: "You'll pay for this! Each and every one of you! He was worth fifty thousand of your miserable lives!"

O'Hare grabbed her mouth with his gloved hand; she bit it hard; he cried out in pain. The bodyguards bundled Constanza out of the shop and dragged her all the way to the car.

Slick turned to Walter Meyer.

"Your own family fooled you with their stupid offer."

Walter stood, very pale and still. "Well, they've paid for it," he said.

"And the Book?"

"It must still be in the library. Where that dull librarian hid it."

Robert's cheeks burned. Slick approached Walter.

"The President has weeks to live. The gate must be opened for him. We will return to Brava tomorrow and you will find the Book. Or you will meet the same fate as the old man."

Slick gently touched the dead body of Theodore Glimpf with his toe. Then he walked out. Walter Meyer paused a second. Looked at his dead uncle. Then raised his eyes towards the ceiling.

Robert held his breath. Was Walter looking up in Robert's direction, through the books?

Robert kept every muscle very still. Walter took a draw on his cigarette, flicked the ash from the end on to the wooden floorboards, then turned and strolled out of the door.

Robert waited for a few seconds.

He crawled out of his hiding place. He tiptoed slowly down the stairs. He reached halfway and saw the body of Theodore Glimpf staring up at him.

Then the phone on the counter rang. Robert jumped two feet in the air. He had to stop it ringing. He flew down the stairs, across the floor and lifted the receiver.

A voice on the line. Male. Old.

"Theodore? What happened? I hear terrible things on the news."

Robert knew the voice. It was Lucius Meyer.

"This isn't Theodore. This is Robert Klein."

"Robert? What are you doing there? What happened?!"

"We were betrayed. Everything has gone wrong. Marie and the others were caught. And Herr Glimpf...they..."

Robert found himself unable to say it...

"Is Theodore dead, Robert?"

"Yes."

"And my sister Constanza?"

"They've taken her."

"I see." Lucius sounded suddenly very tired, as if all hope had bled from him.

"Wait," said Robert. "I have something else to tell you. I have the Book. It's hidden here in the city, but I'm alone and I don't know what to do with it."

There was a pause on the line. Lucius's voice changed.

"You have the Book?"

"Yes."

"Are you at the bookstore now, Robert?"

"Yes."

"When you put the phone down, leave the store immediately! Have you told anyone where you are staying in the city?"

"No. No one."

"Good. Go back there and wait with the Book. Give me the address, please."

Robert did so. Grimaldi Street. Third floor. The special hiding place.

"I'm going to send someone to find you and help you. Just lay low. Everything will be all right."

"Yes, okay."

"Good luck, Robert."

Robert Klein hung up.

Then he turned to see a figure standing at the door.

It was Walter Meyer.

"I forgot my lighter." He smiled. "And who, pray, are you?"

15

George

Rachel and Laetitia lay low behind the front seats of the lice inspector's car. They were passing meadows and fields of cows. Wide rivers banked by marshland, flat and endless.

Rachel was right behind the lice inspector. She could see the black medical bag sitting on the rear seat. The lice inspector had turned on the radio and was whistling along to a patriotic tune. Interrupting the music of the military bands were regular news items referring to President Malstain's heroic defeat of the cowardly assassination plot in Port Clement. It was said the President had personally overcome thirteen assailants in a brutal fist fight and that he was in great health and looking forward to coming home across the ocean to his beloved people.

There was, the radio said, still no news of the unusually freckled boy.

The car drove on. Rachel and Laetitia had hoped that the lice inspector might stop for a toilet break or a cup of coffee and this would give them the opportunity to slip from the car and escape. But she drove for miles without pause. Rachel began to worry. Her leg was cramping and she saw that Laetitia, squashed behind the other seat, taller than Rachel and longer-limbed, was in significant pain.

Rachel needed a plan.

Another patriotic song came on the radio. The lice inspector knew this one well and sang out loud.

"Oh, green and great our land.
And blue and bright our sky…
Oh, President, President,
We love you till we die.
We love you till we die!"

The last line was belted out with a terrific force and then a second verse began. Rachel knew this was her chance.

"Oh, Krasnia, land of war
We fight with sword held high…"

Rachel reached up one hand and quietly opened the clasp of the lice inspector's bag.

"Oh, President. Oh, President…"

She reached inside and found what she was looking for.

"We love you till we die…"

She took out a brand-new bottle of toxic lice lotion.

"We love you…"

She unscrewed the lid.

"Till we…"

And in one quick movement Rachel leaped up behind the lice inspector and poured the entire bottle of chemical on her head.

There are screams and there are screams. The lice inspector screamed a scream the like of which Rachel had never heard. The lotion poured down her matted hair on to her face. There it mixed with eyeliner and rouge and combined with the bright pink lipstick into a foul-smelling glue. The lice inspector's eyes were streaming, she could barely see the road; the car swerved; the lice inspector tried to brake; the car skidded; the lice inspector howled as the chemical started to do its dreadful work on her tongue…and the car left the road and hurtled at some speed into a roadside ditch.

Fortunately the ditch was soft and marshy. The car plunged in, its wheels sinking into the dank and moist reeds.

The inspector was howling "Murder! Murder!" at the top of her voice. The radio still blared out with gusto and it looked for a moment to Rachel as if the tears streaming down the lice inspector's face were due to the sheer patriotic emotion of it all.

"We love you till we die!"

"Rachel!" It was Laetitia who awoke Rachel from her slight reverie. Together they forced open the rear door and tumbled out.

It was quiet in the marshy landscape, but they could hear a distant car approaching.

"Run!"

They ducked down and sprinted, their feet splashing through pools of stagnant water. Rachel turned back to see the lice inspector, still inside the car, stare at her with hatred and horror, her face like a child's painting that had gone horribly wrong. Behind her a car came closer, but as the road was higher than the site of the crash, it passed without noticing the black car half-sunk in the bog, with the radio playing and the lice inspector's face hot with rage, her make-up melting into her lap.

Rachel ran on, following Laetitia through the fields.

They walked for hours across wide open meadows and over small waterways. The flat marshland spread on all sides, with safety from detection only offered by sparse trees and the odd hawthorn hedgerow in late spring bloom.

Eventually they reached a local train station. They sat on a grey wooden bench until the train for Brava arrived. They got on without a ticket. They looked up and down the carriages, almost certain that one of Malstain's secret police would board any minute and demand their reason for travel and identification. But no one came.

They sat still and silent, their hair refusing to dry, their orphanage clogs mud-soaked from the marshland. It was a sleepy suburban carriage, mid-afternoon. A poor family of four were coming into the city, perhaps to work, perhaps to meet relatives. A single old lady read her newspaper and avoided looking at the two muddy girls. A young man with a bird in a cage slept. They reached Brava Central Station without a hiccup.

At the station they made sure to walk close to the family of four, to make it seem like they might be two of the sisters. They held their dark coats tight to their chests so that no one would see the orphanage smocks underneath. They walked proudly past the guards at the barrier and only when they were safely sitting in a square a few hundred yards from the station did they dare pause and speak.

"We did it. We did it!"

Laetitia seemed utterly emboldened by the escape. Rachel was caught between a deep relief that they hadn't been caught and an awareness that her journey was only just beginning.

They sat and discussed. Laetitia knew that Rachel wanted to get to Port Clement. For that she needed money. As for Laetitia, she wanted only to see her dear mother, who was, as far as she knew, still staying with Uncle Bruno and his family in the west of the city.

What had happened was this. Laetitia's father Mikel had, on leaving his doctor's surgery one evening, been greeted by an unmarked van waiting outside. Three men got out and, without explanation, forced Mikel into the back of the van and drove off. In the back of the van he was roughed up and told that he was a traitor to the state for suggesting that the President might not be cured of his current disease.

On arrival at a preliminary detention centre, he was struck off the medical register and told he would never see his family again. His two children Laetitia and Gustav were judged to be enemies of the state, as they were bound to have been influenced by his subversive mind. They were taken away from their horrified mother and placed at St Cecilia's Home for Forgotten Children until such time as they were "cleansed of his thinking".

Laetitia's mother was only given a reprieve for her own behaviour on condition she never saw her husband or children again and moved in with her brother Bruno, who, it so happened, was a high-ranking government official. Laetitia suspected that Uncle Bruno had "pulled strings" to avoid his sister being imprisoned also.

Uncle Bruno lived in the most comfortable area of town, in the west. It was where all Charles Malstain's cronies lived. It had tree-lined avenues and perfect gardens. No one from "the city" was supposed to go there. Laetitia knew the address. They decided to wait until dark.

Rachel was nervous. If Uncle Bruno really was a government official, surely he would immediately report them? And wouldn't the orphanage have called him to say Laetitia was missing? Laetitia was bullish on this point.

"Uncle Bruno adores me," she said with total confidence. "Even if they did call him, he would never betray me." Rachel was not wholly convinced, but what choice did she have? She had no home of her own to go to, no money. She had nothing. And she had to get to Robert.

They left at dusk and walked the whole way. They hadn't eaten for hours, but the terror of being picked up meant they barely noticed their empty stomachs. Occasionally a police van with lights flashing would turn a corner towards them. Rachel's instinct was to duck down but Laetitia said it was best to walk head held high, without shame, "like we own the place". Laetitia did this effortlessly. Rachel tried her best.

At a quarter to nine they turned into what Laetitia said was "almost certainly Uncle Bruno's road". Rachel thought "almost certainly" wasn't quite certain enough, but seconds later her friend jumped for joy and pointed.

"There! That's it! I recognise the cherry blossom! No one has cherry blossom like Uncle Bruno!"

It was number twenty-three. It was indeed a beautiful house, tall and white, set back from the road behind an old stone wall. The short driveway snaked up through fruit trees and exotic plants. But at the driveway's entrance was a security guard and a metal barrier.

Laetitia paused under a cypress as they observed the guard. "Stay here. Let me go first," she said quietly. "I think that's George Polder, in which case we're okay. He always bought me fruit chews without telling my parents."

She walked out from the shadow of the cypress tree and crossed the road with a confident swagger.

"George!" she cried out.

The guard turned in astonishment. "Miss Laetitia…?"

"I know, I know. You're thinking I should be at the orphanage? Well, guess what! They let me out for good behaviour. I was a perfect prisoner!"

Clearly George wasn't sure about that at all. He looked anxiously around.

Laetitia moved swiftly on: "Is my mother in?"

"Yes, she's talking to your uncle. They had a phone call an hour ago. I think it may have been about you."

At this, Laetitia's confidence slipped a little. "Oh yes?"

"Yes. And they're now with a member of the police force. He just arrived." George pointed up the driveway to a small black car by the front door.

Laetitia's face changed completely. She spoke in a hush. "All right, George. Listen to me very carefully. I am in the deepest and most terrible trouble. I need you to get me and my friend inside and upstairs. We have to stay undetected until the police have gone."

"Your friend?"

"Yes. My very dear friend."

Laetitia fixed him with her firmest look as a thin little girl walked out from under the cypress tree. George stared at her in horror. Her muddy coat. Her soaked shoes.

"George. Meet Rachel Klein."

DREAM 28

This Life is Stolen

We have met every night as I sleep
Darkness becomes day
And my room becomes the garden
Where the sun kisses the soil
But every morning you return
Through the gate
To your world of shadows
And I wake to mine
Is there no way through the gate for the living?
Or should the living become the dead?

16

The Petronellis

Rachel followed her friend and George around the side of the house.

They could hear voices in the living room and a woman in tears. From Laetitia's face, Rachel knew it was her mother crying. A man's voice was reassuring her.

"Francesca, listen to me. Laetitia has been very foolish, but they will find her and they will return her. The police have kindly agreed that she will receive no further punishment. She has clearly been led astray by this Klein girl. It's her the chief inspector wants to find. Laetitia has become involved with the wrong type, that's all."

Rachel tried to calm her heart as they reached the rear door to the house. George unlocked it and they entered a beautiful conservatory that looked out on to the immense and perfectly manicured back garden.

George shook his head at Laetitia as if to say, *The trouble you'll get me in*, then turned, slipped back through the door and locked it again. Quickly, his face etched with anxiety, he retraced his steps.

The two girls tiptoed through the house. They reached the hallway, at the foot of a large staircase, not far from the front door. Then they heard more conversation:

"Well, Mr Petronelli, I'll leave you. You hear anything from your niece, you call me. And if you speak to her, she's to give herself up immediately. This will be her very last chance."

"Quite understood, officer. Thank you for your understanding."

And the door to the hallway opened.

Laetitia turned. "Quick!"

In a flash Laetitia grabbed Rachel, opened a large door under the staircase, and dragged her inside. It turned out to be a coat cupboard, very spacious, reaching back behind the coats to a rear area where cardboard boxes of unwanted hats and umbrellas lay gathering dust in the dark.

They heard voices in the hall.

"And thank you so much for coming. We appreciate the discretion."

"Not at all. Government employees must help each other when they can. My coat, if you don't mind."

"Of course. Let me get it for you."

Rachel froze. The door opened and a tall, elegant man in his forties, his hair neatly combed, a thin moustache on his lip, lounge suit and shirt nicely pressed, stood before them and looked straight at them. He saw Laetitia first, then saw Rachel.

There was a pause that Rachel felt lasted the full length of time, from the ancient Egyptians to all imaginable futures.

Uncle Bruno cleared his throat. He nodded quietly. Then he very slowly took a dark coat from the rail, and quietly closed the door.

"Here you are, officer."

"Thank you. And my gloves?"

"Of course. I'll get them."

The door opened again. Uncle Bruno casually reached in for the gloves that were resting on a small shelf. Laetitia helpfully handed them to him. Their eyes met and the door closed once more.

"There you are, inspector."

"Thank you. Do call if you hear anything. Anything at all. That Klein girl is dangerous. There's people high up who want her found very badly."

"You have my word."

A front door closing had never sounded so beautiful. Then the sound of a car starting and drawing off down the road. Then silence in the hallway.

Rachel almost collapsed. Laetitia burst into tears.

The door opened and Uncle Bruno stood with Laetitia's mother beside him.

Laetitia's mother took one look and threw herself into the cupboard. She poured kisses on to her daughter – no mean feat, as Laetitia was surrounded by coats, scarves and all kinds of outdoor paraphernalia.

"Francesca, please. We need to talk!"

Uncle Bruno's voice was quiet and carried an authority. But Francesca was overwhelmed, by emotion, hats and wellington boots. She hugged Laetitia as if to let go might kill her.

"Oh, my darling, I'm so sorry! I'm so sorry. I should have tried to find you. I don't blame you for escaping, and I'll never let you go again!" she said. She was in floods.

"Francesca! Come out of that cupboard at once!"

Laetitia's mother calmed herself a little and they extracted themselves from the coats. Uncle Bruno insisted they went into the living room, as the hallway had windows opening on to the street. He ushered them into a huge room with enormous French windows. Uncle Bruno drew the curtains, sent the servants away, and they all sat down.

The girls swiftly explained how they had got to the city, into the house, and the heroic role played by the gate-man George. Laetitia insisted George be given a raise in his salary for what he had done. Rachel had no idea how Bruno would take any of this. This was a man who worked for Charles Malstain at a high level. Might he not turn them all in, including George? But Laetitia had no such doubts.

"And so you see, Uncle Bruno, we have to help Rachel get to Port Clement. Her brother is in terrible trouble there, and it's all the President's doing. Now I know you've had to work for nasty Charles Malstain to keep your lovely house and garden, and I know you're not a man who likes to cause trouble, but trouble this is! And we have a duty to help. A duty to Daddy, to Rachel and Robert, and a duty to Krasnia!"

This last bit was delivered in particularly patriotic style and it occurred to Rachel that a future on the stage beckoned for Laetitia, should they get through this. She could turn on the taps like nobody's business.

Rachel looked around the room. She couldn't help noticing the small metal tray of buns that lay on the sideboard. She suddenly felt inexpressibly hungry.

Laetitia's mother noticed and jumped up. "But my goodness, when did you last eat?"

"Breakfast," said Laetitia proudly. "And that was just a rotten bit of stale bread."

"But that's awful! Then you shall have a feast tonight while we work out what to do. I will make my best stew. We have pork sausage in the larder and all the spices!"

"Mother, there is no time. Though I will have a currant bun. Thank you. And one for Rachel. Actually, make that two each. Rachel has to get to Port Clement tonight!

Her brother has been involved in the most incredible assassination attempt."

At this, Bruno became suddenly alert. He studied Rachel's nose, her cheeks. His face seemed to fall.

"The boy with the freckles. He's your brother. Oh God."

Rachel nibbled her bun and said nothing.

Bruno slowly put his head in his hands. "Oh, Laetitia, what have you got us all involved in?"

"Revolution, Uncle, there's no two ways of putting it. And you are going to have to help, or hand me in. I would rather die than let those awful mean men take Rachel back to that deadly orphanage!"

Rachel looked at her new friend with a quiet pride. You will remember that children were not allowed to play in Brava, in the streets, or even at school beyond very simple sanctioned games. So friendship had not played a large role in Rachel's life. Family had been everything. But the very first deep, intense friendship in life is a uniquely beautiful thing. It seems, for the first time, that one other soul – picked by the fates at random, with no connection of blood – understands you totally. And would do anything to make you happy. Rachel had that feeling now. And it made her feel strangely wonderful, despite everything being far from safe in her world.

Bruno had turned pale.

Francesca looked at him. "Well, brother. I said it might

come to this. And to be honest, I regret ever heeding your advice. I should have gone to prison rather than let my children fester in that institution. I know you tried to arrange for Laetitia and Gustav to be released, but I don't believe they ever would have been. The President hates children with such passion."

Bruno sat in silence. It was as if his entire life had collapsed in front of him. His rugs, his beautiful tapestries, his garden, all of it looked completely hollow, like a set for a play that no longer had any actors.

"What do you need?" he asked.

"I need money," Rachel said quietly. "And I need a ticket on the first steamship to Port Clement. I must be there tomorrow."

"Then a steamship will be no good, it takes a week to cross the ocean," he said. "You'd best take one of the new airships. They're fast, they do it in eighteen hours."

Rachel nodded.

"I can arrange that." He spoke as quietly as she did. "Laetitia will stay here – we can keep her secret in the house, at least for a while. The truth is the President is very sick. He will die soon. And when he dies, things will change."

They ate with a ravenous hunger as Bruno booked the airship tickets. Rachel asked for a return ticket plus one for her brother. Bruno suggested buying blue single tickets, so that it looked like Rachel was emigrating. He offered her first-class, but she said she would rather have an ordinary second-class ticket. He agreed – it would be more believable and make her less likely to be detected. Bruno knew a friend who would get her false identification papers. Rachel Klein was wanted by the police, so she needed to be someone else.

Rachel was impressed by the calm efficiency of Laetitia's uncle. She tried to understand how a man so apparently good could work for a man so palpably bad.

Grown-ups are just strange, she thought. *Something happens to them. Perhaps it's to do with what mother used to call "the moral compass". Some lose it for a while. Some for ever.*

Bruno turned on the radio to hear the latest on the assassination attempt. The freckly boy was by all accounts still at large in the city of Port Clement. He was referred to as a conspirator and "highly dangerous". There was no further word about any of the assassins.

Then the state newscaster went on to "other news".

"Back in the beautiful city of Brava, everything is perfect. The weather is fine. People live their lives happily."

Francesca was about to turn the radio off. "It's the same news every night. Nothing is ever wrong in Brava," she sighed.

But then the announcer moved on to a new item:

"In sad news just in, renowned book illustrator Lucius Meyer died today of a tragic illness, in his shop in the old centre of the city. He had been ill for some time. Speaking as he left Port

Clement to return home, the President told State News that he mourned a great artist and a close personal friend."

Rachel sat bolt upright. Lucius Meyer dead? Of an illness? Lucius Meyer was old but he hadn't looked ill at all. And he was certainly no close friend of Charles Malstain.

Rachel sensed a truth being concealed, and that it all led back to The Book of Stolen Dreams.

"Uncle Bruno," she said, once everything was ready. "I need to go somewhere on the way to the airfield."

17

The Creak in the Stair

Uncle Bruno's car was the largest Rachel had ever been in. It had sleek runners along both sides, useful for getting into the car when you were Rachel's size. Inside, the seats were red leather and the panelling was, Bruno told her, walnut and brass. The steering wheel was a thing of beauty, shiny and silver, with little grips for Bruno's gloved hands. Rachel thought of her father, who had always loved cars but was never quite able to save up enough to buy one, partly because his pay was always being reduced by Charles Malstain, and partly because Felix had a slight addiction to buying rare editions of poetry.

Rachel looked at herself in the mirror. She had chosen the least glamorous clothes she could find in Laetitia's and Gustav's vast wardrobe. Laetitia's mother had kept everything for when her children returned, but most of the clothes were too colourful for Rachel's covert purposes. In the end she had chosen a pair of dark flannel trousers that belonged to Gustav, and Francesca had kindly sewn the hem up so they didn't overflow her feet. She had also chosen a red check shirt and grey jumper that Laetitia had worn when she was quite a bit younger. Laetitia had offered her many coats of different fashions, but Rachel had preferred to keep her own coat. It was simple and dark, would not give her away. And it reminded her who she was.

The biggest issue was the shoes. Rachel's feet were tiny. But she couldn't wear the orphanage clogs – they were a giveaway and caked in mud. She took a black leather school pair that Francesca had kept for sentimental reasons from when Laetitia was six. They were still too big, but once Rachel took off an unnecessary tassel and turned down the offer of a polish, they did the job. Finally she took one of Francesca's small but elegant travelling bags and Bruno put in a toothbrush, pyjamas and other useful items for travel.

Bruno drove smoothly. It seemed to Rachel he did everything smoothly. She asked him about his work. He told her that he worked for the transport division, ensuring trains and city trams ran on time – *Keeping the Nation Moving*, as the advertising billboards put it.

"Have you ever met Charles Malstain?" she asked.

"Only once," Bruno said. "At a party for a colleague of mine who was leaving. The President gave a short speech and then left through a side exit." According to Bruno, the President was not known for being sociable. He dined alone every night. His wife had not been seen for many years and there was a rumour that he had packed her off to a sanatorium because she'd said she wanted children. Charles Malstain did not want children.

"He has no interest in having an heir to his power," Bruno said. "It's unusual in a leader like him."

"In a tyrant, you mean," Rachel said calmly.

Bruno changed the subject. "Why do we need to stop at this Paradise Lane?"

"I left something with a friend there," Rachel lied. She noted how much better at lying she had become since all this had begun that day at the North Brava Public Lending Library.

Bruno stopped the car by the side of the road. He said he would accompany her, but Rachel said he would only get a parking ticket and that she preferred to go alone.

She got out, left the small travelling bag he had packed for her in the back seat, and entered Paradise Lane.

Rachel walked quickly down the narrow passageway. She remembered the shopfront vividly. The boards were still up. She rang at the door. No answer. She rang again and waited, but no one came.

Instead of retracing her steps, she continued to the

end of the passage, which led out on to a small square with a little fountain that must once have been rather pretty but no longer worked.

Rachel's memory kicked in. She remembered the back door of Meyer and Sons, through which she and Robert had escaped, covered in flour. It must be down a parallel street. She found the street and made her way back, looking at each of the rear doors as she went. Very few had any identifying signs. And the windows were too high in the wall for her to see in.

She searched her memory to recall the colour of the rear door, but unusually it refused to come back to her. Then she paused.

And then it came to her.

It was the lock! The lock that Robert had thrust the key into to keep their pursuers at bay. It had been carved in the shape of a bird.

In seconds she found it. It was a grey door. And there was the bird, right in front of her. It was a phoenix, rising from flames to be reborn.

Rachel thought about knocking, and then a moment of daring overcame her. She grabbed the handle of the door, turned it and walked straight in.

The kitchen was empty. No lights were on. Rachel muttered a "Hello" so quiet she barely heard it herself. She walked through into the rear study. There wasn't anyone there, only the clock ticking, the desk, the pictures of unicorns and queens, of forests filled with mystery and rivers of the brightest blue. The exotic bird with one eye.

Then she heard a creak above. A very quiet creak. Someone was there.

Rachel walked into the hallway and looked up the oak stairs. *Private. Artists Only.* She was worried the steps would make all sorts of noises when she went up them. But she was here now. Rachel took off Laetitia's shoes, left them at the bottom of the stairs, and climbed.

She took it slowly, step by step, testing every stair as she went. A corner-step halfway up proved treacherous but before it could cry out "Intruder!" she had nimbly taken her foot away and leaped past it to the next. Thus Rachel reached the landing. She breathed. Ahead of her were two doors, one in the right-hand wall, one straight ahead. Then the stairs continued up another flight.

Rachel tried both doors but they were locked. She looked up the next flight of stairs. She could just hear voices. She turned to climb, but there was another sign on the wall. It read:

Second Floor is Absolutely PRIVATE. Strictly NO ADMITTANCE to Visitors.

Rachel stopped for a moment but took strength from her mission. She must find out what had happened to

Lucius Meyer. She must help Robert. If she had to break rules to do so, so be it.

She climbed slowly. The walls were lined with more illustrations. They seemed to be as old as the house. She looked closer and realised they were plates from The Book of Stolen Dreams. Individual dreams were represented: one was a woman playing the harp, one a man in a walled garden, one a bird of prey hanging in the sky.

They were exquisitely beautiful. But there were no words.

Rachel reached the second and final landing. A small thin corridor. Again, two doors coming off it. It was even darker here, the air musty and full of mould. The floor was not polished. The walls were unpainted. It all felt as if from another time. It was colder too. Rachel shivered.

Then she heard talking coming from the room straight ahead.

"The army will be here soon." It was a male voice. Rachel thought maybe she recognised it. "They intend to search the house and take everything."

"But what about us? They'll find us!" said another voice, much older. This voice Rachel did not know.

An equally aged female voice joined in. "We'll have to hide! Or they'll know everything!"

More voices called out, high and strange. "What will happen to us? It's a disaster!"

"I don't know what to do. But someone needs to go to

Port Clement," replied the first man's voice. She recognised it for sure but couldn't place it. It was low and hoarse.

Rachel crept along the landing towards the door. Then suddenly an old floorboard gave way beneath her with a crack. It rang out like a gunshot.

"Who's that?!"

"Someone's there!"

"Catch them! Kill them! They might have heard!"

Cold fear gripped Rachel. She turned to flee, but there was no time to get back down the stairs; she slipped quickly through the side door and closed it behind her. Then she turned to see where she was, hoping for a window to climb out of.

And stopped dead.

The room she had entered was a working attic. It was filled with paints, paper, ink bottles, brushes and quills. It smelled of white spirit and damp.

In the corner of the room sat the old woman who had first let Robert and Rachel into the Meyer workshops, who had cried "Murder!" and chased after them with a kitchen knife. But now she was sitting still on a small chair, her eyes closed, either asleep or in such deep contemplation that she had not noticed Rachel enter.

In the middle of the room was a long worktable. It had scratches, daubs of turmeric paint dye and black ink, patches of oil. But it had been cleared in a hurry. And along the middle of the table stood a very long, rectangular wooden box. The box had no lid. Something was inside, but Rachel could not see from the door.

Rachel quietly approached the box. She stood on tiptoe and looked in.

She gasped.

Inside the box lay the body of Lucius Meyer.

He was dressed in the same clothes he'd worn when Rachel first met him in the downstairs office; his shoes were polished. He had coins on his eyes. And his mouth was open, showing pale yellow teeth.

He was dead.

Rachel shrank back in horror. The old woman started from her reverie; her eyes opened. She pointed and clutched her heart.

Rachel stifled a scream; for a moment she was sure she saw Lucius Meyer rise up from the coffin, shouting, "Murderess! Kill her!"

But it was only herself falling.

She saw blackness.

Then she heard voices. Hushed murmurs.

"Who is she?"

"A traitor!"

"No! She is the Klein girl."

"Wake her! Maybe she knows something!"

"Her father was a good man. Remember?"

Rachel looked up from the floor.

Above her were twenty faces staring back at her. People

who were mostly very old and dressed in all manner of strange clothes. The men had smocks and neckerchiefs and white beards, the women had plain skirts and blouses and coverings over their hair. Rachel recognised the faces. They were from the paintings in the hallway below. But those paintings were so old – how was it possible for these people to be standing here in front of her? Was she dreaming?

Then the door was hurled open behind her, and a figure burst through.

"Look who it is, Solomon," said a thin woman in the group. "It's the Klein girl. Now we'll need to tell her everything!"

Rachel stared up in terror.

For standing there above her, tall and skeletal, was the dark-haired man who had come to the apartment door that long-ago morning, enquiring after The Book of Stolen Dreams.

The man she knew as Barrabus Clinch.

DREAM 31

The Key

Many times I've thought myself a key
I enter the lock of the gate that divides us
I turn myself neatly to the left
I sense the metal give
I hear the wood creaking
And feel the cold as the gate swings open
Now I can see into the Hinterland
There you are
Why don't you welcome me in?

18

The Meyers

"We apologise for not telling you all this earlier. But Lucius didn't want to get you involved. He was worried you would be arrested like your father."

An old man was speaking. He was short, he had a long beard and wore a smock and black boots. Rachel was convinced she recognised him from a portrait that was hundreds of years old... She felt faint and feverish. What on earth was going on? Was it possible?

They were in the same upstairs workroom of Meyer and Sons. The dead illustrator lay cold in the coffin on the rough oak table. In the corner of the room, the old serving woman sat once again quiet and solemn, mourning her dead master. The group of staggeringly old men and women stood along the wall as Rachel sat on a small stool and drank a glass of water to steady her nerves.

"Who…who are you?" Rachel stammered.

They smiled sweetly.

"We are the Meyers," they said in unison and then they laughed lightly. The first man stepped forward again. "I am Benjamin Meyer. And these are my descendants."

If Rachel had been standing, she would have fallen over. Instead she gripped the stool.

"We have been living here in secret all this time!" they tittered.

"I don't understand," Rachel said. "Benjamin Meyer illustrated the Book. But the Book was made five hundred years ago…"

"Five hundred and sixteen," the old man said proudly. "It was my finest work."

This claim was contested by some of the other Meyers.

"So you're…" Rachel interrupted.

"Ghosts! Spirits! The Reborn!" they all cried out, and one old woman did a little jig.

Rachel felt dizzy. She was worried she might be sick.

"You know about the gate, my dear," said Benjamin. "The Hinterland. Your father showed you the Book. Perhaps you did not take it seriously?"

Rachel dropped her glass. It rolled on the floor but did not shatter. One old man leaned down and picked it up. Rachel remembered the feeling of heat, her mother walking, the ghosts of the dead… *This Book contains more secrets than you know…*

"Perhaps, Solomon, you should explain. The poor thing's terrified," said an old woman in a black dress and four petticoats.

Rachel turned. The tall figure of Barrabus Clinch was leaning against the door. His eyes were hollow with grief. He nodded and approached Rachel. And Rachel's mind flashed back to that cold morning in the family apartment, with her mother dead. The visitor at the door.

Rachel looked at the clock on the wall, aware Bruno was waiting in the car and might leave at any moment. But this was too important. It felt like this might be the key to everything.

"My name is Solomon Rose," explained the man previously known as Barrabus Clinch. And Rachel remembered her father's instruction in the basement of the lending library. *A man called Solomon will be there reading a newspaper and wearing a white flower in his lapel. Give the Book ONLY to him.*

"What you are about to hear is the biggest secret in all Krasnia," Solomon said. "I beg of you to tell no one."

Rachel nodded her agreement. The old men and women whispered "Good girl" in chorus, and Solomon continued.

"You remember that shortly after your mother's death I came to visit your family apartment. I used the false name Barrabus Clinch for my own and your safety. But you refused me entry and, besides, you were not alone."

The old men and women tittered slightly. "She refused him entry! Ha!"

Solomon glared at them and went on.

"I came back later to try to explain who I was. But by the time I did, you'd already left with your brother. I tried to find you here at Meyer's offices, but you slipped away. Then your brother Robert disappeared and you were sent to the orphanage. I missed my chance."

Solomon sighed.

"Not your fault, Solomon," said Benjamin Meyer. "We all wanted to keep the secret."

"Tell her the whole story, Solomon," said an old woman who held Benjamin's hand tightly.

"Yes, tell her!" they all echoed.

Solomon nodded. "The tragedy you find yourself involved in is at its heart the tragedy of a family. A family with a secret kept for centuries. The secret of the Hinterland. It is also the battle between a father and a son – Lucius and Walter Meyer."

The group of men and women nodded sagely.

"First I must tell you about myself," Solomon continued. "I am the son of immigrant labourers. We lived on the outskirts of Brava. My father tilled the Emperor's fields, my mother washed the linen of wealthy households. My life looked destined to be the same as theirs – hard work and little reward.

"Then one day, when I was eight years old, my mother found me stealing the coloured chalk that she used to mark the washing of different households. She was about to tell me off when she saw the drawing I had made on the back of a wooden box. It was of her, as she washed the clothes on the banks of the river, her back bent, her face creased by the sun.

"'Did you do this?' she asked me.

"I nodded. She looked at the drawing, then reached out and clasped me close, like she was holding something precious.

"My mother was a clever woman. The next day she used the wooden box to deliver clothes to the households in the centre of the city. She happened to let the box drop within the eyesight of one particular household – this one here. The house of the great artist and illustrator Lucius Meyer."

The old men and women made a "hmmm" and "haw" sound which was meant to be encouraging. Solomon continued.

"Lucius saw the drawing and picked the box up. According to my mother, he stared at it for a long time. Then he enquired in a calm voice, as if nothing at all strange had happened, as to who had done the drawing.

"'My son Solomon. He's only eight,' my mother said proudly and she made to take the box back. But Lucius held it firm.

"'May I take it for a day?' he asked.

"My mother knew then she had him hooked."

"She did!" agreed the chorus of ghostly old men and women. "Lucius showed it to all of us."

"Quiet! Go on, Solomon," urged Benjamin Meyer.

"Lucius arranged that I should go to the finest school in the city, where he sent his own son Walter. Walter and I were the same age. We had art classes together. I loved Walter – he was funny and rather free-spirited. And he was a Meyer! The most famous family of artists in Krasnia!"

The old men and women looked serious now. Rachel felt the temperature in the room drop.

"We spent more and more time together," Solomon continued. "Of course we were the top two pupils in the school. The only problem was that I was always first and Walter was always second. Walter had always assumed that as the son of a great artist, he would be the best. But life is not so simple."

Solomon paused as if what he was about to say would hurt him deeply.

"Go on, boy," said one of the old men seriously, "she needs to know."

They all nodded their agreement.

Solomon turned again to Rachel. "It was as we approached the end of our schooling that Walter changed. He started to get angry at his schoolteachers, at his friends, even at me, his closest friend. He missed lessons. He seemed unlikely to finish his final exams.

"I got him through it. I helped him revise. I even cheated in one art exam on his behalf, slipping him an answer about Roman frescoes. I'm not proud of that, Rachel, but he was a friend and in need."

Benjamin Meyer shook his head.

"Shame!" cried out an old man with a pipe.

"After we finished school," Solomon said, "we both started working here in the workshops of Meyer and Sons. I was the only non-Meyer allowed in. An immigrant's son in the greatest artist's studio in the city! I was in heaven! Surrounded by paint dyes, carmine and gold and ochre, and the best paper man can buy, with great artists to learn from! Only one thing confused me. Neither Walter nor I were allowed up to the top floor. Every now and then I heard voices and footsteps, but Lucius would not tell me who they belonged to. And when I asked Walter, he said that I would never be allowed up, but that one day he would."

"Arrogant boy!" cried out an old woman in a bodice crossly, but Benjamin said, "Hush, Mathilda, be quiet!"

"Walter was increasingly distracted," Solomon continued. "He was often late into the shop and early out. His breath smelled of beer. And still he had not been invited to the top floor. I could feel him losing his grip on life, like a young man who has climbed a wooden ladder above a fire."

The old men and women muttered their agreement. The Meyer with the pipe shook his head silently.

"Inside Walter there began to burn an anger and a shame that he did not fully understand. One day it broke. He failed to come to work. He had got drunk in a city bar and ended up in a fight.

"It was a terrible scandal. Lucius was shaken. Within a year they were barely talking to each other. Walter stopped coming to work at all. I knew Lucius was beginning to have doubts about whether his son was in any fit state to take over Meyer and Sons when he should retire.

"I remember Lucius looking across at me as I worked each day. There was a sadness in his eyes – a sadness that I was not Walter, and Walter was not I.

"And then one evening, just over a year ago now, Lucius came over to my desk. 'Come with me, Solomon,' he said. And as I followed him, he led me up the stairs to the top floor. To this very room."

"That's when you met us," chirruped a woman in a white apron and very strange red shoes.

They all smiled and nodded.

Rachel was beginning to understand now. She checked the clock. She had just over an hour to get to the airfield. But she sensed that what Solomon was about to tell her was the centre of everything. She had to hear it.

"In this room, Lucius told me about The Book of Stolen Dreams."

"He told us too," Rachel said quietly. "The old King Ludovic. He commissioned the Book to open the gates of the dead."

The Meyers all nodded and made "yes" noises. Solomon raised his hand. The room fell silent.

"But he didn't tell you that the Meyer family have been using it ever since."

Rachel felt her skin tingle. She looked at the strange chorus. "You've come back from the Hinterland," she said. "From the land of the dead."

They all nodded like little ghostly puppets. "Clever girl," said a whiskered one. "She understands."

Benjamin Meyer walked forward. "I must take the blame, Rachel. When I made the Book for King Ludovic to bring back his queen, I realised the power of what I had created. The King soon regretted his decision, his wife and he quickly got bored of each other and three months later she asked to return to the dead. But I knew by then that the Book worked. And when my wife Rosica died, I used it to bring her back so we could be together again."

The old woman next to him smiled sweetly. She held Benjamin's hand. "And we've been happy ever since," she said. "Four hundred and eighty years!"

"So our secret began," Benjamin continued. "Every generation of the Meyers has called its loved ones back from the dead, using The Book of Stolen Dreams. Lovers. Children. Grandchildren. Great-grandchildren. Twenty generations of Meyers!" They all smiled. It was like looking at a living family tree.

"We have strict rules. We keep it only to family. We never leave the house," Benjamin continued. "We trust each other to stay secret, to work here quietly on the top floor of the shop, drawing and painting, and to tell no one. Because we all know how dangerous our secret could be in the wrong hands. You see, Rachel, we will never die. And that is not a secret to share with everyone."

Rachel felt a strange fear at these words. *Not a secret to share with everyone.*

Benjamin looked with a deep intensity across at Solomon, who took up the story again.

"The next day Lucius took me to the North Brava Lending Library. To the Rare Books section. He told me he no longer trusted Walter, his own son, and so instead he was telling me the secret. I knew then that I was being chosen to continue the line instead of Walter.

"I remember the feeling, Rachel, the feeling of being chosen, of being special. But I also felt I was betraying my best friend, and so I was terribly confused. Do you understand that?"

Rachel nodded. "I do."

"Lucius showed me the Book and then pointed out one thing I had not noticed before. There are only forty-nine dreams. Why forty-nine, he asked?"

Rachel looked into Solomon's haunted eyes and felt a

quiet inner glimmer of understanding. Her mind went back to the Book, the page that was torn out, the pensive expression on Robert's face.

She spoke quietly. "The Book has a missing page."

He smiled. "And Lucius told me why. He said the Meyer family were always concerned someone would discover their secret and abuse it for their own power. So they created an insurance policy. The Book itself was public property and must stay in the library. But they tore out one page of the Book. The very last dream, Rachel. To complete the words that you must say for the gate to open. They kept it hidden in this very room."

Rachel looked around. She saw a little black safe in the corner of the room.

Solomon smiled. "Lucius said that he would give me and only me the passcode to that safe. And he told me it that very evening. 2469. Try it."

Rachel got up and walked to the safe. She opened it. It was empty. She looked around. The old men and women looked very grave indeed.

"There's nothing here."

"That's because someone stole it."

Rachel began to piece everything together. "Walter."

"Yes. You see just as Lucius told me the passcode to the safe, we heard a noise outside the Rare Books Room. The door handle turned and Walter entered. He stared at his father with a terrible rage. He had followed us! He had been listening all that time outside the door. What neither of us knew was how much Walter had heard.

"Soon we got our answer.

"The next morning this office was found ransacked. Papers were thrown everywhere. The safe was open and empty. And Walter had disappeared. With the missing page."

Rachel didn't move. The old men and women turned almost transparent in anger and disappointment. "Call himself a Meyer?! The boy's a traitor!"

Solomon spoke quickly now, as if aware time was not on their side. "At that moment I knew that Walter must not get his hands on The Book of Stolen Dreams. If he had the Book and the missing page, why, he could read the whole Book aloud, and open the gates for ever and for anyone! He could, for example, open the gates for Charles Malstain."

Rachel's heart froze. This all confirmed her worst fears. Malstain's illness. His desperate desire to get his hands on the Book.

Solomon looked grave. The old men and women hissed. "Shame! Villainy! The rascal!"

"I searched for Walter in the city. I found him easily enough – I knew his favourite haunts. He was sitting in the corner booth of an old tavern in the east of the city. His face was like death.

"I begged him to return the missing page and reconcile with his father. He refused. I tried everything. I threatened,

I cajoled. When you are older, Rachel, you will recognise the look that someone has when they are about to destroy everything they love. Well, Walter had that look in his eyes that night. In his mind I had deliberately replaced him in his father's affections. He leaned into me and said something I will never forget:

"'I am going to sell what I have to the devil.'

"And Walter laughed at me. Well, I knew exactly who he meant. He was going to sell the Book to the most powerful man in Krasnia – *to cure him*."

The old men and women wailed.

"We all knew Malstain was ill and dying. He was trying every remedy available to man, but none of them had worked. He was hiring and firing a doctor every week. But if he could open the gates between life and death, what would he pay for that?"

Solomon was grabbing breaths as he spoke. His eyes were ablaze.

"I begged Walter to rethink, but he said it was too late. He told me that Johannes Slick, the President's Head of Secrecy and Communications, was coming to the tavern that very night. Walter warned me with deadly seriousness that if I valued my life, I should leave now and pretend I had never found him."

Solomon wheezed for a moment, and Rachel wondered if he might be sick, or whether it was just fear and sorrow getting to him.

The old man with the pipe leaned forward. "Finish the story. She must know everything!"

Solomon looked up at Rachel. "To my great shame I did as Walter asked. I went home. The next day the announcement came that The Book of Stolen Dreams was officially listed as a dangerous book and would be taken from the library and destroyed. I knew what that really meant. Charles Malstain was going to take the Book for himself and open the gate. Not for a lost love to return, a parent or a child, no. For himself. *So he could become immortal.*"

Solomon paused, his eyes cast down to the table where Lucius Meyer lay.

"And if he can become immortal, he can rule Krasnia *for ever.*"

The men and women moaned a chorus of "No! It cannot be!"

Solomon raised his hand. His forehead was sweating. There was a deadly silence in the room.

It was Rachel who spoke next. "So you asked my father to steal the Book. It was you."

"I called your father at the library. We had become acquaintances during my visits there. I told him he had to steal the Book that very day and smuggle it out."

Rachel looked into his sorrowful eyes. The sadder they were, the hotter and more angry she felt.

"I am so sorry, Rachel, that I ever got you and your family involved in this."

"You had no choice. If rotten Charles Malstain gets the Book and has the missing page…" She couldn't finish her sentence. The anger was choking her. Anger at Malstain, at Walter, at what they'd done to her father…

Then Benjamin Meyer spoke. His five-hundred-year-old eyes bore into Rachel's.

"Rachel, listen to me. There is one thing that Walter does not know. There is a way to lock the gates for ever. I wrote it into the Book. No one will ever be able to cross over any more. But we need the whole Book, missing page and all. We have to have the Book!"

Rachel felt the silence of the room. The clock said half past five now. She had to leave.

"Mr Meyer. Solomon. Do you trust me?"

"Yes of course!" said Benjamin.

Solomon nodded.

"Of course we do! Of course we do!" echoed the room.

"Then I am going to leave now. And when I return, it will be with the Book. Missing page and all."

The men and women leaped with joy at the promise. "Wonderful girl! What courage! That's the stuff!" they cried out. "Someone give her a medal!" "Not yet! She hasn't done it yet!"

Solomon hushed them and fixed her with a feverish look. "If you can do that, you will be saving your country."

Rachel looked out into the cool night air. A new determination was filling her. "I must go."

"Let her through!" cried Benjamin Meyer. "No time to waste!"

The generations of Meyers parted like a ghostly sea as Solomon helped Rachel down the stairs.

"Goodbye and good luck!" she heard them cry from their hiding place on the top floor. "The future of Krasnia depends…"

Solomon and Rachel crossed the hallway and he opened the front door.

"Good luck, Rachel. I will bury Lucius Meyer. He was a great man and deserves a decent funeral. They interrogated him but he told them nothing."

Rachel nodded. She shook his hand.

Solomon looked around cautiously and took a piece of paper from his pocket.

"When I found Lucius dying in his office, he had this in his hand. He couldn't speak. Do you understand it?"

Rachel read the message.

> *CG gone. TG dead.*
> *KRF broken.*
> *Only RK.*
> *He has hidden the BSD.*

And then a strange word.

IDLAMIRG 342. 3rd.

19
Spotted

When Rachel returned to the car, Bruno Petronelli did not ask her where she had been or why she had taken so long. She wondered if this was to protect her or himself, but she was relieved. Rachel was in a state of shock. What strange things she had seen and heard on the second floor of Meyer and Sons. A family of ghosts? A door to the dead? A Book that, if wrongly used, could allow a tyrant to rule Krasnia for ever? But if rightly used could bring her mother back to life?

Bruno drove without speaking a word, without seeming to hurry, and in such a way that would not draw attention. A light drizzle had started up and he quietly turned on the windscreen wipers. They made an elegant rhythmic swish as the car purred down the road towards the airfield. Rachel sat back and allowed herself to breathe.

She admired this neutral quality of Bruno's. He was like a windscreen wiper himself, she thought. Doing his job with efficiency and style. Rachel wasn't sure she would ever possess this coolness. It wasn't in her veins. She was too beset by worries and guilt. And perhaps being like Bruno had its drawbacks. Perhaps it was one reason why you could work for the devil and not seem to mind. A windscreen wiper does not ask who is driving the car.

As Bruno changed gear with a smooth tan-gloved hand, Rachel felt the piece of paper Solomon had given her in her coat pocket. She hadn't had time to consider fully what it meant. But surely the RK must refer to her brother? And the BSD to The Book of Stolen Dreams? Then had Robert told Lucius he had the Book? And if so, how? Either way, it was vital that if the airship security searched her as she boarded, they did not find the paper.

Rachel reached down, pretended to itch her ankle, and slipped the paper into her left sock. It fitted nicely. If Bruno noticed, he didn't say. But then, of course, he wouldn't.

As they approached the airfield, Rachel saw the vast form of the *Pegasus* waiting on the grey horizon. Large crowds were gathering. Bruno turned on the radio. The news was on. President Malstain had just confirmed that in light of the attempt on his life in Port Clement, he was closing all Krasnian borders in two days' time. Rachel sensed that was why the airfield was packed with last-minute travellers, people desperate to get out and join family or friends abroad.

"Rachel." Bruno spoke at last. "There will be secret police watching every passenger. Keep your head up, never look like you're hiding. Your identification papers will get you past almost any standard customs officer. Just act—"

"Like I own the place." She finished his sentence for him.

"Yes, exactly." He smiled and stopped the car a few hundred yards from the entrance. "You'll forgive me if I don't take you the whole way."

She nodded. "Thank you, Bruno. I am sorry to have involved you in my troubles."

"Rachel, let me tell you something," he said thoughtfully. "I am by nature conservative. Do you know what that means?"

"You like things as they are?"

"I don't trust radical change. It almost always ends worse than it started. I trust in time. President Malstain is a bad man. He is a cancer in our country's blood. But he will die. That much we know."

"Maybe we do. Maybe we don't." She looked at him steadily.

"What do you mean? Everyone dies, my dear."

"When it comes to a person like Charles Malstain, nothing is guaranteed."

She said no more but Bruno sensed a hidden knowledge.

"You are a strange child. You have secrets."

"But you don't want to know them. Please give Laetitia a hug from me. She is a true friend."

"I know she feels the same."

Rachel grabbed the elegant travelling bag and got out of the car. Bruno performed a neat three-point turn and drove back the way he'd come. Rachel saw a tan-gloved hand wave a brief farewell through the rear windscreen.

Then he was gone.

Rachel joined the crowds queuing to board. The light drizzle was developing into a rain. The sky was low. She felt safe in numbers; she was smaller than most of the travellers and could barely be seen amidst the chaos of suitcases, hats and umbrellas. Laetitia might hold her head high, but Rachel felt safer at low level.

She heard music and saw a distant figure sitting on the pavement, playing his violin for money. He had a strange hat, but she couldn't see his face. The occasional coin fell in his violin case that lay open in front of him.

Rachel's gaze scanned the crowds, then the vast ship itself. Once intended for the most glamorous of journeys, it now was an escape craft for a twelve-year-old girl trying to save her brother, her father and her country. If only it knew. If only it could help her get aboard undetected.

Rachel took a small woollen hat from her coat pocket and put it on. She chose the shortest queue and stood in line. Slowly the queue moved forward. People seemed anxious, as if afraid the ship would suddenly be declared full and they would be turned away. Rachel looked around and caught the eye of a little boy, maybe four years old. He was eating a small doughnut and had jam on his nose.

Then Rachel's eyes alighted for a moment on three figures standing slightly apart; one was female, tall and elegant, with a folder in her hand. Rachel knew the woman's face. And it filled her with cold dread.

It was the orphanage director.

The director was standing with two police officers by the side of the queuing travellers. They had black umbrellas up to protect them from the rain. And they were examining the crowd. The director's face was lined with anger. She was a woman who knew she had "let the side down" and was determined to make up for her mistake.

Rachel breathed deep. No question – they were looking for her, trying to stop her from reaching her brother.

It was at this moment that she remembered Bruno's clear instructions. Head high. Own the place. But however hard she tried, Rachel couldn't do it. Her head kept bowing, dropping back to the safety of the ground. In terror she approached the turnstile and the waiting ticket collectors.

The violin player continued to play his folk rhythms. The orphanage director watched. The ticket collectors barked instructions: "Tickets out! First class to the left! All second class to turnstiles one to five! Single file! Hats off!"

Rachel approached. She was leaving it to the last minute to take off her hat.

Then suddenly a kerfuffle broke out at gate five, to her left. A couple were trying to smuggle a third small person on to the ship and had been caught hiding him under a coat. It was the little boy with the doughnut and he was screaming, "Mummy!"

"Get back!" shouted the customs officials. Police whistles sounded. Rachel seized the moment. She took her hat off, held her head as high as she ever had, and called out to her ticket collector, "Isabella von Gurning." She handed over the false identification papers and fixed the official with an imperious gaze.

"Reason for travel?"

"Emigration to join my family the von Gurnings in their Port Clement residence."

A pause. He looked her hard in the eye. "Travelling alone?"

"Yes. I was at finishing school here in Brava but due to the recent presidential decree, wish to return to the bosom of my family."

Another pause. He perused the papers. "All in order. Rudolf, let her through."

Rudolf was a young man of thickset appearance, whose job was to buzz the gate open on instruction. This he duly did. Rachel marched through and strode towards the ship. The rain was falling fast now.

"Don't look back," she murmured to herself. "Don't look back."

But doubt is a hungry little weasel. With every step towards the *Pegasus*, it gnawed at Rachel's anxious imagination. Shouldn't she look back and check, just to make sure, just to be absolutely sure they hadn't seen her?

She heard Uncle Bruno and Laetitia in unison saying: *No! Head high! Don't look back! Own the place!*

Rachel looked back.

For a moment all seemed fine. She saw only the huge crowd and the rain and the odd little violin player offering another tune.

But then the orphanage director turned her head in Rachel's direction.

Their eyes met for the briefest moment.

Rachel turned back fast. She lowered her head and hurried into the bowels of the airship *Pegasus* as fast as her legs could carry her.

Back by the emigration turnstiles, the elegant orphanage director paused under her umbrella. She gazed at the airship for a moment, at the little figure scurrying across the gangway. She spoke to the man next to her. Together they discussed the best course of action.

Then the orphanage director walked through the crowd of screaming women, bustling men and crying children, to where the violin-playing busker sat with his strange bird-shaped hat.

The violin stopped in the rain-spattered wind, as the orphanage director explained very clearly to Josef Centurion what she wanted him to do.

END OF
BOOK ONE

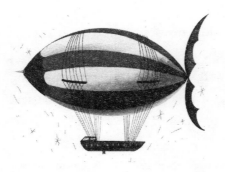

20

The Childhood of
Josef Centurion

Rachel woke just before dawn on the deck of the airship *Pegasus* to find the strange man with the penguin-shaped hat looking at her.

"My, Isabella, you slept well! We need to get you breakfast – we'll be there in an hour." Josef Centurion smiled. The air above the clouds was clean and fresh. The *Pegasus* was making good progress across the brightening skies.

Rachel shook herself awake. Quietly, quickly she reached down to her left sock, pretending to itch her ankle. Yes, the paper was still there. A small wave of relief went through her.

Most of the other passengers were still sleeping, huddled under blankets, families clinging to each other for warmth. Josef stretched his little arms, shook himself awake, and suddenly bounced to his knees and did twenty press-ups.

Rachel watched and couldn't help giggling.

"Every morning for twenty years!" he said proudly as he put back on his bird-shaped hat. "The secret to eternal youth."

Rachel smiled. She didn't say what she was thinking – that Josef really didn't look eternally youthful at all. Instead she jumped down herself and did ten press-ups, keeping her knees on the ground as she was told young people were allowed to do.

Josef watched and nodded sagely, as if he was training an Olympic athlete. "Good, my dear Isabella, but keep the back rigid. We'll do more later."

"Tell me more about your sister Lotte, Josef," Rachel asked casually as they sat eating bagels for breakfast.

Josef paused for a moment. "But I told you about her last night. An absolute angel. What more do you want to know?"

"Where is she now?"

Josef's face seemed to fall for a moment. "Ah. The truth is I don't know."

"You don't know?"

"No. We...mislaid each other. Many years ago."

"Mislaid? But how? How could you lose someone you love so much?" Rachel thought of Robert and how painful even a few weeks apart had been.

A cloud passed over Josef's face. Not a real one, but Rachel felt the temperature plummet in Josef's heart. "No one has ever asked me that before."

"Why not?"

"Because they didn't want to know, I suppose." He smiled sadly. It was the smile you offer when you know you have lost something and there is no hope of getting it back.

"I want to know." Rachel gave him one of her direct gazes.

He breathed deep.

"It was all because of Charles Malstain." Josef looked around the airship's deck, as if checking for people watching. Rachel's heart clenched. Was Malstain at the centre of his story too?

Josef spoke quietly, half into his bagel. "I told you my family lived in the countryside in the East. It really was a wonderful childhood. But then everything changed one spring day.

"I returned home to find soldiers at the house. They said they suspected my father of thievery. They searched every room and found money, jewels, a lady's hat, a wristwatch, two bottles of vintage wine, several cravats and a stuffed penguin. My father made no attempt to defend himself. Ha! Such a rogue! He even invited the soldiers in for tea before they took him away. We had cake and sang hearty songs while my father packed a small bag for prison. It was a lovely farewell.

"We were left in the care of my uncle Leonard, my father's brother. A very different proposition, Isabella my dear. He claimed to be an inventor, but he never invented anything. What he really was, was a close personal friend of the local landowner and governor of the region – a man called Charles Malstain."

Rachel gasped.

"Ah yes, my dear. The very same. Malstain put Leonard in charge of our house. Within weeks Leonard sent my mother to a local sanatorium, claiming she was unwell. We were alone, Lotte and I, with this terrible man. And we had to do everything he told us.

"Even then Charles Malstain hated children. He hated the sound of their laughter. He started to create local laws. Children were forced to work all day and stay inside their own homes after dark. We could not meet any other children, could not swim in the river, could not walk free in the fields.

"My uncle Leonard ruled our house like a mini-Malstain. He drank all day – cider in the daylight and brandy in the dark. He sat in the kitchen, drawing in his leather-bound book, pretending to be inventing a wingless aeroplane. But when he fell asleep, Lotte and I sneaked a secret look at what he had drawn. And you know what? The page was empty – but for a few words scrawled in one corner.

"I hate Josef. He is a devil that stops me working. I must deal with him once and for all.

"We were terrified. Lotte said I should run away but I wanted to stay with her. You can imagine – my father in prison, my mother locked in the sanatorium 'for her health' with no visitors allowed! Lotte was all I had left. I clung to her as to a lifeboat. I said that if I was to run away, she was coming with me.

"We began to plan our escape together.

"My first plan was to poison Uncle Leonard's brandy but Lotte said that although she hated Leonard to the bottom of her heart, she could not kill another human being. So we decided instead to introduce a sleeping potion into his night-time drink, strong enough to make him sleep but not enough to kill him. Then we would leave the house, jump on to one of the express trains that came through our village at night, and by the time he woke we would be far away.

"Everything went to plan. We sneaked off from the cottage one day, took the back roads to the apothecary's and asked him for a sleeping draught, claiming that Lotte was suffering from a sore tooth. The apothecary dispensed a strong potion and told Lotte to take one teaspoon before bed and no more.

"We went home and while Leonard was busy 'inventing', we slipped seven teaspoons of potion into his bottle of brandy.

"That night Leonard started drinking early. We waited for the potion to take effect.

"But then, as he drank, there came into Leonard's head a particularly twisted idea, one that spelled disaster to our plan.

"He offered us both a drink.

"He had never done this before, my dear Isabella! Never in Leonard's life had he even once dreamed of wasting his precious brandy on two such reprehensible villains as his nephew and niece. But tonight, of all nights, the idea tickled him.

"'Have a drink with me, children,' he said with a smile.

"I believe the impulse behind it was to make me become tipsy so that I might knock over something precious, a glass perhaps, and thus justify him 'dealing with me once and for all'.

"Quietly Leonard placed two small glasses on the table and poured brandy into them to the brim. Then he raised his own glass.

"'A toast! To you both!'

"And then he commanded us to drink.

"We tried to protest that we were only children, that he shouldn't waste such valuable liquor on us, we wouldn't appreciate it, but he was not to be dissuaded.

"'Drink!'

"He grabbed Lotte hard, forced her mouth open and poured the liquid down her throat.

"I stood speechless. What could I say, my dear? Then

Leonard turned to me. He approached me with my glass, his smile beaming.

"'Open your mouth, boy.'

"His teeth glowed yellow in the candlelight; I could see the decay as his tongue licked his livery lips.

"'Open your mouth!'

"I kept my mouth clamped shut. He went to force the liquid down my throat.

"But then, before he could do anything, Lotte grabbed my glass from his hand and, in one gulp, drank it too!

"I looked at her in horror. What had she done? She had deliberately damned herself! But she kept a steady eye on me as if to say: *Don't worry, Josef. Everything will be all right*.

"Then suddenly her bright blue eyes rolled up in her head, her knees buckled, and she passed out on the floor. She lay there quietly breathing.

"Leonard cursed her and tried to revive her from her deep sleep, but she was too far gone. He hurled the glass at the wall in fury; it smashed into a thousand pieces. He roared like a wounded beast.

"'Children of the devil!'

"Then he turned his eye upon me and grabbed the stick from the wall.

"'Well, boy, you will take the punishment for her impudence. Given you love her so much, I suppose that won't be hard for you. Eh, my boy?'"

"I refused to cry, refused to lower my gaze, I felt a bravery, my dear, that I had never felt before.

"Leonard downed another glass of brandy, then approached me. I held out my hand. He raised his cane. I closed my eyes…waited for the flash of agony…

"And felt nothing.

"I heard only a swish of air pass my ear, and then the crash of a great weight falling. The smash of china, the tinkle of glass.

"I looked up. I saw that Uncle Leonard had passed out, mid-blow, on to his work desk. He had knocked over the inkwell, had hurled ink across his empty pages, had smashed the brandy bottle, and had fallen amongst the shards of glass, where he lay, his arm bleeding, his mind dead to the world.

"But not dead. His nostrils flared as he lay there, brandy-breath hissing from his lips like steam off an exhausted horse.

"I moved fast. I dashed to Lotte. I tried to wake her, but she was deeply asleep. I tried to lift her, but cursed my weak arms!

"All I could do was drag her to the kitchen, where the rusty bucket was kept for water which we fetched from the well. The bucket was empty. I ran with it to the well, filled it as deep as I could carry, dragged it back into the kitchen of the cottage, and, with a slight apology to my sleeping sister, poured its freezing contents all over her.

"She woke, spluttering.

"I cried for joy. I grabbed her soaked body; I told her we had to run now!

"She staggered up, woozy, unbalanced. I held her tight and carried her to the cart.

"Oh, how I wished Ludwig the faithful ass had been there! But he was long sold and I had no choice now but to pull the cart myself. I strained every sinew and eventually – yes eventually! – the cart moved. I started to run, pulling Lotte behind me. Perhaps one day you will know this feeling, when fear pours through your blood like petrol and makes you do things that seem impossible! I pulled, my dear, I dragged the old cart through the darkness of the night. I knew where I was going, I was going to the railway line where Lotte and I would board a passing train and travel a thousand miles, far from Uncle Leonard and the tyranny of Charles Malstain.

"I reached the track and saw the train was coming just as planned. It was an open goods train. All we needed to do was climb on to it as it trundled past. I stopped the cart and dashed round to the back to help Lotte off.

"But she was once again asleep. And this time I could not wake her. I tried – I shouted at her, I shook her. But nothing could rouse my sister from her slumber.

"That's when I saw soldiers. It was Charles Malstain's night patrol. They were on the hill, enforcing his curfew. No one was allowed out beyond seven o'clock, on pain of death. Least of all children!

"The train was getting closer. The soldiers had not yet seen us. This train was our only chance of escape. If we missed it, the soldiers would find us, take us back to our cottage, find Uncle Leonard sleeping, and discover everything.

"I grabbed Lotte. I made up my mind that I could lift her on to that train. It seems impossible looking at me now to think it. But I just decided. I grabbed her by the waist, I pulled her on to my back. I knew the train always slowed at this point as it crossed the river. The trucks had a crop of carrots and potatoes, a perfect landing mat. I lifted Lotte on my shoulder, I clambered on to the iron runner of the moving train carriage; the wheels turned beneath me, steam rushed through our hair. And, dangling half on the train, half off, I launched Lotte on to the potatoes! She landed with a perfect thud. Unharmed! I leaped with joy.

"Which was my mistake.

"As I landed on the edge of the carriage, I slipped. I fell from the carriage on to the dirty ground; my ankle twisted right round. I could not get up. Oh, how I tried. Oh, how terrible the pain as each wheel rolled past me, just inches from my face, but I had no way to rise, no way to grab the life raft that was slipping away.

"The last carriage passed. The train rolled over the rickety bridge, then started to climb the small hill on the other side. Soon all I could see was a wisp of smoke as it rose over the hill and disappeared down the other side. And with it, my sister Lotte.

"Minutes later the soldiers arrived. They found me lying by the railway tracks. They took me back to the house and Uncle Leonard. And the rest, as they say…is history."

Josef paused. The morning sun was starting to rise across the deck of the *Pegasus*. It made the silver ship burn gold.

Rachel stared at Josef intently. "You had to stay with your uncle? That beast?" Her eyes glowed with sun, sorrow and admiration.

Josef smiled sadly. "I'm afraid so."

"You were so brave, Josef. You saved your sister's life."

Rachel's words, so sincere, cut Josef to the core.

"Yes," he replied. "Since then I have wandered, I have travelled to many lands, but never have I felt as I did that night. As brave as I did that night."

Josef shivered. The truth lingered uncomfortably close to the surface of his mind: that saving Lotte from death was the last heroic thing he had ever done. That, from that moment, bravery had leaked from his soul like water from that rusty bucket.

Questions rose now in Josef's mind. What did the elegant woman who had approached him while he was playing music by the airfield really want? Why did she have such an unfriendly face? Why was Rachel Klein calling herself Isabella von Gurning? Why did the elegant woman very clearly say that Josef must take the Klein girl to the Hotel Excelsior in Port Clement's most expensive district? Why not another hotel?

Was Rachel Klein in danger?

For years Josef had never thought himself "father material". He lost things too easily. He would definitely worry that he would lose a daughter, leave her at the launderette or the theatre. So he had remained wifeless and childless. He had never really loved, not for twenty-five years, not since his sister Lotte.

But now Rachel Klein had come into his life. She had touched his heart.

Was he about to betray her?

"Josef, look!" Rachel's voice was filled with sudden excitement.

He followed her gaze. Below them, beyond the railing, they could see something glimmering beneath the clouds. It was new and shining and magical.

"Port Clement," he whispered. "We're here!"

Rachel looked down on the buildings jutting towards them from the earth, splendid and proud. Metal spears, glass towers and, between them, postage-stamp gardens that joined every building, each office and magnificent department store. And the bright ribbon of the Skyline railway flickering through the city like an electric current.

All of a sudden the face of her brother Robert flashed into Rachel's mind, and her heart filled with hope. Somewhere in the shining city she would find him, and they would hold each other tight after so many weeks apart. She would give him the precious knowledge that had been entrusted to her by Solomon Rose and the Meyers, and together they would defeat Charles Malstain's wicked plan to rule Krasnia for ever.

And maybe, just maybe, they would find their father...

But Josef Centurion looked down on the glittering glass and metal with a tightness in his chest. Because Josef knew that this very evening he would take Rachel Klein to one of the finest and most magnificent hotels in the whole city.

And he would leave her there, at the Hotel Excelsior, to her fate.

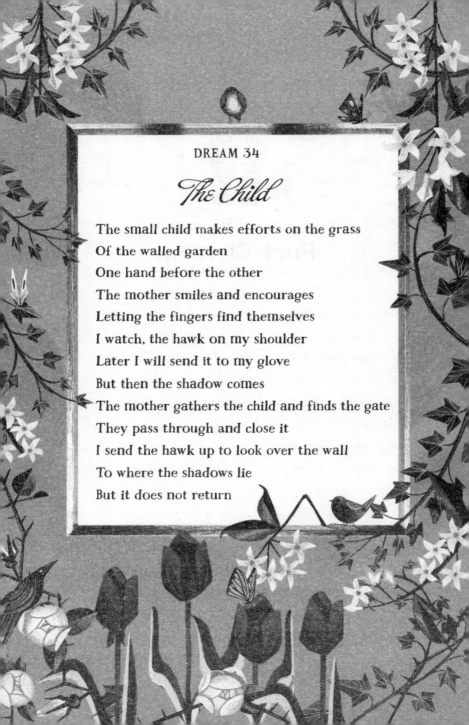

DREAM 34

The Child

The small child makes efforts on the grass
Of the walled garden
One hand before the other
The mother smiles and encourages
Letting the fingers find themselves
I watch, the hawk on my shoulder
Later I will send it to my glove
But then the shadow comes
The mother gathers the child and finds the gate
They pass through and close it
I send the hawk up to look over the wall
To where the shadows lie
But it does not return

21

Port Clement

Around midday, the airship landed on the vast runway of Port Clement International, and the passengers began to disembark. Rachel and Josef lined up and waited their turn, she clutching her elegant travel bag, he his old violin case. The queues were long, with thousands of desperate travellers waiting to rebuild their lives in a new land.

Rachel was aware that Josef, kind though he was, and funny with it, presented her with a problem. The message she had in her sock would take some decoding, but she had to do that alone. She had never considered that a kindly tramp might befriend her, buy her cocoa and tell her stories on the ship to comfort her. Now what was she going to do with him?

Rachel was very well brought up and could not just leave Josef alone without a proper thank you. And Josef seemed entirely content to wait with her in the concourse of the magnificent arrivals hall at Port Clement International. He seemed delighted to have her company as they queued to be signed through the many immigration procedures.

Four hours later they were walking together out of the arrivals hall and staring at the shining city awaiting them. It was late afternoon and the sun was already beginning to set.

"Isabella, my dear," he said. "Shall we share a taxi?"

Rachel wasn't sure. What was important now was to get to cheap and simple lodgings as fast as possible and then set out to find her brother and The Book of Stolen Dreams.

"That's very kind, but I can't waste my money on taxis at this stage," she confessed. "I think I'll walk and find my bearings."

"Nonsense!" said Josef with a broad smile. "The city is far too huge for a little girl to navigate on her own and the light is already fading. I have good contacts here who can help you find your brother. Why, even at the Hotel Excelsior where I'm staying, there's a concierge called Clive who knows the city like the back of his hand! I mean look at it, my dear. It's no village."

Rachel looked and saw he was right. A forest of glass,

vast metal and concrete blocks, stretching away into infinity. Somewhere in there was a thirteen-year-old boy with freckles. But where?

"Would Clive require payment for his help?" she asked anxiously.

"Not at all, my dear! It's his job and, besides, he's basically a cousin of mine. He gives me a room at reduced cost. I'm sure he'll give you one too…"

"Oh no!" she cried out. "I could never stay somewhere as grand as that." Rachel had read in magazines about the Hotel Excelsior. It was a legendary place, with a swimming pool on the twentieth floor and exotic carpets in every room. It had a famously huge breakfast.

"Just for tonight, you shall. I will pay, Clive will listen to your needs and then we will go our separate ways. Tomorrow I have a business meeting to attend, but today, my dear, I feel a duty to help you."

He looked into her eyes with a sincere kindness Rachel had rarely seen outside of her own family. And although she had sworn not to tell anyone about the true nature of her journey, and not to trust anyone who offered help, Rachel felt she could accept Josef's charity. It would mean finding Robert quicker, and that could only be a good thing.

"Josef, can I tell you something?" Her voice became a whisper. "My name isn't really Isabella von Gurning. That is the assumed name I am travelling under. My real name is Rachel Klein. And my brother is called Robert. Robert Klein."

"Oh really?" said Josef quietly. "Well, you had me fooled."

Rachel reached down and took the piece of paper from her sock. Handed it to Josef. He read it calmly.

CG gone. TG dead.
KRF broken.
Only RK.
He has hidden the BSD.
IDLAMIRG 342. 3rd.

"A coded message," he said solemnly.

"I am hoping RK might be my brother. But what Idlamirg 342 is, I have no idea."

"And BSD?"

"I don't know," Rachel lied sweetly. That was a secret she would tell no one.

Josef paused. "A head-scratcher indeed. But fear not. My friend Clive will know for certain how to help. He is a wizard at solving codes. To the Hotel Excelsior, and not a moment to spare!"

And before Rachel could say anything, and with a youthful bound, Josef stretched his arm out and hailed a taxi.

22

A Boy with Freckles

Rachel and Josef Centurion arrived at the Hotel Excelsior as dusk was falling. The statue of the man on the horse stood in the middle of the square, exactly where Robert had sat with Marie two days before. His sword was still held high.

The trees were gaining their leaves as spring took hold. Light jackets were now in order for the city folk taking their early evening walks, smiling and chatting. The street lights had just come on, the air was fresh, promising the warmer future of summer but not yet delivering it.

Rachel got out of the taxi that Josef had so kindly paid for.

She looked at the finely uniformed doormen: gold brocade on dark green cloth, shiny buttons, ridiculous hats that made her eyes dance with pleasure. Rachel gasped as the spacious revolving doors swept her into the main lobby. Once inside, her eyes were dazzled by the million shards of glass in the chandelier hanging above her head. Her nose tingled at the sweet perfumes that drifted from the hotel's vast array of boutiques, selling things one really didn't need but perhaps might like to have.

It was all so different to Brava, the orphanage, the dreadful grey of her previous life. But how did her strange little travelling companion fit in here?

"I'll find my friend Clive," said Josef with a bright smile. "You stay here, Rachel my dear."

As Josef walked to the reception desk, Rachel noticed a large woman in bright pink silk pants and a feather boa, with a little dog poking its nose out of her handbag. The woman was talking loudly to a nervous-looking concierge. Rachel crept closer.

"If there is fire damage to the portrait, I must insist the hotel perform a full repair. It is a masterpiece and is irreplaceable! I shall not be able to write one line of poetry until it is back on my wall."

The concierge bowed meekly and promised the woman that the hotel would see that the portrait be restored to its previous glory. The woman nodded and tickled the dog under its chin. "Come, Chintzie," she gurgled. "Time for din-dins!" Then she walked grandly across the lobby, stopping only to pluck a newspaper from the hotel magazine rack as she went.

That's when Rachel saw the headline on the newspaper.

It was a daily paper called *The Clementine*. There were several copies in the rack. The headline concerned the assassination attempt on Charles Malstain two days before:

PRESIDENT IN NEAR MISS!
TERRORISTS ARRESTED!
ATTACK FOILED!

Rachel approached and quietly took a copy. She looked up to see Josef in close conversation with a uniformed man behind a desk. Was that Clive? Rachel sat down and looked at the front page of the paper. There was a black and white photograph. Charles Malstain was getting out of a limousine. He was surrounded by men in suits, all with their right hands inside their jackets.

Bodyguards, Rachel thought to herself. She'd seen their type before.

She studied Malstain closely. He had a clenched smile, shoulders hunched. Dark receding hair, slicked back. Tiny eyes that somehow seemed to look both left and right. Beside him was a thin nasty-looking man with a cold stare. Next to him, a giant with a massive moustache. And finally, a young and strangely handsome man stood at the very edge of the photograph, smoking.

Under the photograph, there was a caption: PRESIDENT CHARLES MALSTAIN OF KRASNIA AND HIS HEAD OF SECRECY AND COMMUNICATIONS JOHANNES SLICK ARRIVING FOR TRADE NEGOTIATIONS WITH THE PORT CLEMENT GOVERNMENT, HOTEL EXCELSIOR, SHORTLY BEFORE THE ASSASSINATION ATTEMPT. APRIL 17TH.

The penny dropped. Rachel froze. She looked around at the luxurious foyer. This was the very same hotel where Charles Malstain had nearly been killed two days ago.

Rachel's hand trembled slightly. She felt like she had entered an enemy camp without realising. If this was really where Charles Malstain stayed, how could Rachel be sure that his spies were not still here? And what about the tyrant himself? Where was he?!

Rachel's head went very cold despite the warm, scented air of the lobby. She was about to get up and warn Josef when she saw something in the photograph that made her heart leap with astonishment.

Amongst the crowds that had gathered to welcome Charles Malstain were a group of protestors, with placards saying things like *Justice for Prisoners*, *Brava is a Prison* and *Free Our Friends!*

And among those protestors was a face. A young boy's face. Pale, with many freckles. The sort of face that gave you chocolates for Christmas but with one missing.

Her brother Robert.

He was standing next to a very pretty girl with nice

eyes, and he was looking at Charles Malstain with a deep private loathing.

Rachel gasped. Robert had been here! But where was he now? And why was *she* here – at the very same hotel? Was it just coincidence that Josef had brought her here?

Rachel felt a strange, lingering sense of fear grow inside her.

Then a voice behind her:

"Slightly frustrating, my dear. About my friend Clive."

It was Josef Centurion.

"I'm afraid he isn't here at the moment – his shift isn't until tomorrow morning. But we can settle in for the night and wait; they've given us both rooms on the seventh floor. Here is your key. The views are wonderful."

Rachel turned. Instantly Josef Centurion knew something was wrong.

"What is it?"

Rachel did not reply. Joseph looked beyond her at the newspaper in the rack. His eyes focused on the photograph of the squat figure of Charles Malstain and the headline above it. For a moment Josef said nothing. Then he turned his sad eyes to Rachel.

"Oh, my dear. I'm so sorry, I had no idea that *he* stayed here. But he left two days ago. Shall we take the elevator? Trust me. A good night's sleep, and we will meet up with Clive tomorrow. Clive will help us find your brother."

Rachel looked up at Josef slowly. Her eyes floated past him, to the photograph of the freckly boy – her brother Robert, the very person she was seeking in this city of seventeen million people.

Should she mention him? Show his freckly face to Josef? Point out the coincidence?

Rachel opened her mouth.

But then she paused. Nodded to Josef politely.

And said nothing.

DREAM 36

The Blade of Grass

And if I became a blade of grass
Would you hide me in your hair?
Would you take me beyond the gate?
Then I could see the Hinterland
I would be with you as you walked
Lie with you as you slept
And from my hiding place
I would whisper love into your ear
But oh I had forgot
How much you love to brush your hair
And send the bits of grass flying

23

Sleepless Nights at the Hotel Excelsior

The Hotel Excelsior's bedroom was by far the biggest and most luxurious that Rachel Klein had ever seen. It had a super-king-sized double-sprung bed. The goose-down pillows were deep and welcoming, the sheets smelled of fresh fields, the cotton was soft, the air cool, the night quiet and still.

But Rachel could not sleep.

For a while she wondered whether it was because she missed her mother and her father. Or perhaps the fact that she felt she was suddenly close to Robert was putting her on edge.

But there was another reason and she knew it. She was scared. Here she was, lying in a bed in the very same hotel where Charles Malstain had so very nearly been killed. It was like being in the grip of the tiger's claws.

Questions once again buzzed around her brain. Where was Malstain? Where were his cronies? What had happened to the would-be killers who had been caught? What role had her brother played in the affair? Where was Robert now? Did he still have the Book? Might he have found the missing page? Or was all lost? Was Robert caught? Was Malstain triumphant?

And if so, why was she here?

Was it mere chance that Josef had chosen this hotel? Come to think of it, was he really the sort of man who could afford to stay in it? But surely he could be trusted! He had bought her hot chocolate and paid for the taxi, he was giggly and sweet and kind. He had offered the help of Clive.

So why did Rachel's heart feel like a knot had been tied in its middle?

In the next-door room Josef Centurion wasn't sleeping either.

Josef had only once in his life been in a bed as comfortable as this. It was nine years ago. He was a committed thief by that time. He had set his heart upon stealing some rather fine diamonds from a rich spice-trader's townhouse in West Brava. He had done his homework. The trader and his wife would be away for the weekend at their countryside retreat, with all their servants. The house would be empty – the perfect occasion for a bit of breaking and entering.

Josef had waited until nightfall and then quietly smashed a rear window on the ground floor. He climbed the servants' staircase to the first-floor master bedroom where the trader's wife kept her famous gem collection. As expected, the room was empty. Josef got to work.

But there was something Josef didn't know.

What he didn't know was that the spice trader had a ninety-year-old mother, a woman of fierce temper and very poor eyesight, who lived with her son and daughter-in-law. What Josef also didn't know was that as a result of an unfortunate argument with her daughter-in-law, whom she loathed, the old lady had not been invited to the countryside residence that weekend. She had been left behind on her own.

In an act of petty revenge, the old woman decided to take advantage of her son's absence to use his huge master bedroom to sleep in. Her daughter-in-law had only ever given her a small attic bedroom and she was very angry about it. That evening she prepared a large bowl of her favourite chocolate ice cream (with sprinkles) and climbed the stairs.

The old woman walked in on Josef mid-robbery – diamond necklaces and bracelets in both his hands, gold rings and trinkets stuffed into all his pockets. But thanks to her poor eyesight, she simply didn't see him. The old woman was anxious about burglars so locked the bedroom door from the inside, thus locking Josef in with her. Then, without seeing the young thief standing glittering like a chandelier right in front of her, she undressed and climbed into the vast bed opposite the huge main window. She finished the ice cream, licking the bowl clean. Then she settled down to sleep.

Being a woman of nervous disposition, she kept the room key in her hand.

Josef Centurion now had a dilemma. He was inside the room and in his pocket were gems worth millions. But how to leave? The windows had locks on them so offered no way out. The only exit was the door. But the key was in a wrinkled, sleeping hand.

Then he heard a snoring. The old woman had entered the deep land of dreams.

Now was his chance to get the key.

Josef reached towards the old crone's hand to extract the key. But the more he tried, the harder the sleeping woman clenched her fist.

Josef tried tickling her arm, squeezing, pinching, but nothing worked. He tried lying beside her, singing to her reassuringly to keep her asleep, using his fingers to release the grip of the elderly dowager, who was snoring like a tiger.

It began to work. The ancient hand began to relax.

Still singing, he slowly unclenched the gnarly fingers and extracted the key. The snoring was deep now, reassuring. Josef had the key in his hand. He lay back in relief. He kept singing.

Then something terrible happened. Josef, to his horror, found himself getting sleepy from his own singing. The sheer comfort of the bed, the softness of the sheets, the rhythmic purr of the old woman, all conspired to send him into a profound and lasting slumber.

He fought it in vain…in vain…

In vain…

Josef awoke seven hours later to find the old woman standing with a knife, screaming in her nightdress, police rushing in, diamonds everywhere, and his own prospects for escape looking very slim indeed.

The bed in the Hotel Excelsior was just as comfortable, maybe more so. But did Josef feel himself slip into that gorgeous state where we are neither waking nor sleeping, floating as if between day and night, the land of the dead and the land of the living?

No. Josef was the widest awake he had ever been.

Because Josef knew that at seven in the morning his instructions were to get up from his heavenly bed, walk out of the Hotel Excelsior without paying, take a taxi to Port Clement International and use his pink return ticket on the last ever airship back to Brava to collect his dirty earnings.

Leaving Rachel Klein alone and unprotected.

Josef had realised very quickly on arriving at the hotel that it was the same one where Charles Malstain had nearly been murdered. It didn't take a genius to see the girl and her brother were somehow caught up in this. Josef was embroiled in a plot of deepening intrigue. His usual reaction in such a situation would be to get out as fast as possible, wash his hands of the whole rotten business. But there was something about the little girl in the room next door that tugged at his heart and prevented any rest from entering his troubled soul.

The clock said a quarter past four. Those who find sleep difficult will know that the worst hour of the night is between four and five o'clock. It is then that the mind will be the unwilling recipient of a thousand thoughts, fears and anxieties. A first draft of a letter to Father Christmas will combine with concerns about the political future of Brava, anxieties about homework will slide into a fanciful thought about using rum to power a petrol engine, crosswords will be solved, a football score remembered, a resolution made to be kinder to one's parents, and a decision taken to repaint one's bedroom as soon as possible.

Ah, the mind. It has mountains. As a poet once said.

But Josef's mind tonight had only one thought. Was he really going to leave Rachel to her fate?

You will remember that Judith Klein talked to Rachel

about a moral compass. That we have some kind of device or mechanism in us that tells us whether something is right or wrong. And we say that someone "lacks a moral compass" as if somehow God or whoever forgot to put it into certain people, like a factory forgetting to put a steering wheel in a car.

But of course the truth is more complicated. Josef felt very strongly that he was born with a moral compass but somewhere along the way, what with losing his father to prison, his mother to the sanatorium, his sister to who knows what fate, what with all the ensuing beatings and arrests, he had mislaid that solid feeling we all need in ourselves, that calm composure that enables us to judge what is the right and what is the wrong thing to do.

So Josef had become a piece of driftwood, floating with the tide and lacking the strength to say, *No, that is wrong, and this is the way I wish to go.*

And tonight was no different.

He knew what he wanted to do, deep down, in the night-time darkness. Josef saw very clearly that he shouldn't leave Rachel alone in the hotel, but that he should help her.

But Josef Centurion also knew that he wouldn't.

And now as Josef lay looking up at the high white ceiling of the hotel bedroom, he glimpsed a simple but painful truth. Josef had been chosen by the elegant woman at Brava airfield precisely because he was the sort of man who would do her bidding without asking questions. Precisely because he was a man without roots, accountable to no one. Precisely because ever since he had lost touch with his lovely sister Lotte, he was utterly alone. And he was incapable of loving anyone.

Josef's cheeks flushed from a deep shame.

He heard a knock at the door.

Was he mistaken? No, there it was again. Could it be Malstain's men coming early to take the girl? No. Their knock would be loud and unpleasant. This knock was gentle and nervous.

He got up, walked over in his long undergarments (Josef had no pyjamas to speak of) and opened the door very slightly. Two sad-looking, twelve-year-old eyes stared at him from the dark hotel corridor.

"I can't sleep."

Josef sighed deeply.

Rachel thought about the sigh. It might mean: *Oh great, there I was in the middle of the deepest sleep, dreaming of sunny meadows, blue skies and iced drinks, and now you've woken me and I'm going to have to talk to you.* Or it might mean something very different.

"Come in, dear."

"I'm sorry. I'll go back to my room."

"No, no. Come in. I wasn't sleeping either."

This casual confession stopped Rachel in her tracks. She saw Josef's hotel bed. It looked just as comfortable as hers. Why wouldn't Josef be sleeping?

"Are you anxious about tomorrow's business meeting?" she asked.

He looked blank for a moment and then stuttered, "Oh that, yes, maybe. Maybe I am." He smiled a thin smile.

Rachel sat on the small sofa that faced the bed. *He lied to me*, she thought to herself. *He has no meeting tomorrow.* Rachel's heart began to feel strangely heavy. Then she looked up. "Are you all right, Josef?" she asked.

Josef was standing in the middle of the room. He seemed to have stopped breathing. His eyes didn't blink, just stared out the window. In fact his entire being seemed suspended between two points.

Rachel grew scared. "Josef?"

Another pause. Then: "My dear, since neither of us can sleep, what say you? Shall we get dressed and go for a walk together? The city is so beautiful and never more so than at night when no one is around."

Rachel considered this. On the one hand she loved cities at night, but on the other hand it was a slightly odd idea. Should she trust him?

"I suppose we could walk for an hour or so, and then return to talk to your friend Clive."

"That's it!" In seconds he had dressed and packed all his things.

"But aren't we coming back?"

"Of course we are. Of course we are. But I hear that in Port Clement thieves operate more in the rich hotels than anywhere else. Best to be safe, my dear! Get your bag and I'll meet you in the corridor."

Nine minutes later they were taking the lift down. They walked silently across the dark lobby. The chandelier was unlit. A night-porter snoozed in a velvet corner seat. A bellboy lay on the stone. Other than that, the place was deserted.

Rachel noticed Josef's eyes dart furtively from side to side as they walked through the revolving doors on to the street. *He's looking for someone*, she thought.

And for the first time, Rachel began to feel sure that Josef Centurion was not telling her the whole truth about why he was in Port Clement.

24
Josef Makes a Decision

They walked together into the vast park at the heart of the city. Birds were up early, impatiently welcoming the coming day. Otherwise the two figures were alone.

Rachel was thinking fast. Why was Josef not telling her everything? What did he know? How could she get him to talk? She turned to him and spoke softly as they walked. "What happened to you, Josef? After Lotte left?"

"Not much to tell, my dear. Years alone, missing my sister, whom I'm afraid to say I never saw again. Is she dead or alive? I don't even know."

Josef's eyes stared into the darkness of the park, the oncoming dawn, the spring air. Rachel waited for him to continue, then, when he failed to do so, gave him a little nudge.

"But you didn't stay with Uncle Leonard."

"No. Eventually I left and drifted on my way. I took nothing but my clothes and the stuffed penguin to remember my father by."

"Where did you go?"

"Hmm? Oh, to the city. Where else?"

"To do what?"

"Oh, you know. This and that. That and this."

"Music?"

"Yes, music! That sort of thing."

Josef shivered awkwardly in the cool of the dawn. He looked up at the clock on the old zoological building. It said 5.30 a.m. In an hour and a half the people he was working for would arrive at the hotel and they would expect to find Rachel Klein in it.

But Josef just stood there, saying nothing. Going nowhere. Like he was stuck in mud.

Seconds passed in silence. Finally Rachel spoke again.

"Josef? This has been a lovely walk. But shouldn't we be going back to the hotel to talk to your friend Clive? I'm sure he'll arrive for work soon. And he can help me find my brother."

Rachel looked at Josef steadily. As if she was really asking him a different question.

There was another long pause.

"Rachel, I have something to tell you," Josef said without looking at her.

He saw a bench ahead of them and gestured her towards it. Rachel sat, placing her travelling bag beside her. A few dawn birds approached, hoping for early breakfast, but Josef shooed them away. There followed another long and very difficult silence. Then:

"You must never go back to the Hotel Excelsior."

Rachel's face was very still. "What about your friend Clive? Isn't he expecting us?"

"No, he's not."

Her wide eyes stared up at his. "Why not? Where is he?"

"He isn't anywhere. I lied to you. There is no friend Clive."

Rachel said nothing for a moment.

"Why…did you lie?"

"For money. I was supposed to take you to the hotel and leave you there. I was hired for that purpose back in Brava."

Rachel's mind went quietly to work. The orphanage director at the airfield. Josef playing his violin…

Again, a silence.

"Say something, Rachel. Tell me I'm a terrible person."

But Rachel just stood up. The city was still. The park empty.

"I understand. Thank you for telling me the truth. Goodbye, Josef." She said his name perfectly, with a "y", like yesterday. She grabbed her bag and started to walk away.

"No, wait! Where are you going?" He got up to follow.

"I have to find my brother."

"But where will you go? This city is enormous... he could be anywhere."

She continued walking away.

"Rachel, come back! It's dangerous! Let me help you!"

But Rachel Klein turned with eyes of such deep disappointment that Josef's heart almost broke.

"I think you've helped enough. Don't you?"

Then she disappeared amidst the trees of the park.

25

Captive

It was just before dawn and Robert Klein was also not sleeping. Ever since Walter Meyer returned for his cigarette lighter at the Behind the Eyes Bookstore and found Robert over the dead body of Theodore Glimpf, Robert had been furious at himself. Why had he been caught so off guard? Why hadn't he run straight out the back of the bookshop? How could he have been so stupid?

Now, if Lucius Meyer did manage to send someone to Port Clement to help him, he wouldn't be at the rented room to meet them. Would they even find the Book in the hiding place he'd so cleverly chosen? He knew that his sister Rachel would have found it – she was always so good at hide-and-seek in the apartment – but Rachel was stuck in an orphanage back in Krasnia, alone and friendless.

Robert realised that his entire mission had been a disaster. He kicked the radiator in frustration.

The house Walter had taken him to was outside Port Clement, near the airfield. From his locked window, Robert could see the airships land and take off. Port Clement was the busiest airfield in the world. Flights from all over came in daily, packed with sightseers, cameras at the ready, to enjoy all the fun that a successful modern city had to offer. Not one of those tourists knew there was a boy locked inside a small house just a mile from the airfield, nor why he was there.

Robert was not allowed out of his room. Walter and Johannes Slick took turns to visit him to try to persuade him to tell them what he knew. Robert stayed silent, only saying that he had come to Port Clement because he didn't want to be sent to an orphanage. He had refused to say how he had met Herr Glimpf. Robert had eaten a couple of meals, tried to sleep without success, and waited.

He had been in the room for nearly two days now.

The sound of a key in the door. The handle turned. Walter Meyer walked in. He was elegantly dressed as usual, had already shaved and smelled of citrus. He brought with him a tray of breakfast, which he put down on the side table. Robert stayed looking out the window.

"Did you sleep?"

Robert did not reply.

Walter smiled, as if enjoying Robert's performance.

"I've brought you food. I'd eat the toast while it's hot if I were you. Toast is never the same cold."

Robert didn't even turn, though he was starving.

Walter sat on the edge of the bed. He nibbled a bit of toast himself. Then he leaned casually back on the pillow and gazed at the ceiling. "Oh, by the way, I have some news. Someone you know is in Port Clement."

Robert felt his back stiffen. He didn't turn, in case his face showed Walter what he was thinking.

"Yes," Walter continued listlessly. "She's staying at the Hotel Excelsior."

Robert breathed. Walter had said "she". Robert mustn't ask who. He must stay strong and silent.

Walter smiled. "Are you sure you're not going to have this toast? It's terribly good."

Robert almost bit his tongue off to stop it from speaking.

Walter waited for a moment, then continued. "Of course, your sister couldn't afford the hotel on her own. But we've helped her with that. Rachel doesn't know it's us who are paying. She doesn't know anything. She's only young, after all. She thinks she's looking for you. She's totally unaware she's walked into our trap."

Walter smiled. He cut a neat piece of Robert's toast and slipped it between his thin lips. "Very nice and buttery."

Robert turned, his eyes flashing. "You're lying."

Walter smiled, then took something from his pocket. It was a guest registration form from the Hotel Excelsior. The name on the form was Isabella von Gurning, but the copy of Isabella's passport photograph very clearly showed a twelve-year-old girl. And the twelve-year-old girl was very clearly Rachel Klein.

There was a silence in the room as Walter quietly finished his sliver of toast.

Robert flushed red. He wanted to fly at Walter and tear his smug face open, but he knew that Johannes Slick and his heavies were down below. Only the injured Rufus O'Hare had returned with Charles Malstain to Brava the day before. The rest were still here. And all of them were waiting for Robert Klein to talk.

"Your sister is a very determined young woman," Walter continued. "According to our spy, she is going to try and find you in Port Clement despite having no idea where you live."

Robert said nothing.

"Of course, her problem is that *we* know where *she* is. So unless you agree to help us, Robert, we will abandon our efforts to persuade you to tell us what you know, and focus on her instead."

Robert threw himself at Walter. "You touch her, I'll kill you! I'll kill you!"

The door flew open. Two heavies came in and pushed Robert back as Walter tidied his jacket and removed a crumb from his lapel. Walter nodded and the heavies left.

"Calm down, boy," Walter said. "And stop being stupid. It's beneath you. Your sister is at this very moment sleeping in a bed that is far too big for her in the Hotel Excelsior. Unless you tell me right now why you are here and what you know, I will send men to the hotel and they will force her to tell us instead. Now I am a very civilised man, but I'm afraid the same cannot be said for some of the President's retinue."

He glanced at the door. Then turned back to Robert. "So I would very much advise you to tell me everything now."

Robert paused. What choice did he have? Rachel must have escaped the orphanage and come to Port Clement to find him. Maybe she had even spoken to Lucius Meyer! In which case she knew much too much. Robert had to say something. "I came here to help the KRF kill Charles Malstain."

"And what do you know of The Book of Stolen Dreams?"

"Nothing."

"You're lying. Constanza Glimpf is my aunt. She knows all about the Book. And I think that means you do too."

"Then why don't you ask her?"

"Oh, we're trying to persuade her. We've taken her back to Brava specially for that purpose. The President has an excellent interrogation chamber, right under his palace. But she is stubborn and old. She'd rather die than speak. Whereas you...are young and sensible."

A pause in the room. When Walter spoke again his voice was almost a whisper.

"We know your father stole the Book, Robert. Did he give it to you? Do you know where it is? Just tell me, and your sister will be safe."

Robert shook his head. He felt hot tears sting his eyes.

Walter turned to the door. "Herr Slick."

Almost instantly Johannes Slick slithered into the room. "Yes?"

"The boy is not cooperating. I think it's best you go to the hotel now, get the girl, and ask her to tell us what we need to know."

"Very well."

Slick left the room. Robert heard steps descending the stairs – Slick's sliding shuffle followed by heavy boots.

"No, wait!" Robert cried out, the tears now running down his cheeks. "Rachel knows nothing! She doesn't know I met the Glimpfs or that I was in the KRF or where the Book is! She doesn't know anything!"

"But you do?" Walter smiled at him. "Where is it, boy? Where?"

26

Lox and Eggs

Rachel walked fast through the city. This was no time to wallow in self-pity. Okay, so Josef Centurion was a liar and a toad, but the world was full of them. It was clear that you couldn't trust anyone except family. Maybe Laetitia too, but she was far away. Rachel was alone in a foreign land and would have to deal with it. She had to think. And she had to find Robert!

Dawn was breaking; a large clock said the time was nine minutes to six. Rachel needed to find somewhere safe and quiet to study Lucius Meyer's note and try to decipher it. But everything was shut. The streets were empty apart from road-cleaners making their way home from their night's work.

Then she turned a corner and saw a small cafe. *Mitzie's*

Fine Dining – Lox and Eggs, the sign said, with a picture of a fish and a chicken. It had three small windows to the street and seemed, to Rachel's surprise, to be open, even at this early hour.

She walked in. She half expected to be thrown out immediately, but no one so much as turned to look at her. The place was small and low-ceilinged. It felt like a train carriage. There were little booths with red leather seating all along one wall. Mirrors lined every booth, wooden and painted. The lighting was soft and warm. There were menus in plastic folders on every table. The room was half full, almost entirely men – tall, short, fat, skinny, all wearing slightly shabby work clothes – whether overalls, aprons or heavy boots. Working men, Rachel thought, maybe from the shipyards, some delivery men and market traders. There was not much chatter. The focus was on the eating – huge plates of eggs and bacon and waffles, bowls of steaming porridge, and jugs of hot coffee.

"Looking for someone?"

A woman's voice rang loudly in Rachel's ear. She stood at the cash desk like a wonderful bird. She was about sixty, Rachel thought, tall and very upright, with long white hair pulled back off her face and clipped to avoid getting in the food. Her nose was like a great beak, over which two sparkling eyes studied Rachel as you might look at a worm. Her skin was white, like she had never gone out in the sun. She had on a clean white apron over a smart dark two-piece suit and a high white blouse pinned with a gold brooch. A pair of glasses hung round her neck. She held a stick in her left hand.

"I'd just like to eat, please."

"Then sit down, why don't you, instead of prevaricating? You want eggs, sunny side, coffee, juice? You want lox, oatmeal, honey waffles, blueberry pancakes?"

"Yes, please."

"Yes what, please?"

"Yes, blueberry pancakes, please."

"Four? Eight? Twelve?"

"Four, please."

"With syrup, with cream?"

"Yes."

"Coffee? Tea?"

"Tea, please."

"Juice? Orange? Grapefruit? Comes with."

"Orange. Thank you."

The woman nodded briskly, wrote it all on a pad, tore the paper off the pad, pinned it to a board. She shouted, "Hassan! Meal six, tea, orange, with all the sweets!" Behind her, through an opening Rachel could see two small men, one dark, one fair, working in the steam and sweat of the kitchen. There were hundreds of eggs piled high, flour particles dancing in the morning light. The smell of butter and bacon tickled Rachel's nostrils.

"Sit down. Rest your tush."

Rachel sat in an alcove as ordered, wondered what a tush was, and waited.

Seconds later, eight steaming pancakes arrived, with a bowl of fresh blueberries and a jug of cream. Seconds after that a mug of tea slammed itself down on the table.

"That's eight blueberry pancakes with syrup and cream, tea's there, juice on the counter. Pay now."

"Oh. Of course." Rachel had only ordered four pancakes but decided not to make a thing of it. She fumbled inside her travelling bag, found her money, handed it over. The woman paused. Eyeballed Rachel hard.

"What's this?"

"Money?" Rachel said hopefully.

"I know it's money, baby. I got eyes in my head. But this is Krasnian currency. In case you hadn't noticed, sugar, we're in Port Clement."

Rachel stopped dead. Her heart tightened in her chest. "Is Krasnian money not still money?"

"Krasnian groschen aren't worth nothing here now. Borders are shutting. No one wants it."

How could she be so stupid? Uncle Bruno had told her she must change the money on arrival in Port Clement, but what with Josef Centurion appearing and paying for everything, she had forgotten. And now she was unable to pay, and doubtless any second the delicious pancakes would be whisked away and the police called. And she would be in prison for stealing food, when she should be looking for Robert.

Rachel nodded. She gulped down a tear or two, and got up to leave.

"Where are you going?" the woman barked.

"Well, I can't pay."

"Sit down!"

The woman seemed angrier than ever. Rachel wondered whether to bolt. But there were men looking at her now. And some of them looked strong and fast.

"You don't like the look of my pancakes?" The woman spoke again.

"No, I love the look of them!"

"Then eat them!" She was almost shouting now.

One of the customers yelled across: "Mitzie, give the girl a break!"

"I am giving her a break!" the woman screamed back. It was a competition in loudness. "My pancakes are the best in town, and don't let anyone tell you different!"

"Mitzie, don't hassle the kid, let her eat."

"She can eat and have a conversation."

"But I can't eat your food without paying." Rachel spoke quietly.

"You'll find a way to pay me. You can wash up the dishes today, give my back a break."

"No, but I can't…"

The woman leaned in, glowering. "Afraid to work? Too fancy for it, are you? Too hoity-toity?"

"No, not at all!"

"She's got airs and graces, this one!"

"Leave the girl alone!"

"I'm giving her the best pancakes in Port Clement. I'm giving her my very own juice. My very own tea and milk. What more does she want?"

Rachel tried to explain. "I didn't mean I was afraid to work. It's just, I have to find someone. It's really important. So I can't stay."

"Find who?"

An air of curiosity filled the room, as if everyone sensed a story in the young girl with the strange case and the threadbare woollen coat.

"My brother." Rachel said it without thinking. Was this wise? She didn't know. But there was something about the dining room that seemed so loud and open. It reassured her after the stuffy menace of the Hotel Excelsior.

"Tell Mitzie the truth. Who is this brother?"

"Mitzie, stop sticking your big honk of a nose in other people's business."

"You shut up, Bernie. This is my joint. Anyway, she brought him into the conversation!"

"Let her eat!"

"Let us all eat!" Laughter filled the dining room.

"Eat, girl. Those pancakes are best hot." Mitzie sat

opposite her. "You want lox? I got fresh smoked lox right off the truck."

Rachel said she was very happy with the pancakes, which was true. They were the sweetest, butteriest pancakes she had ever tasted. The blueberries stained her fingers and mouth. And she had no idea what lox was.

"So come on, spill. Who is this brother?"

"He's called Robert. I think he's in trouble."

"You know where he is?"

Rachel shook her head.

"No clue?"

Rachel looked up. She thought for a moment. And then on an impulse she took the small piece of paper from her sock. She handed it to Mitzie.

"What's this?"

"It's my only clue as to where my brother might be."

Mitzie took the pair of glasses from around her neck and placed them on her nose. She read the note out loud:

"*CG gone. TG dead.*

KRF broken.

Only RK.

He has hidden the BSD.

IDLAMIRG 342. 3rd.

"What the hell does this mean any given Saturday?"

Men left their tables and gathered. Rachel was no longer sure this had been a good idea at all.

"What is this?"

"Looks like code!"

"Don't be stupid, Vinnie."

"Who's calling me stupid?"

Mitzie slammed her stick down on the counter. "Hey, what is this? A chicken coop? Pipe down, all of you! Now let's have a look at this." She read the note again.

"*CG gone. TG dead.* These are people, right?"

Rachel nodded.

"*KRF broken.* What's the K?"

Suggestions were offered.

"Might be king."

"Or kettle."

"Or kindergarten."

"How can a kindergarten be broken, you schmuck?"

"It could be Krasnia." A low male voice spoke from the back. "Girl's from Krasnia."

"Very good, Femi!" Mitzie applauded. "He's a smart one is Femi."

Rachel agreed. Femi was smart. Krasnia made sense.

"You only ate five pancakes," Mitzie observed. "Don't you like them?"

Rachel kept eating as Mitzie studied the note.

"Okay, so something belonging to Krasnia is broken. Hand me that newspaper. Didn't I read about Krasnia only yesterday?"

Someone hurled her *The Clementine*. It was the same edition Rachel had seen in the hotel. Mitzie looked at the front page then slammed her stick down in triumph.

"Look here! Femi, you're a bona fide genius! *The assassins are thought to come from the Krasnian Resistance Front.*"

A roar of triumph filled the room. Femi had his back slapped several times. He smiled, embarrassed.

"Okay, so what's RK?"

Rachel spoke first. "That's my brother. Robert. Robert Klein."

"Oh, that's him, is it? And he has the BSD. Whatever that is."

Rachel nodded. She knew exactly what the BSD was, but that she dared not say. It could get all of these innocent people into terrible trouble.

"Okay, so the last bit. Idlamirg 342."

Another voice came from the alcoves. "How do you spell that word?"

Mitzie spelled it out. "I-D-L-A-M-I-R-G."

"That's a weird word."

"That's not a word at all!"

A murmur of agreement. Then another voice from the bar.

"Hey, Mitzie, is it like one of those...one of those Hanna Grams?"

"A Hanna Gram? What's a Hanna Gram when it's at home?"

Rachel spoke up. "I think he means an anagram."

"Could be, Nuri. Could be a Hanna Gram. Where's my pen?"

Mitzie wrote the word up on the order board with a blue marker pen. The room gathered round it, some holding cups of coffee, some with mouths stuffed with moist bacon and waffles.

"Idlamirg. I can't see anything in it."

"There's something there, boys. There's something there. Mix the letters! Mix the letters!"

"Maid girl!"

"Dig llama!"

"Grid mail!"

"Any of those mean anything to you, sugar?"

Rachel shook her head as she started the seventh pancake.

"Ah, I don't think it's a Hanna Gram at all."

Another murmur of agreement and some of the men returned to their food. But Mitzie stayed looking at the word. Her beak seemed to get a little longer, her eyes a little more bright.

"I'm thinking it must be a street name," she said. "Because look, he says *3rd* after it. That means third floor or my name's not Mitzie McConnell. He's telling you where he is."

Rachel nodded. It made sense.

"Honey, you got blueberry on your chin." Mitzie handed her a napkin from a large box.

Rachel turned to the mirror to check what a mess she had made. She wiped the blue goo from her face. She saw Mitzie in the mirror behind her, still looking at the note.

Then Rachel stopped. "Wait." Rachel turned and looked at the letters, then looked back at the mirror. Her heart leaped. "Look!" She showed Mitzie the mirror.

Mitzie looked in amazement. "GRIMALDI! Boys, look at this! If you look backwards, it kind of says Grimaldi."

The boys looked too. Mitzie was turning to them in excitement.

"I'll be damned! Grimaldi Street! That's in the South District. Nelson, isn't Grimaldi Street in the South District?"

"Sure, it's by the harbour."

"Yeah, it's where some of the port boys live. Cheap rooms in Grimaldi Street!"

Rachel and Mitzie exchanged a look.

"That's it, sugar. 342 Grimaldi Street. Third floor. That's where he is."

Rachel's face flushed red. She stood, her mouth still full of the seventh pancake. "Can I walk it?"

"Sure you can. Fifteen minutes at most. I'll come with you."

"No, please. I'll only…"

"Only what?"

Rachel spoke quietly. "I'll put you in danger."

"Danger? What danger?" Mitzie lowered her voice. "Believe me I've seen danger full in the face in my time."

She moved fast to the back of the cafe, grabbed a maroon coat and a dark scarf.

"Hassan, look after the place! I'm going with the tutz. And she's eating the last pancake on the way!"

DREAM 38

The Glimpse

I found a gap in the wall
And looked into the Hinterland
Where my love was planting seeds
In the welcoming soil
I looked into her face
To try to find the pain I feel
But maybe pain is not the same
On the other side of the wall
In the place of shadows
Where she crouches planting

27

Grimaldi Street

Mitzie and Rachel strode through the city. At every corner Mitzie greeted a shopkeeper or a trader with a "Morning, Omar my love" or "You still owe me for those cauliflowers, Becky!" It was barely half past six but the city was alive with colours and smells. The meat and vegetable markets were open, cars roared by, and the Skyline was already in motion, bringing the working people of Port Clement to their offices and factories.

They turned south towards the harbour.

Grimaldi Street was a little row of tenement houses, nicely kept, almost all used by shipyard workers, Mitzie said, some with families abroad, earning money to send home. The street was long, running parallel to the beach and only a few hundred yards from the roar of the ocean.

Rachel glimpsed the sky behind the houses, the sun rising in the east, where far away her home country lay. In Krasnia it would already be lunchtime, she thought. Laetitia would still be in hiding in Bruno's huge house. And her father? Where would he be?

They found number 342 without difficulty. It had several bells; Mitzie rang all of them. There was a small pause and then a man answered.

"Who is it?"

"We are friends of the gentleman on floor three."

There was a pause and then they were buzzed in. Rachel turned to Mitzie.

"If you don't mind, I'd prefer to go alone. I feel rude to ask, but I have my reasons."

Mitzie scrutinised the young girl. "You're a right box of surprises, you are. I'll wait outside. Anyone comes, they'll have me to deal with."

Rachel nodded and walked in. She climbed the narrow staircase.

A man approached her. "Hey! You friends with the boy in room three?"

"Yes."

"Well, tell him he's late with the rent. It should have been yesterday. I don't throw him out seeing as he's been prompt with payment up until now, but consider this a warning. Staying out all night isn't good for a kid his age."

"He stayed out last night?"

"For two nights. Not seen hide nor hair of him."

Rachel thanked the man and continued up. Then she turned. "Is his door locked?"

"I should say so."

"I am his sister. I have come from Krasnia to visit him. May I stay inside and wait?"

The man looked at her, unsure. "He never mentioned a sister."

"I *am* his sister. Please believe me. I know, for example, that he has a coat with a hole in the left sleeve, and a grey suitcase with string for a handle because the handle fell off last winter, and his face is very freckly and his hair is brown—"

"All right, you made your point."

The man led her up the stairs. Through the landing window, Rachel glimpsed Mitzie waiting outside.

The landlord opened the door and let her in. It was a tiny room, nothing more than a bed and basin. A small window looked straight out on to the wall of the next building. At this early hour the room was still dark though the curtains were pulled back. The room was empty but for a few of Robert's things, including his magnifying glass, his book of insects and his toothbrush.

"If you want a drink, kitchen's below. You pay for everything before you take it."

Rachel nodded, the man walked out and closed the door. She was alone at last. For a second she looked at

Robert's things and felt a little tug of love, as if she had just got that little bit closer to him. Then she got to work.

She looked under the bed and found the grey suitcase. She opened it; it was empty. She lifted the false bottom. Nothing there.

Rachel felt a little shiver of fear pass through her. Had Robert been caught? Had they taken the Book from him?

Rachel looked again. She looked up at the ceiling, hoping that a similar panel to the one at home might reveal a hiding place. But the ceiling was just plasterboard. The walls were bare. There wasn't even a cupboard, just a chair placed against the wall on which Robert had hung a change of clothes. Rachel checked the mattress and the dirty sheet. She looked under the pillow. But she did all this already knowing that if Robert had hidden the Book, he would do it properly. The Book was either gone, or she hadn't yet solved the puzzle.

She thought herself into Robert's mind. She sat on the bed, just as he would have done, to consider the best hiding place. She looked at the floor. Floorboards. Yes, that was possible. But when she pulled them, none came up. She sat again. She lay back on the bed, looked up. She looked at the window, then back at the door.

Then Rachel had a simple moment of clarity. There was nowhere in the room to hide the Book. So Robert had not hidden the Book in the room.

She looked again at the note.

IDLAMIRG 3rd.

And then she understood. There was a reason the word *GRIMALDI* was reflected like in a mirror.

"A mirror," Rachel murmured to herself. And got up.

Rachel quietly opened the door of the room and looked outside. The landing was empty. It was small, with stairs leading up to it from the ground floor and on up to the top floor and roof. It had a rug and a window that looked out to the front.

And a wooden mirror on the wall.

Rachel approached the mirror. It was too high up for her to look into it. She walked back into the room and grabbed the chair, throwing Robert's change of clothes to the floor.

She put the chair under the mirror and climbed on to it. She held the mirror in both hands and started to lift it carefully from its hooks.

Beneath her she could hear the landlord shouting at someone to "Pull yourself together!"

The mirror was heavier than she expected. She had to brace her arms against the wall and push up with her legs. The chair creaked and nearly gave way. Rachel lifted the mirror just enough to see that behind it two bricks had been removed from the wall and, instead of the bricks, tucked into the wall was a dusty leather-bound book.

Rachel gasped. And lost her balance. The chair swayed on to two legs, both legs snapped and Rachel fell.

The mirror slipped from her grasp and smashed on the floor.

Now she heard cars outside.

She kept low and crept over broken glass to the window. Rachel looked out to see two black cars park outside the house.

And out of one car came a tall thin pencil of a man. Rachel recognised him from the newspaper – it was Johannes Slick. He was with two other men in dark suits. They walked calmly towards the house, where Mitzie was sitting on the step, correcting her lipstick.

Mitzie eyed Slick, who told her to "Go find another place to fix your face" and pushed past her.

Or tried to. Instantly Mitzie was on her feet and giving him both barrels. "How dare you push me, gumshoe? You learn your manners in the pigpen? You know who Mitzie McConnell is? You're about to find out!" As she did so, Mitzie glanced up at the window where Rachel was watching. Their eyes met. And in that look was a clear understanding. *They're here for you.*

Mitzie started to argue with Slick and barred the door. She talked very loudly, saying she owned the place and they couldn't come in without a warrant. She even threatened to call the Port Clement police and said she knew several high-ranking government officials personally.

Rachel moved fast. She took the half-broken chair, leaned the two remaining legs against the wall, jumped up and, in the seconds before those legs also broke, she grabbed the Book and fell to the floor holding it.

It was The Book of Stolen Dreams.

In seconds she was up. The door downstairs was being hammered at. Mitzie was screaming, "Call the cops! Call the cops!" One of Slick's men shoved Mitzie hard; the door smashed open. The landlord came rushing from the basement, but Slick pushed past him, sending him sprawling.

Mitzie dived after them, grabbing the ankles of two of the men and biting them hard. They shouted and kicked but her teeth clung on.

Meanwhile, gun out, Slick started to climb the staircase.

Rachel quickly opened her travelling bag, threw the Book inside, and dashed up the stairs. She ran out on to the roof. She could still hear Mitzie out front, holding on to the two heavies and screaming blue murder.

Rachel ran across the roof. She slipped, lost her footing, almost fell, but grabbed a TV aerial at the last moment. Finally she reached a thin fire-escape ladder leading vertically down the back of the building to an alleyway at the rear of the house. Across the alleyway behind a wall there was a large refuse dump belonging to the harbour warehouses, filled with plastic, rotten vegetables and meat carcasses. The disgusting smell lingered on the wind.

It was dizzyingly high but Rachel had no choice. Gripping the travelling bag in one hand, she slowly let herself down the ladder with the other.

Rung by rung she descended. She was halfway down when she heard the fire-exit door open above her and the sound of Johannes Slick's black leather shoes on the tiles. Within seconds he would be at the top of the ladder and would see her climbing down. Rachel had to move fast. She let the bag drop from her fingers. It hit the pavement below with a thud. Then she let herself follow, sliding her hands down the ladder at high speed until just above the ground she let go, and hit the alleyway hard. Then she grabbed the bag and ducked back against the rear of the house, just as Johannes Slick stuck his head out to look down.

He could see no one.

At the bottom of the ladder, Rachel pinned herself against the brickwork as Slick peered over and started to climb down. Rachel heard his steps approach. The only way out was down the alleyway. But she knew that if she made a run for it, Slick would see her.

Now Slick was halfway down the ladder. With both hands free, he was much quicker than she had been. Any minute now he would discover her. She would have to run. And with the bag in her hand she would be too slow and he would catch her and with her The Book of Stolen Dreams. And Malstain would get the Book, and all her and Robert's hopes would be dashed.

Then Rachel heard distant footsteps to her right. She looked round. A figure was running up the alleyway from where it joined the road by the sea. At first she thought it might be one of Slick's men coming round from the front, but he was too small and thin for that. And he ran in a way that clearly showed running to be a stranger to him.

The figure was silhouetted against the morning sun as it rose in the east over the ocean. Rachel's eyes strained against the sunlight; the figure was closing now, soon Johannes Slick would see him...

Then Rachel looked in amazement.

The silhouetted figure clearly had a penguin on his head.

For a moment Rachel's blood froze. Was Josef with Johannes Slick? But as he approached, Josef's eyes searched hers out, and she saw him shake his head as if to say, *Don't move!*

Then with a courage and strength that he had not shown for twenty-five years, Josef Centurion reached the ladder and, with a terrific tug, started to pull at it, wrenching it from the wall.

Halfway down the building, Johannes Slick felt the ladder being pulled from under him. He tried to grab the bricks of the house, his fingernails digging into the cement.

Then Josef Centurion gave a huge animal roar and, with one last tug, the ladder came away. The Krasnian Head of Secrecy and Communications felt the ladder leave the wall and start to fall. His fingers came away from the brick. Rachel watched in shock as the ladder toppled like a tree in a beautiful curve across the alleyway above her, hit the wall opposite and catapulted Slick over the wall into the huge refuse dump on the other side. Rachel heard the sound of bone meeting metal, the soft thud of human flesh plunging into rotten turnip and cabbage. Then silence.

"Let's go," said Josef Centurion. Their eyes met. Then he pulled Rachel fast down the alleyway.

28
The Plan

They took refuge by the ocean, in an area of mud flats where abandoned ship-containers were left rusting on the sand. One container had a small gap in it made by the sea, which allowed them to sneak inside. It was empty but for a few old wooden crates, three drunk cans of "soda" and a few sand spiders.

Josef sat down on a crate, checked Rachel for injuries, then wiped his brow with a filthy rag. He was exhausted.

"Why were you there?" she asked, still holding tight to her small travelling bag. "Why did you come?"

"Followed you. To that diner. Then followed you to the house." He spoke in spurts, still getting his breath back. "Brave woman," he continued. "That cafe owner."

"I hope she's all right," Rachel said.

"It'll take more than a few heavies to hurt her." Josef nodded. "She's no coward."

The word "coward" hung on the ocean breeze. Rachel smelled the salt of the sea. The air was tense. Josef spoke again.

"I know why you're angry, Rachel. You have every right to be. But I took you away from that hotel for a reason. Didn't want them to get you. Grew to like you, you see."

Josef said all this looking at the ground, like Robert had back in Brava after Rachel and her mother had discovered the chocolate was missing.

"I'm very sorry, Rachel. I want to make amends."

Rachel paused. She felt a strange pity for this little man, beaten by life like a piece of wood in the waves. She studied his sad, shattered face.

"You did make amends, Josef. You saved my life."

He nodded. The sea murmured. Gulls pondered overhead. Then Josef looked at the travelling bag.

"Why didn't you throw that away? Would have made you faster."

Rachel looked at the bag. Then she looked at Josef. She was searching for something, but it wasn't a real thing; it was the moral compass she had thought Josef had but then thought maybe he hadn't. Josef could feel her scrutiny, could sense that Rachel Klein was making a decision about him, about what sort of man he was and whether, at the end of the day, he could be trusted. And he knew that she had to make that decision alone, and whatever decision she made he would have to accept it.

Then Rachel suddenly kneeled down and opened the bag. She took out of it a dusty old leather book.

"What's that?" he asked.

"It's what I've been looking for," she said. "It's what they're all looking for."

And so, with the roar of the sea distant in their ears and the gulls circling above, Rachel told Josef all about The Book of Stolen Dreams: about her father and her brother, about the North Brava Public Lending Library, about Lucius Meyer and the gate to the Hinterland, and Barrabus Clinch now known to be Solomon Rose, and the Meyer ghosts, and Walter Meyer and the missing page, and Charles Malstain's illness, and Lucius's note, and Mitzie's pancakes, and why she was here in Port Clement.

Josef sat very still as he listened. Then when Rachel had told him about Grimaldi Street and the gap behind the mirror, he nodded.

"So you need to find Robert."

She nodded. "I think he's in trouble. I think Charles Malstain is holding him. Robert must have sent the message to Lucius Meyer but couldn't get back to Grimaldi Street himself."

"But you also need to get the Book back to Brava."

She nodded again. "Yes. Benjamin Meyer knows how to close the gate. But he needs the Book and the missing page to do so. And I think Walter has the missing page."

Josef looked through the gap that the rust had made in the container. He was studying the sun. "Must be nearly seven," he said. A pause. He was thinking.

Then: "Rachel, my dear. Did they see you in that house back there?"

"No."

"And would old Mitzie tell them you were there?"

"No. She would never betray me."

"So as far as Malstain and his cronies are concerned, you're still asleep in the Hotel Excelsior."

"Yes, I suppose."

He chewed his mouth.

"What are you thinking, Josef?"

"Well, you might not agree to it." He paused.

"Go on," she said.

"Well, I was thinking that if you were to return secretly now to the Hotel Excelsior, and if you were to be in your room at 7 a.m. as they expect, and if I was to return home to Brava with my pink ticket, as they expect, then they would think nothing had gone wrong with their plan. And they would never suspect you of having been at the house just now. Or that you had found the Book."

"But how does that help us? They would take me to Robert. But I'd have the Book with me, so they'd get their hands on it. And that would spell disaster."

"Not necessarily."

"What do you mean, Josef?"

"I mean you might not have the Book with you in the hotel. It might be on an airship going back to Brava."

Rachel looked at him.

"No one will search me. They think I'm on their side," Josef said. "I'd get back to Brava. Collect my money for betraying you. It would look like I'd done my job perfectly. Like a true coward." He smiled a little sadly.

Rachel's eyes lit up. "And then you could take the Book to Benjamin Meyer in Paradise Alley!"

"Yes, exactly. And you could find Robert and the missing page, see? And then you can escape and get back too."

"Oh, it's brilliant, Josef! We really could do it, together Robert and I could, I'm sure!"

"There's only one thing." He stopped.

Rachel's face fell. "What? Josef. What?"

"You would have to trust me with the Book. You'd have to give it to me now, and you'd have no guarantee I wouldn't betray you again."

A wind blew through the container, picking up the sand and rustling the pages of the Book.

"I would understand if you didn't trust me, Rachel. You have no reason to."

Rachel nodded. "Josef, I do trust you. I believe at heart you are a good man."

He gave a little nod and cleared his throat. The ocean

rumbled gently in the distance. And Rachel saw that a bit of salt must have got into Josef's eyes, because he took a dirty old hanky out of his pocket and wiped a tear from his cheek.

At precisely seven o'clock that morning, Walter Meyer entered the Hotel Excelsior. He looked behind him to see two of Charles Malstain's retinue waiting outside. It was Walter who had insisted it be done this way. The girl was only twelve, she would hardly put up a fight. It was beginning to frustrate Walter how vulgar some of Malstain's men were. Why did everything have to involve muscle?

Once Robert had told them where he had hidden the Book, Johannes Slick and Walter had separated. Slick insisted he go to Grimaldi Street to get the Book. He sent Walter to the hotel to pick up the girl. Walter wondered if Slick trusted him. After all he had done for them, he was still seen as an outsider. When he was back in Brava he would talk to the President. He would remind the President that he still had the fiftieth dream in his possession and only he knew where. Without that, the Book was worthless. He would demand a proper reward for his loyalty.

Led by a chambermaid, Walter took the elevator to the seventh floor, took out the room-key that the hotel management had, after some persuasion, given him, and opened the door.

"Rachel? Rachel Klein?" he called out.

He walked in.

It was a huge room, with white curtains billowing in the morning breeze, a thick cream carpet, and gold fittings on white built-in wardrobes. A mirror was hung over the giant bed.

And in the bed, as expected, a small girl was sleeping under the covers. Walter looked at her. There she was, so unaware of everything that was happening. Walter almost laughed.

"Miss Klein." He tapped her gently on the face. "Did you have a good sleep?" he asked.

Rachel Klein turned, still sleepy and confused. "Who are you?"

"I'm Walter Meyer. I'm a friend of your brother Robert's," he replied. "Do you want to see him?"

DREAM 43

Questions

For who is to say that life is not a dream
And when we think we sleep we wake?
For when I dream is your hair not more lustrous
Is your skin not softer
Is your eye not clearer
Is your love not more true?
Then why must I wake each morning?

29

The Safe House

Rachel sat in the back of the limousine as it headed out of the city. Walter was beside her. A thick-necked bodyguard drove. They approached a street of abandoned houses near the airfield.

As the car turned into the street, Rachel saw an airship in the distance lifting from the ground. The fires burned fiercely as the metal creature slowly rose into the sky.

"That's the *Pegasus*," said Walter. "Making its last trip back to Brava before the borders close. Wouldn't you like to go back home soon, my dear? With your brother?"

Rachel said nothing, imagining Josef on board with his special cargo.

The limousine stopped outside an isolated house at the end of the street. There was no one around.

Walter slid out and approached the front door. He knocked. Rachel held on to her case and followed.

When the door opened, all hell broke loose. Johannes Slick was standing there covered in vegetable slime and bits of rotten meat. He was screaming in Walter's ear. "Someone got there before us! Who could it have been? WHO?"

Walter stammered, "That's impossible, no one else knows about the Book!" then turned to Rachel. He flew across the pavement and grabbed her elegant travelling bag, hurled it on to the hood of the car and forced it open. Like a maniac he searched through Rachel's travel items, as chosen by Bruno Petronelli. A washbag that had belonged to Laetitia, a change of socks and underwear, a yellow towel, all went flying into the morning air as Walter wrestled the case like some crazed enemy. He tore at the bottom looking for a secret compartment but there was none.

Then he turned in astonishment and dismay and sprinted into the house.

"Where is it? WHERE IS IT, BOY?"

She heard a scuffle and Rachel's cheeks burned in anger. Without thinking, she dashed through the front door. The wretched Slick tried to bar her way but she darted between his slime-spattered legs and into the hall. She could see Walter Meyer taking hold of a small figure, who was biting and scratching and giving as good as he got.

"ROBERT!" Rachel cried out and ran, her arms outstretched towards him.

"RACHEL!" he cried out in return.

Walter let go of the boy, astonished by the sheer joy in Robert's voice.

Robert flew towards his sister, grabbed her, held her tight. "You're all right! You're alive."

"*You're* alive!" she replied, holding him as if letting go might mean losing him for ever.

Then they slowly released.

Two furious pale faces greeted them.

"Who took it, boy? Who took the Book?"

Robert looked genuinely perplexed and glanced very slightly at Rachel. Rachel's face didn't move, but something in it told Robert that he should be very careful about what he said.

"I don't know. I swear."

"There was a hiding place behind the mirror, but it was empty!" said Slick. "Who did you tell where you lived? Who?"

Robert said nothing. It was as if he was obeying his sister's silent instructions.

"Did you tell your sister?" Slick looked across at Rachel. "Is that why you're here?"

"I am here because Robert disappeared and I decided to find him!" Rachel said proudly.

"And how did you find him?"

"I didn't. A kind man with a violin offered to help me stay the night in a very nice hotel and then he disappeared and then this man appeared and brought me here." Rachel's face shone. And even a teacher or the holiest of nuns would have believed her.

"SO WHO TOOK THE BOOK?" screamed Johannes Slick. "WHO PULLED THAT LADDER OFF THE BUILDING, SENDING ME INTO A HEAP OF GARBAGE? WHO, BOY?"

Rachel stayed very quiet. Slick approached Robert, nostrils flaring.

"I assume someone from the KRF must have taken it," Robert said calmly. "I told them where I was staying."

"Who? WHO? We have arrested them all! We have interrogated Constanza Glimpf," shrieked Johannes Slick, still visibly shaking. "She said she knew nothing! And believe me, our questioning was VERY persuasive!"

Walter turned to Slick. He spoke smoothly. "I think my father is behind this. He must have sent someone before he died." Robert looked astonished at the news of Lucius's death but saw that Rachel didn't flinch. "In which case," Walter continued, "that person may already be on their way back to Krasnia with the Book."

Slick turned a strange colour, something close to celery. "I am going to take a shower. Get those two ready. Then arrange a private flight back to Brava."

He reached the door and turned. His customary

deadly whisper returned. Hushed was his rage now, like a lion put back in its cage before the next devouring.

"We have two hostages now." He smiled. "I will make sure Constanza Glimpf knows that either we receive the Book or our hostages will pay."

He walked out and closed the door.

Instantly Robert was turning to Walter. "How could you do that to Constanza? How could you betray her! She's your aunt! How could you be so cruel?"

Walter took out a cigarette and placed it in his holder. He sighed as if bored by the whole affair.

"Save your breath and rest. We fly home this afternoon."

Walter walked to a window, and watched the light build in the sky. Robert stood fuming, about to make one last angry retort.

But then Rachel Klein turned to her brother and very quietly put her finger to her lips.

30

Two Hundred Groschen

The *Pegasus* landed at Brava airfield early on Tuesday morning. The flight had been over eighteen hours and Josef had not slept for one minute of it. He had hugged the violin case close to him like it was his lost sister Lotte. Why was Lotte in his head so much these days? How he missed her and wished he could see her face once more.

Inside the violin case there was no longer any violin. It had been discarded in the rusty ship container back in Port Clement. Instead, safely wrapped in the jumper that Laetitia had given Rachel for the journey, was The Book of Stolen Dreams. Around the jumper Josef had wound an old scarf, and a sheet that he had "borrowed" from a washing line near Port Clement International airfield. And all were packed tightly in the violin case.

Josef travelled under his own passport, using the pink ticket given to him by the director of the orphanage. He passed through immigration without a hitch. Then a tall man in a dark suit and with a pencil moustache approached him.

"Centurion?"

"Yes."

"You took the girl to the hotel?"

"Yes, that's right. I left her there in the morning."

"Anything strange to report?"

"Nothing. Why? Was she not there?"

The man did not reply. He looked Josef up and down, then stared at his violin case. "What's in there?"

"Just the fiddle. I was playing it when your boss approached me. Want me to play you a tune?" Josef smiled sweetly and made to open it. Inside, his heart was racing.

"No, that's all right." The man reached into his pocket and took out a small cloth bag. Inside were twenty coins, each one ten groschen.

"That's for you. Say nothing about this. You hear me? If anyone asks, you never met that girl."

His eyes searched Josef's for a moment. Josef nodded, and the man turned and walked to his black saloon car. Josef watched the car drive away. He breathed slowly.

Then he took one of the coins out of the bag and waved at the first taxi he could find.

Josef knew he must do exactly as Rachel had asked. Even though he was exceptionally hungry and the coins in his pocket screamed *Bagel!* and *Tartine!* at him with every passing restaurant, he directed the taxi driver straight to the junction of Goethe Street and Paradise Lane.

He got out and saw the entrance to the narrow passageway. Grabbing the violin case, he paid the taxi then crossed the road. Josef felt a strange leap of joy in his heart. Firstly, he was back in Brava and that pleased him more than he expected. It felt like home. And secondly, for all that what he was doing was probably intensely foolish and highly dangerous, he was doing it for *the right reasons*, and this lifted Josef's spirits enormously.

He took a quick look around then ducked down the passageway. He hummed a little tune to himself to keep calm. It was a dance piece he played often on the violin.

"*Dum de dum dum de de dum dum de diddle diddle deeee.*"

Keeping his head low and pulling his coat tight against the increasing cold, he skipped past the offices of lawyers and merchant venturers.

"*Dum de dum dum de de dum dum de deeee.*"

Then he saw the sign:

MEYER AND SONS. ILLUSTRATING THE STRANGE AND THE FANCIFUL.

Josef paused. It was just as Rachel had said. She had told him also about the note beneath.

MEYER AND SONS REGRETFULLY ANNOUNCES THAT IT HAS CEASED TO OPERATE IN BRAVA.

Nothing was different to how Rachel had described it. So why did Josef feel strange?

He took courage and knocked on the door. There was a silence, then the door opened. It was an old woman with a large nose, just as Rachel had said it would be. Her face seemed stained with tears. This Rachel had not mentioned.

Josef smiled at her politely but got nothing in return. He cleared his throat and quietly intoned, "Let the true dreamer wake."

The old woman stared at him impassively. Did she nod just slightly?

Josef continued. "I am looking for Solomon Rose."

The old woman nodded again, then opened the door. Josef walked in. He saw the candelabra and the visitors' book and the portraits on the walls. The old woman was already halfway across the dark hallway, heading to the back room.

"In here."

She opened the door to the back room. Everything was exactly as Rachel Klein had said it would be. Josef was about to cross the hallway. But then he paused.

When one has been a minor thief for as long as Josef Centurion, one gains a certain instinct for trouble. Josef would often be walking down a street towards a corner when he would feel a strange pain in his side. He would immediately know that a policeman was approaching on the other side of the corner. Seconds later the policeman would appear but by then Josef Centurion would be gone. It was a useful skill on many occasions, but never as useful as it proved right now in the hallway of Meyer and Sons.

Josef Centurion felt a clear stabbing pain in his side.

He looked at the old woman, who turned in the hallway, wondering why the man with the violin case had not followed her.

"This way."

He looked into her tear-stained eyes. And in her eyes he saw a fear. He saw fear also in the fingers that were clutching her apron a little tighter than was necessary. He saw it in the toes of her house slippers that were gripping the oak floor as if for dear life.

And Josef sensed that whoever was in that back room, it was not Solomon Rose.

Josef ran.

As he did, figures burst from the back room of Meyer and Sons and flew after him. Soldiers. Holding the violin case tight, Josef dashed back out of the house, sprinted down the passageway, burst out into the square where the fountain no longer worked, and hurtled across the square and over a small wall at the far side.

All the time his mind was whirring.

He had to hide the case, it didn't matter about him, *but he had to hide the case.*

Josef found himself in a small old cemetery, walled off and hidden away, with dozens of graves from the Emperor's time and earlier. He heard feet behind him, uniformed men climbing the wall, screaming, "Stop or we'll shoot!" But Josef was in no mood for stopping. He reached the far side of the graveyard and climbed a metal gate, bullets pinging past his ears on to the metal. He vaulted over and landed in a cobbled alleyway filled with what had once been bars and cafes, now all closed under the Malstain regime. He ran on, desperate for one empty doorway, one open window. But everything was boarded and shut.

The soldiers had vaulted out of the graveyard too and were in hot pursuit. Josef took a sharp left down another alleyway, into the heart of the medieval city, under stone arches cracked with lack of care, past old abandoned shrines with little statuettes to the dead. He cut another left, but the soldiers were younger and faster and Josef cursed his life of wine and song that had in no way prepared him for such a test of stamina.

They were going to get him. It was inevitable.

Then he saw the open door. It was the only open door on the street. An angelic-looking child with blond locks was alone on the step playing a game involving a spinning top. Josef rushed to the doorway, hurdled the child in one leap. The child turned in wonder. Inside the courtyard Josef saw a stone staircase heading up. He had to get up there! But now a woman was descending and calling the child. "Josef, what are you doing? Come in for your supper."

Josef Centurion barely had time to consider the strange chance that this lovely little blond-haired boy should share his name. He approached the woman who was coming down the staircase to fetch her son; he held out the violin case, and said, "Take this! The future of Krasnia depends on you!" Then he stopped dead and stared into the eyes of a woman two years younger than him, a woman whom he had not seen for twenty-five years, but whose blue eyes and little mole on her left cheek took him instantly back to a trainline and a river and the last time he had seen her.

"Lotte!" he cried.

31

The Palace

Rachel and Robert were together for the whole flight home. They were locked in a first-class private cabin. The entire plane had been paid for by the Krasnian government. The cabin had comfortable bunk beds, soft carpets, fruit bowls and a small bar with chocolates and soda drinks. This would normally have been a source of unbelievable pleasure and excitement to both children, but nothing at this moment was further from their minds.

All Robert wanted was an opportunity to talk to Rachel privately, to tell her about Constanza and Walter Meyer and the Book. And all Rachel wanted to do was tell Robert about Solomon Rose and the Meyer ancestors, and Walter's missing page and Josef Centurion and the Book. But they were never alone, guarded at all times by

Johannes Slick and his band of silent officers.

Every now and then Walter Meyer would drift into the cabin where they were being held. He would say nothing, just look at both children then leave. It occurred to Rachel that some strange private conversation was taking place in Walter's head.

The hours passed. Rachel grew hungry. But she knew that to accept even one sherbet would admit defeat. Robert seemed to feel the same. He sat silent and sullen, eating and drinking nothing.

Then, with just an hour left of the journey, Walter entered again. He had the same listless smile. Walter approached the guard on duty.

"Get me some food, old boy. Kitchen will close soon."

The burly fellow shook his head. "Got to stay with these two," he said, pointing at the Kleins. "Orders from the top."

"Oh, don't be such an ass. I'll watch them. We're six thousand feet up in the air, where exactly are they going to go? On to a passing cloud?" Walter waited for a reply that he knew wouldn't come. "Get me a pastrami roll with extra salad and a half-bottle of brandy. Make sure it's Baron Lafleur."

The guard grumbled for a moment and then sloped out, muttering that it was more than his job was worth.

Walter turned immediately. The children suddenly felt a danger. The guards were muscular but stupid, like a heavy axe with no edge, easily avoided. Here was a razor, sharpened and primed.

Walter smiled. "So I've just learned something interesting. Early this morning, a man knocked on the door of my father's offices in Paradise Lane. He had a violin case in his hand. The state police were waiting. They've been watching the offices for a while. He asked after Solomon Rose."

Rachel and Robert stayed very still.

"The man escaped. But it left me wondering about my old friend Solomon. And his connection with you two."

"Never heard of him," replied Rachel. "Who is he?"

Walter studied them closely. "Oh, come now, children. Let's stop these games. I've watched you run rings around Slick and his morons, but I'm a different proposition. I know you met my father. It was you he sent to Port Clement. And you met Solomon too. He told you everything. Didn't he?"

Rachel said nothing. Robert once again looked confused. Walter checked the door was shut. Then came closer.

"What did he tell you? That I was a bad man, rotten to the core? That I had betrayed my family?"

"That you were angry," Rachel said quietly. Robert glanced at her, as if to ask politely what the hell she was doing. But Rachel seemed calm. She sat very small, watching Walter, waiting for his next move.

Walter glanced out the window of the airship at the delicate clouds passing. "I am angry with good reason. My father…" He paused for a moment.

"Your father was killed," Rachel said softly.

"I know."

"Soldiers killed him," she continued, watching Walter. "I saw his body."

Robert stared, deeply shocked. Walter took a long drag from his white cigarette. His thin frame gave a small shiver.

"Well, serves him right. I gave him every chance to change his mind. He could have given me the secret to the Book, but he chose…another path." The words burst from him and his face went red.

"I met the rest of your family," said Rachel. "All of them. In the house."

Walter looked at Rachel sharply.

Now Robert was completely lost. "What family?" he said. "What house?"

"I met all the Meyers in Paradise Lane," Rachel explained despite Walter's increasingly hostile glare. "Benjamin Meyer and all his descendants. They all live in the house. The Meyers kept the secret of the Book all these years." Robert looked bewildered. "The gate, Robert. The gate to the Hinterland."

Robert was getting it, slowly. "You mean…? You don't mean? You mean…they're…?"

Rachel nodded.

Robert's eyes widened. "But that's impossible. It's completely unscientific."

"You remember the noises we heard in the house that day we visited? The voices up the stairs? It was them. They use the Book to bring back those they love most in the world from the Hinterland. Only they know the secret of how to do it. And Lucius Meyer was supposed to give Walter the secret, but he changed his mind."

"Why?" asked Robert.

"Because he didn't trust him."

Robert turned to look at Walter. Walter took another draw of his cigarette then stubbed it out on a saucer as if the taste had suddenly become foul. Rachel felt Walter was slowly losing that poise that she found so frightening.

"This is my father's fault," Walter said. "If he had passed the secret on to me, none of this would have happened. Instead, he chose to give it to that...nobody... Solomon..."

"He didn't trust you, Walter," said Rachel quietly. "And he was right. The Book is only to be used by people who respect its power. People who respect the dead. But you are about to give it to a man who has no respect for anything."

"I was the one who was not respected!" Walter's eyes flashed.

"And so you're going to give the keys to the dead to the worst man in the world? Charles Malstain loves no one! He has no one to call back from the dead. He cannot love anyone! He wants the Book so that when he dies HE can be called back – to live for ever. To rule Krasnia for all time!"

Robert stared in astonishment. Was this really his sister? Her eyes were fierce.

"Enough of this pointless talk!" Walter snapped. "Do you know what happens when we reach Brava? You are to be taken to the palace for questioning. President Malstain will do terrible things to you if you refuse to cooperate. He does not spare children. Quite the opposite. So if you know where the Book is, you'd better tell me now."

Rachel felt her insides shake with anger. Robert gulped. Walter waited. Then Rachel spoke.

"We have nothing to tell you. But if you tell us where the missing page is, then maybe we can help you."

Walter's face seemed to fall off a cliff. His eyes turned a strange colour, his forehead began to moisten. Robert watched him, now more lost than he could have thought possible.

"Solomon says you have it," Rachel continued, her eyes fixed on Walter. "If you give it to me, I will get it to the Meyers and they can close the gate for ever. Krasnia will be safe."

Walter glanced around; his breath shortened. Robert looked at Rachel in total disbelief. Rachel continued to stare at Walter, daring him to look away.

"Do you still have it? Or did you give it to the President? Is it too late?"

Walter shook his head. "Stop asking stupid questions!"

"I will if you answer them. Is it too late, Walter? Have you betrayed all Krasnia to that man?"

"You understand nothing!" All the calm, all the elegance fled Walter. His face was red-hot, sweating. He was almost in tears. And in that moment Rachel saw a young boy, not much older than her, a boy who had discovered he was not the chosen one as he had always assumed. And who did not know how to deal with his rage.

"It is you, Walter, who understand nothing." She spoke very quietly. And as Rachel looked Walter hard in the eye, it seemed just for a moment that he might agree.

At Brava airfield, there was a limousine waiting with a police escort. Rachel was surprised to see the airfield was empty. No passengers were waiting to board. Robert quietly reminded her that all flights had stopped. Brava and the whole of Krasnia was now officially cut off. No escape. No return.

They sat in the back seat as the presidential convoy sped through the streets. Johannes Slick was in the front seat, Walter in the car behind. A police escort scattered the few vehicles that dared be in their way, like leaves in a wind. Brava was so quiet compared to the life and bustle of Port Clement. It did indeed feel like a ghost town – a city of the dead.

Rachel considered their options. According to Walter, Josef had nearly been caught at Meyer and Sons but he'd escaped. Did he still have the Book? Or had he dropped it in his flight? Did he manage to circle back and give it to Solomon? And what about Walter? Did he still have the missing page? Or had he handed it over to Malstain? All she had were questions but no answers. She had no way of knowing anything.

The convoy reached a large ugly dual carriageway in the city centre. It had been made especially for the President to reach the palace at high speed. Malstain was always convinced someone would shoot him if his car was forced to slow down even for a second. Several old churches and houses had been demolished and the residents evicted without compensation.

The limousine swept up the two-laned presidential avenue towards the palace gates.

Rachel looked out in awe. She had never been this close to the palace – ordinary Bravans were not allowed anywhere near. The gates were pure gold with dozens of burning spears reaching to the heavens. There were uniformed sentries outside, armed with rifles. The police escort drove fast towards them. The sentries turned to open the gates so that the motorcade could pass through without stopping. Rachel felt Robert grip her hand. They were entering the palace of the most powerful and hated man in Krasnia.

The convoy stopped outside a side door. The children were pulled roughly from the car and bundled through the door into a vestibule. There they were searched by two guards while Johannes Slick went straight to a telephone and made a call. Walter stood in the doorway, pallid and silent. Rachel tried to catch his eyes but felt he was deliberately avoiding her.

Slick put the phone down and spoke quietly to Walter, who nodded. Slick left through a side door and Walter turned to the guards.

"Second-floor reception room. Now."

They were hurried along a corridor, up a small flight of steps to a lift with a modern metal door. The lift took them up two floors. They were pushed out and along more corridors and through more anonymous rooms. Everywhere, the palace showed evidence of Malstain's state of mind. Rachel saw cameras on every wall, she saw steel security doors that had been built in front of old archways, she saw paintings from the Imperial times taken down and left in piles in corners of rooms. She saw guards everywhere, with guns and radios, and secretaries and administrators scurrying past them to offices that lay deep within the building, heads down as if to avoid detection.

"Move!" a particularly unpleasant guard screamed at them, as they were shoved around a corner into a waiting room with a glass-fronted admissions desk. A flag of Malstain's own invention languished in a sad flowerpot.

Behind the desk sat a man who looked a little like a rat with glasses.

The guard shouted to present them: "Rachel and Robert Klein. Here for interrogation!"

"Then why not take them down to the basement area?" the rat replied with a sneer. "That's where interrogations take place. They took the Glimpf woman there yesterday. O'Hare is with her now, doing what O'Hare does."

Robert and Rachel exchanged glances. Walter Meyer stepped in.

"The President has requested a private audience with the prisoners." He smiled casually.

"I will need to confirm that." The rat got on the phone and made a call, shutting the glass window for privacy. After a few seconds, without speaking to Walter or the guard, he pressed a button and the glass barrier opened.

Walter nodded and the guard pushed the children down another corridor, towards a pair of tall double doors. The guard threw open the doors, and Rachel and Robert entered the largest room they had ever seen in their lives.

It was a throne room. The floor was wooden and polished, the walls decorated in gold and marble. There were double doors at both ends of the room. At the far end stood the old Imperial throne, gem-studded, on a marble platform. The room had three vast portraits of the President, one on each wall. In one painting Malstain was in military uniform astride a horse. In another he was with the "people of Krasnia", who were throwing flowers at his feet while he smiled and waved. In the final picture he was sitting on the very throne Rachel was looking at, in ceremonial clothes.

The room was empty.

Walter had followed them in. He stationed himself in one corner of the room, took out a cigarette but did not light it. The guard stood to attention for no one in particular.

Then Rachel heard footsteps coming from behind the double doors at the far end. The doors flew open and several footmen filed in, polishing the floor as they came.

Behind them marched four armed soldiers, who carefully checked the room. And behind them walked a small figure with carrot legs, who Robert immediately recognised. It was President Charles Malstain. He was in military clothes. His shoes sparkled. His face was powdered white. His lips had a touch of red added to them. His oil-slick hair was combed slightly to the right. He carried a black cane in his left hand, which he used to support himself.

He's changed, Robert thought. *He looks unwell.*

Malstain saw the children and stopped in his tracks. For a moment he seemed like he might be violently sick. Then he composed himself.

Walter spoke from the corner of the room. "These are the Klein children, Your Excellency."

"I know…who they are."

Malstain surveyed them, then nodded to his retinue, who immediately fetched two small chairs from the side of the room and placed them in front of the throne.

The President climbed the marble pedestal and sat on the throne, his legs stretched out, his shiny feet not quite touching the ground. His black cane was propped up between his thighs.

"So. Children. Let's have a little talk, shall we?"

His voice was higher pitched and thinner than Rachel had expected. He seemed to be speaking in a "children's" voice for their sake. The way he said "little talk" irritated her immensely.

Rachel and Robert were pushed hard in the back and sent sprawling towards the chairs. Robert turned angrily. "That's enough! If you want us to sit you just need to ask!"

There was a silence as they sat.

"And if I ask you something else?" The reedy voice of the President filled the room. "Will you answer me that?"

They stayed silent. They knew what was coming.

"I am looking for the Book." Malstain spoke quietly.

Rachel studied him from the low chair she had been given. He was very white indeed. His skin was puffy, his forehead was glowing with sweat under all the powder. His breath struggled to escape his throat. *Yes. He's ill*, she thought. *And he doesn't have the Book*.

"I am tired, children, and my usual patience will soon

be exhausted. So. You can either tell me where the Book is, or you can join Constanza Glimpf and her other associates in my basement dungeon. Rufus O'Hare will get everything out of you, I can assure you."

"We don't know where the Book is," Rachel said defiantly, and it was true. She really had no idea. It might be with Josef, it might be with Solomon…

The President seemed to read her mind. He paused and smiled. "Don't think Solomon Rose will help you." He eyed Rachel with disdain.

All Rachel's bravery evaporated in one moment. What had happened?

"Rose is a dreamer and a fool. After you left Brava, he insisted on burying that dumb old goat Lucius Meyer."

In the corner of the room Walter Meyer directed his eyes studiously to the floor as Malstain gave a hollow laugh.

"It was just so easy to follow the funeral cortège to the grave and arrest him! Oh, he tried to run, but one thing I can tell you, Solomon Rose is no sprinter." Malstain cackled. "So if you were hoping to get the Book to him, then you can think again, my dear. He is in my dungeon, right beneath our feet, and receiving very special treatment indeed."

Rachel looked down to the ground, imagining Solomon in agony in the darkness beneath. And what about the Meyers? Had they been found too? She felt her blood pumping in helpless anger.

Malstain's laugh turned to a deep cough. He breathed heavily. His eyes sagged deep into his face. "So. I'm giving you one…last…chance. My little children." He looked at them and tried a sweet smile. "I don't want to hurt you…"

"We're not your children! We don't know where the Book is and we wouldn't tell you if we did!" shouted Robert.

Malstain stiffened. A sort of hiss seemed to come from his lips. A froth formed on his chin and out of his nose. He gasped, then slammed his stick down on the ground. "Get Slick," he whispered.

The guards sprinted to the doors and ran out. Walter still had not lit his cigarette. Malstain leaned heavily on his cane and rose to gain more height over the Kleins.

"You…will…regret…crossing me." He forced the words from his throat like unwanted flies. "You may think…that because you are…children…the rules are different. That I will be easy on you. That I will show…pity…" He spat the word out with contempt. "But I will make it doubly worse for you. Just because you are children. I will…do things…" He left the words hanging in the air.

Rachel felt her resolve weaken for a second but looked across at Robert and saw he had a fire of rage in his eyes.

"There is nothing you can do," said Robert. "You have killed our mother and sent our father to endless torture. There is nothing you can do!"

Malstain slammed the black cane on the ground. It

echoed through the hall. Then he fixed them both with a glare of pure hate, and spoke in a whisper, like a kettle's hiss. "Don't…be…so…sure…"

At this, there was a commotion outside the doorway.

"Slick?" screamed Malstain, fearing imminent assassination. And indeed Johannes Slick came storming into the room. But he was dragging someone with him. And Rachel gasped in horror when she saw who it was.

Josef Centurion was sent sprawling at the feet of President Charles Malstain.

32

Block K

Josef groaned. A giant boot had just made use of his stomach as a football.

"Leave him alone!" A young girl's voice rang out. It was Rachel, and he looked up at her gratefully from the vast palace floor.

"Silence that child!" The thin flute-like voice of President Malstain filled the room. "Ask him again."

Johannes Slick approached. Rufus O'Hare, he with the giant boot, stood waiting, eager for another go.

"Where did you hide the Book?" Johannes asked quietly, his voice no more than a whisper in the grass.

"What…book?" Josef said, for what he thought must have been the seventh time. He waited for another kick in the belly.

This had been going on for a while. Rachel and Robert were being held by two guards as Slick and O'Hare went about their business. Malstain remained on his throne, clutching his black cane, his eyes glaring – first at Josef, then at the children who had dared to imperil his dreams of immortality.

In the corner of the room Walter Meyer stood, very still, watching it all, not taking part, not saying anything. The cigarette was between his lips but still he had not lit it.

Josef squirmed in pain as the next kick came in. It occurred to him that the desperate life he had led was now coming in useful. Josef was used to being beaten. He'd been beaten by Uncle Leonard, by local police, by national guards, by soldiers, shopkeepers, market traders, bar owners, drinkers, thieves, and even once by a group of deeply unpleasant car salesmen. Josef had been bruised in so many parts of his body that the pain now just washed over him. He lay on the ground and thought about the pattern of the wooden floor, the nice little rectangles, and how it must have taken someone a good while to lay it down.

"Where is your violin case! Where is it, Centurion?!"

"I lost it. Silly me."

Slick approached. "Centurion, let me explain something. I will give you one more chance and then O'Hare and I will take you down to the basement under the palace. And there you won't find life so easy."

"Don't you dare!" cried out Robert.

"Then get him to tell us where he's hidden the Book!" cried out Malstain.

Rachel looked across at Josef, who managed to peer up from the parquet floor and meet her gaze. His sad eyes said a very simple thing. *I won't tell.* Rachel understood them clearly and gave him a look back that said, *I know. And I am very proud of you.*

Josef grinned like you do when you receive a present you've always wanted. And then he put his right finger to his left cheek as if to scratch it.

Rachel studied him carefully.

"One last chance, Centurion!"

It was Slick who screamed at him again.

But Josef was too busy scratching his left cheek. Rachel watched him silently. He was using the first finger of his right hand. And she understood.

He was trying to tell her something.

At the same time and with the skill of a true fiddle player, he was turning his thumb at ninety degrees flat across his cheek. So that the two fingers together formed a kind of half a square. Or more correctly a letter.

The letter L.

He made the letter once. Then relaxed his fingers. Then made it again. Then relaxed. Then made it a third and last time.

"You ungrateful wretch!" Malstain stood and his fury

was unrestrained. He hobbled down from the podium and spat on Centurion's prostrate body. "I want every torture known to man exercised on this piece of vermin! I want his arms torn from his shoulders! I want him placed on the rack and electricity pumped through him! He will submit! He will submit!"

A noise came from the floor. It came from the body of Josef Centurion. Rachel looked across to see his stomach moving back and forth. For a moment Rachel was convinced that he was having some kind of fit. "Help him!" she called out. But then Josef raised his face from the floor and she saw that Josef was not having a fit at all. He was laughing.

Malstain stepped back in horror. Josef's laugh became louder.

"Your legs!" he said. "They're like carrots."

Malstain clutched his chest and faltered. "Get him out of here!" he sputtered.

Slick nodded; O'Hare moved forward and grabbed Josef, who had tears pouring down his cheeks and was holding his sides like they might fall out. In one movement O'Hare picked up the laughing thief, hurled him over his shoulder and strode from the room.

"Get those children out of my sight! Imprison them! No food! No books! Nothing! NOTHING!" Malstain was screaming now. He looked suddenly very small in the middle of the huge room.

Slick nodded to Walter Meyer, who had not moved from his position in the corner. "Meyer!" he hissed. "Take the children to Accommodation Block K. Say I sent you. Bread and water only. No visits. No records they were ever here."

Then Slick hurried to Malstain, who was wheezing heavily, as if suffering some kind of minor attack.

"Fetch the doctors!" he called. "Get the President to his rooms!"

There was a flurry of action as officials and soldiers all rushed to help the struggling President and ushered him from the hall.

A moment's silence. Walter Meyer stood very still. Suddenly he let his unlit cigarette drop on to the elegant wooden floor. Then he slowly approached the children. One guard remained, armed, his gun trained on them. Walter spoke quietly, without emotion.

"This way."

Walter took them through a side door and along a corridor. At first the corridor was as ornately decorated as the room they had come from, but soon it turned into a dark grey stone. The windows became gradually smaller, the light dimmed and the silence grew. There were no longer views out to the palace gardens or the great city beyond. Light peeped from narrow slits high in the wall. It was like disappearing into the heart of a mountain.

Meyer walked in front, followed by the children, then

the armed guard behind, his gun pointed at their backs. Meyer turned left then right, down a small grey flight of stairs and into a new area labelled *Accommodation Block K*. Rachel heard distant screaming. She saw that Robert had heard it too. He shuddered.

Walter turned at the doors to Block K. He spoke to the guard wearily.

"All right, I'll take them from here. Get back to the prisoner, make sure he tells us what we need to know."

The guard nodded and continued down the stairs. Walter made to enter the double doors into Block K, and paused. He waited for the guard's steps to fade, then he looked around at the children. His eyes were strangely blank.

Walter said nothing, waited a few more seconds. He looked back up the stairs, then turned and said one word: "Hurry."

They followed him back up the stairs and through another door into a new part of the palace. He led them up and down, left and right. Twice they had to duck into small alcoves, as administrative officials passed the other way clutching files and briefcases. Rachel was completely lost now. She had no idea if they might end up in the President's bathroom or just as easily in the dark dungeons where poor Josef had been sent.

Walter moved nimbly, still with a kind of ease but with more speed than she had seen him use before. Once, an official came around the corner before they could hide but Walter just paused and had a light-hearted chat about the weather and the need for better snacks in the staff canteen. Then they continued. Walter was always in front, his head high, his step confident.

A green door beckoned. In through the door went Walter, and the children found themselves in a kitchen area. Walter approached the cook, a small, anxious-looking man who was responsible for the President's extremely bizarre and demanding diet. Walter explained that the children were relatives of the President's dentist and wanted a brief tour of the palace before they were sent back to their home in the countryside. The cook ushered them through and Walter said loudly, "I'm going to show you a side of the palace that few visitors get to see. As the descendants of dentists, I think you will find it very interesting."

They walked through plastic-sheeted doors and daylight hit them.

They were now in a yard where the food deliveries for the palace arrived. Trucks were lined up to deliver enormous amounts of red meat, white fish, brown eggs and green beans – everything that the President had demanded in his endless search for health.

Walter kept talking very loudly about why this delivery yard was of particular interest, as it was the largest delivery yard in the whole of Krasnia and possibly the world. At the same time, he was walking the children to one of the meat trucks, quickly and quietly opening the back of the truck, and helping both children climb up and inside the freezer compartment. Then, still talking, but now to thin air, Walter watched carefully as the driver of the truck finished his coffee and ambled back towards his vehicle. Walter sidled over, had a quiet word with him, and handed him something. The man nodded, walked to the driver's door, climbed in and started the engine.

Inside the truck's container, Rachel shivered from fear and cold. She was crammed between blocks of ice, under huge legs of frozen lamb and sides of beef that hung from hooks nailed to the roof of the container. As the truck started to move, through the plastic rear window she saw Walter standing in the yard. He watched very carefully as the truck approached the palace security. Only when it was waved out through the presidential gates and into the city, did Rachel see Walter Meyer turn on his heel and return into the palace.

DREAM 48

The Secret

I have found it, the secret
It is in words
Words will keep you in the walled garden
And no gate will dare to send you back
No door will separate us
We will lie for ever here
And the roses will not wither
Nor the grass turn brown
There will be no winter in this garden
When the secret has been spoken

33

The Bottom Drawer

The meat truck clattered through the city. Inside the rear container the temperature had plummeted. Robert and Rachel were sandwiched between blocks of ice. They had ice in their hair and ice in their clothes. They sat close together to avoid being hit by swaying legs of meat.

Rachel looked across at her brother. His teeth were chattering, his lips were blue. His eyebrows had spawned little flakes of frost. Rachel felt her whole body shaking. She began to wonder how long they could take this.

The truck suddenly turned; the meat swayed violently. A leg of beef clocked Robert on the side of the head as the brakes squealed and the truck came to a shuddering halt.

The engine was turned off. Frozen air stopped pumping

through the vents. Rachel looked at Robert, who was shivering and nursing a bruise on his temple. They listened as the driver's door opened then slammed. Steps on the ground. Then a loud clunk – metal on metal.

The doors opened and the rear of the truck flooded with daylight.

The driver stood open-mouthed in astonishment. Two small yetis greeted him, coats covered in snow, faces blue and bodies shaking as they almost fell out of the container like ice cubes into a glass of lemonade.

"What the blinking…?" he said quietly.

"D-d-d-d-d-d-d-d…" said Robert.

Rachel saw through half-frozen eyelids that they had stopped in a rather elegant and quiet mews alleyway.

"B-b-b-b-b-b-b…" said Robert.

"How the hell did you get in there?"

"G-g-g-g-g-g-g…"

"All right, son, let's warm you up." The man grabbed Robert and held him tight. He was a large man and enveloped Robert with ease.

"W-w-w-w-w-w…" said Robert as the driver hugged him hard and bounced him up and down. Then he grabbed Rachel too and all three bounced up and down. It would have been a curious sight if anyone had seen it, but as usual the streets of Brava were quiet and the mews deserted.

"Whe-whe-where-where…where are we?" Robert finally managed.

"We're where the gentleman sent me, that's where," said the driver. "Gave me fifty groschen to deliver two fresh young lambs to this address. Even gave me some keys." The driver laughed. "Now I know what lambs he meant."

The driver held out the keys. "I'm guessing these are for you."

"Th-th-th-thank…"

"Don't thank me. I don't know what's going on and I don't want to. It's every man for himself in this country these days. Here's the keys and good luck, I say."

He laughed. Robert somehow managed to take the keys without dropping them.

"Apartment 27b," the driver called out. "Gentleman said I should leave the lambs in the front room. But I think you can find your own way. This crazy country!" He laughed again, then closed the back of the truck, jumped in the front and drove off.

Robert held the keys tight in his hand. There were two keys, one iron, one silver. The iron one let them in the front door.

Inside, the children found an elegant apartment, heated and warm. There were carvings and unusual silks on the walls. The wooden floors were covered with rich woollen carpets. There were three letters waiting on the doormat. The letters were addressed to Walter Meyer.

"It's W-w-w-walter's apartment," Rachel stuttered.

They brushed half the ice off themselves and waited for the rest to melt. They opened the letters, but they were only reminders of bills not paid. The kitchen had bread and chocolate biscuits, which they devoured. They drank hot "Peruvian" coffee, which almost scalded their tongues. Then they got to work.

"There's a reason he sent us here, I'm sure!" Rachel was trying to place herself in Walter's mind. Why had he sent them here?

"The driver said he was to leave us in the front room," Robert pointed out.

Rachel nodded. They looked in the front room. It had a bed but nothing hidden under it. It had pictures on the wall but nothing behind them.

"This is no good! Why did he want us to come here?" Rachel was frustrated.

"Maybe just to keep us safe."

"No. There's another reason. I saw Walter's face when Malstain was insulting his father. Walter has realised his mistake. He wants to stop him."

Rachel continued searching. She looked under the beautiful rugs and behind the ornate Indian silks that hung on the walls. Nothing.

Then she looked at the small desk in the corner.

On the desk were various papers. Rachel found only unpaid bills and tax demands.

Then she tried the drawers of the desk. The top two

were open and had pens and letters, mostly from a woman called Giselle.

But the bottom drawer was locked.

Rachel turned to Robert. "The keys."

He handed them to her. She took the silver one, slipped it into the lock. It fitted perfectly. The drawer slid open.

Inside was just one very old, folded piece of paper. Even folded it was staggeringly beautiful.

"Now I know why he sent us here," she said quietly.

Robert looked over Rachel's shoulder as she opened the paper. And read.

DREAM 50

Now we have come this far
Let us vow
To live for ever in this garden
Say the words
"Forever More"
And nothing
Not even death, my love
Can stand between us
We will live
Eternal in this land of dreams
I say it now
"Forever More"

34

L

"What I don't understand is this." Rachel was walking fast along a cobbled street in the middle of Brava. "The dream says what you need to say if you want to open the gates for ever. You say 'Forever more'. Fine – that's clear. So if Charles Malstain has the Book and says those words then he lives forever more. That's obvious."

"Rachel, slow down."

"But what it doesn't say, is what I thought it would say. It doesn't say what you have to say to lock the gate for ever. It doesn't say anything about locking the gate at all! Benjamin Meyer clearly said that he could lock the gate. But how?"

"Rachel, I said slow down."

"Even if we find the Book – which has got something to

do with the letter L, because that's the sign Josef made three times on his cheek while he was being brutally beaten by those monsters – even if we find the Book, I'm not sure I know the right words to say. But we have to try!"

"Rachel, listen to me for once in your bloody life!"

Rachel turned. Robert was fuming with anger.

"Robert. Firstly, don't swear, it's beneath you. Secondly, and with respect, I don't have time to go over everything now. Suffice it to say, the missing page is the key. We have to lock the gate so Malstain can't ever open it again. There'll be soldiers all over Paradise Lane, so we can't go there. And Malstain will soon know we are missing. He'll start looking for us. We have to find the Book before they find us! And I have to work out what to say to lock the gate!"

Robert paused, taken aback by his sister's new-found authority. *She's grown up*, he thought to himself. *And not just because she's had a birthday since I last saw her.*

"But, Rachel, and with respect, if we're going to find the Book, we have to know where we are going. There's no point walking in circles. We've been through this square four times in the last hour."

Rachel looked around. He was right. The cobbles did look familiar.

"All right then. Let's sit and think."

She walked to a bench and sat down. Robert checked for police.

"What does L mean?" Rachel mused out loud. "Why did Josef make that sign? And why three times?"

"Don't ask me. You know him better than I do," said Robert and kicked the ground.

Rachel paused. It was true, she did know Josef much better than her brother, who had barely met him. But more than that, she knew Josef better than anyone did. Josef had come to trust her. Rachel realised that must be the key to everything. She needed to think about everything they had shared together. All their secrets.

And suddenly everything became wonderfully clear!

"You're right, Robert. I do know Josef. And he told me something very important about his life. L is for someone very special to him, the most special person he's ever known, maybe the only person he's ever loved. L is for Lotte."

"Lotte?"

"His sister. He lost touch with her. But somehow – and don't ask me how, Robert, please, don't even ask – he has found her. And she has the Book."

"How can you be sure?"

"I just am."

"But L could be for anything, Rachel. Lion or linctus…"

"No, it's for Lotte."

"Or lemonade or llama or lending library…"

"No, Robert!" she called out and then she stopped. "What did you just say?"

"I said llama."

"No, before that."

"Lemonade."

"No!"

"Before llama I said lemonade!"

"Then after!"

"After llama? I said lending library."

"Why?"

"Because walking through these endless squares reminds me of our father and that afternoon we went with him to the library. So what?" Robert looked at her, upset and confused.

"Robert Klein, you are a genius," Rachel said quietly.

"Am I?" he sulked, but with a little bit of hope that it might be true.

"Yes, you are. You see I also told Josef about the lending library! I told him we stole the Book from there with our father. I even told him about the Rare Books Room."

Rachel's mind was flying now, the hot Peruvian coffee and the chocolate biscuits and the adrenaline of having the missing page tucked into her coat pocket all combining into a fury of thought that poured out of her.

"What if Josef told Lotte to go to the lending library? I told him all about it, I told him that was where the Book came from! That's why he made the sign three times! I think he told Lotte to go to the lending library and wait for us!"

She shouted this so loud that two passers-by turned and stared at the children. Robert waved at them and implied with a mime that his sister was eccentric and to be ignored.

"Keep your voice down!" he whispered.

The passers-by passed by.

Rachel spoke more quietly. "Which way is the library, Robert? Which way?"

Robert, relieved to be needed, flicked on his internal navigation switch and looked around. "It's north, of course. This way."

They ducked through narrow streets. Robert was leading now. Rachel knew that this was when to be quiet and let the Klein compass do its work. Robert took them down alleys, across small hidden squares, over bridges, under arches. His nose was raised slightly; his freckles seemed to be alert to every turn. He was like a tracker hunting seal.

Rachel watched the back of her brother's head as she followed. She thought about the compass in his head that was currently on overdrive and the moral compass that Josef had found and how life in so many ways was a kind of maze of narrow streets and passageways, some dangerous, some beautiful. And that what mattered was who you travelled with, and the choices you made along the way.

"Keep up, Rachel, or I'll lose you," Robert whispered sternly.

They walked on. They saw two state policemen coming the other way and stole down an alley until they'd passed. They heard a siren and paled with fear, but it was only a fire engine rattling through the quiet streets. Rachel tried to check the time on a clock tower but it was broken. How long before Josef could bear the pain no longer and would tell Johannes Slick everything he knew? How long did they have before Charles Malstain came after them?

"Rachel, look."

Robert was peering through a small gap between two dull office blocks. In the distance Rachel made out a high building. It had three towers reaching towards the sky. Rachel's heart skipped a beat.

Neither of them could help it. They started running. They ran through a courtyard, around two corners, and down a once busy shopping avenue. They turned another corner, and into the square where their father had worked so happily for so long in the years before President Malstain has made his terrible presence felt.

As the Klein children moved closer, Rachel saw stone angels carrying a ribbon. And on the ribbon it still said proudly: *The North Brava Public Lending Library.*

Robert ran ahead now, reaching the main gates. But the gates to the library were locked, the steps were deserted, the windows were boarded on the inside. There was no sign of any army, no sign of anyone at all, only empty streets around an empty forgotten relic.

Then Rachel remembered. She had told Josef about the side entrance their father had used to enter the library that fateful afternoon. So she grabbed Robert's hand and together they walked purposefully around the building towards the small arched gate at the eastern side.

And stopped.

Sitting at the step of the little side gate was a boy with blond curly hair, playing with a small red toy soldier. And just a few feet away from the little boy, under the overhanging branch of an apple tree, stood a beautiful and very anxious young woman. She was dark and slight, she wore her hair tied up and had on a simple grey dress and black shoes, with a cardigan over the top for warmth. Her eyes were bright blue. She had a mole on her left cheek. And she carried in her hand a beaten-up black violin case.

As they ran towards her, the woman turned and her son cried, "Mummy! It's them!" And Lotte Centurion broke into a smile of relief and joy.

But as Rachel embraced Lotte, introduced her brother, smiled at Josef Junior, and took the violin case in her hand, what none of them saw was a solitary policeman walk out of the shadows of a nearby alleyway and quietly take out his radio.

Presidential Palace -
Security Log, April 20th

15.14: A routine personnel and prisoner check on all palace accommodation blocks has been carried out. The check identified Prisoners 2457K and 2458K to be missing from Accommodation Block K. Missing Prisoners 2457K and 2458K are confirmed as Robert and Rachel Klein.

15.16: Superintendent Schreiber, when questioned as to why the prisoners are missing from Block K's roll call, says: "I never saw them in my life! They never came to Block K in the first place!"

15.19: Discovery of missing prisoners relayed to Head of Secrecy and Communications Johannes Slick. Slick desires to meet Walter Meyer as a matter of "extreme urgency".

<u>15.21:</u> Walter Meyer found missing from his rooms in the west wing of the palace.

<u>15.45:</u> A search of the palace has resulted in discovery of Walter Meyer trying to escape by climbing the south wall in the presidential orchard. Meyer has been arrested and forcibly taken to the presidential suite. Injuries to Meyer during arrest: a black eye (left) and bruised wrist (right).

<u>15.50:</u> Meeting between President Malstain, Johannes Slick and Walter Meyer. President Malstain requests Meyer to reveal precise location of Prisoners 2457K and 2458K. Meyer declines to do so. The President, exercising his customary patience, asks again. Meyer again declines. Meyer calls the President a "murderer" and says, "You killed my father." Injury to Meyer. Broken finger. The President authorises his Head of Secrecy and Communications to take Meyer to Interrogation Block Q beneath the palace for "further discussion".

<u>15.55:</u> Meyer is taken down to Interrogation Block Q. Further discussion begins.

<u>16.25:</u> Further discussion continues. Meyer still refuses to speak. The tooth extractor is requested.

<u>16.40:</u> Meyer confesses to having helped the prisoners escape. He says he sent them to his apartment to retrieve "the missing page". He says he knows nothing else. On being asked why he did this, he replies that "It was in memory of my wonderful father who I betrayed, to my great shame."

<u>16.45:</u> Further discussion ends as Meyer passes out. He is given a prisoner number (4145M) and is placed into a cell next to Prisoner 3097R. Guard on duty reports that the two men "recognise each other". Prisoner 3097R asks Meyer, "What did you tell them?" Meyer does not reply, though guard on duty reports this may be due to the state of Meyer's mouth, which is bleeding badly. Guard on duty reports: "The two men looked at each other for a

long time through the bars. Then Prisoner 4145M held out his hand to Prisoner 3097R. The hand was taken. Meyer spoke for the first time. Words unclear. Possibly: 'Solomon, dear friend, I beg of you. Forgive me.'"

17.00: The palace infirmary receives a phone call from the presidential rooms. The President has suffered a minor fit and requires immediate attention.

17.05: Fourteen doctors are treating the President, who is in a critical condition. Johannes Slick orders a complete news blackout on the health of the President.

17.30: Update from Interrogation Block Q: Prisoner 4410C (name: Josef Centurion) has still not spoken, despite best efforts to get information from him. Prisoner continues to laugh repeatedly at his guards.

17.37: Update from Interrogation Block Q: Prisoner 2184G (name: Constanza Glimpf) has asked for a fresh pineapple

cocktail. Request denied. Prisoner 4410C
(Josef Centurion) continues to laugh
loudly and other prisoners are now
joining in. The entire block is filled
with laughter.

17.45: The President has been sedated
and is out of danger. However, doctors
suggest that should the President suffer
another fit of rage, it may prove fatal.

18.00: The President awakes. Demands
news of the missing prisoners. When told
they have not been found, he is not
pleased. One guard suffers minor injuries
to face and stomach.

18.10: News from the city - Prisoners
2457K and 2458K have been spotted by
police patrol in Jackdaw Square in the
north of the city! They met a woman who
was carrying a violin case. Johannes
Slick notes the square is home to the
North Brava Public Lending Library.

18.11: All troops are to be sent to
Jackdaw Square immediately. Instructions

are to kill both prisoners and retrieve
the violin case in their possession, at
any cost.

18.12: President has refused medical
advice and is travelling in the
presidential limousine to the square. "I
need the Book," he calls out. "Get me the
Book!"

35

The Garden

Rachel and Robert crawled through the darkness on hands and knees. Rachel held The Book of Stolen Dreams in front of her, just as she had that afternoon when she had escaped from the North Brava Lending Library. This time they were using the same ventilation shaft to get back in.

It was the only way to enter the library. Once the President's troops had finished searching the building without success, they had locked every door and put chains on every gate. The only way in was the secret route they had found with their father.

It was Rachel's idea to return. She knew what she had to do. And she knew she needed peace and quiet to do it. What better place than the library where her father had worked? Where better than the room where the Book had rested for so long?

They reached the grate which overlooked the cellar from which they'd escaped. It was carnage below them. Books and trolleys were scattered across the brick floor, walls had been drilled into and smashed with hammers. Robert kicked the grate in. It fell twelve feet to the ground.

"We'll have to jump," he said.

Robert went first, landing with an awkward thud and a slight wince.

"Are you okay?"

"I'm fine. Just my ankle. Throw me the Book."

Rachel leaned out as much as she dared and dropped the Book towards Robert's waiting arms. It almost slipped through his fingers, but he held on.

"It's fine," he reassured her. "Now you."

Rachel looked down through the darkness towards him. It seemed suddenly much further than it had done when she was looking back at Felix Klein saying his last farewell.

This Book contains more secrets than you know.

Rachel closed her eyes, thought of her wonderful father and everything he had gone through, and jumped.

She flew through space and crashed straight into Robert's chest, sending him flying to the ground, his sister sprawled on top of him. Dust blew up from the ground, covering them both in a thin coating. The Book slid across the floor.

"Rachel, you could have warned me! Whatever happened to one, two, three?"

"Sorry. It was now or never."

Robert pulled himself up and patted himself down. "Come on."

They made their way back through the basement. Rachel noticed that Robert was limping.

"Was that me or you?" she asked.

"Bit of both," he replied.

They climbed the stairs back into the main library. And stopped in horror at the sight that greeted them.

The library was in ruins. Every area had been torn apart in the army's futile attempt to find the Book. Massive bookcases were toppled like dead trees on a forest floor. Thousands of volumes lay trodden on and torn open. Loose pages flapped off empty shelves. The air was thick with dust and glue. It was like a bomb had hit.

"Oh, Robert." Rachel's eyes filled up with tears. "What would Father think?"

"Come on."

Robert led her through the ruins. They stepped carefully over ancient texts and scrolls. Robert used the few signs that remained on the walls to navigate his way.

"Look," he said. "Zoology. Remember? We're going the right way."

Rachel did not remember, but she felt a deep and lasting admiration for a brother who had travelled half the world to save his father's life and was now back where it all began.

"Not far now."

They turned a corner and climbed over a huge flattened bookcase of plant biology and herbalism. Robert paused, his nose twitched, and he took a right, leading Rachel through a small passageway and up a staircase whose steps had been ripped up so they had to balance carefully on the joists beneath.

They paused.

In front of them was a small doorway. The door was hanging diagonally on one hinge. It was old oak, carved with small pictures of grapes, harps and angels. The velvet curtains had been ripped off. They lay at the foot of the door, trampled and torn.

And on the door, it read:

RARE BOOKS ROOM.
BY INVITATION ONLY.

"You are invited," Robert said quietly, and Rachel nodded.

They stepped through, ducking under the broken door.

Rachel gasped. The beautiful little room was devastated. The cabinets were smashed, all the rare books taken out and thrown around the room. The oak panelling had been completely removed and all the wood piled up at one end.

Only the tiny window high in the wall remained undamaged.

Rachel breathed the air. She felt the Book in her hands. It seemed to be very slightly warm.

She turned to her brother. "Robert," she said solemnly. "One of us should guard the door. And this part I need to do alone."

He turned to her. She expected him to argue but he did not. For Robert had come to understand that his sister knew things he would never fully grasp.

"You know what to do?" he asked simply.

She nodded. "I think so."

"I'll be outside. If anyone comes, I'll call. And, Rachel…" He paused for a second. "Good luck."

Robert suddenly held her hand very tight, then he walked quickly out of the room. Rachel heard his steps climb back down the broken staircase.

She looked around the room and saw the cabinet where The Book of Stolen Dreams had lain that fateful afternoon. She remembered her father reaching towards it with his small golden key. Now the cabinet was smashed and turned over on its side.

Rachel approached it, put the Book down and, with all her might, she lifted the cabinet back on to its legs. Then she took the Book and put it back on the damaged velvet surface. She opened the Book and found the place she was looking for. There was the rip where the paper had been torn out. She reached in her pocket and took out the missing page. Carefully she replaced it.

For a moment nothing happened.

Then, as she stared at the Book, it glowed, like coal. And, in front of Rachel's astonished eyes, the missing page resealed itself into the Book as if it had never been away.

Rachel breathed deep. She nodded. Yes. It might just work.

She leafed back to the beginning of the Book.

Let the true dreamer wake...

Then she turned the page and began to read the first dream.

The Walled Garden

**I sleep to find myself waking
I am in a walled garden of a thousand flowers...**

36

Jackdaws

Robert stood alert in the destroyed main room of the library.

He was up close to one of the tall windows along the north wall. The windows had been boarded up by the President's soldiers before leaving, so no one outside could see into the chaos the army had caused. But Robert found a small gap which afforded him a view on to the street. He couldn't believe it. He was standing guard for his twelve-year-old sister while she saved all of Krasnia from the grip of a brutal dictator!

He took stock of the last twenty-four hours. Flown back to Brava, interrogated by the President, escaped in a meat van, frozen half to death, and now standing in the ghostly remains of his father's favourite place on earth.

All sorts of odd feelings flooded through him. There was no silence like a library's. It was as though the broken books were listening; to his breath, to the echoes of the building, the occasional car outside.

Robert was a scientist, to his size-five boots. But something about The Book of Stolen Dreams made him wonder. Was it possible that somehow a king could find a gateway to the land of the dead and bring back his bride? And could a whole family of artists have travelled from the Hinterland for hundreds of years, to live together right here in the middle of Brava? And no one knew? If that was the case, could an evil tyrant use that gate to rule a land for ever? Could a brilliant young girl find that gateway? And close it in order to stop him? Would she be able to? Would something stand in her way?

He suddenly grew afraid. What if Rachel wasn't strong enough? What if she, like Charles Malstain, grew tempted by the power of the Book? What if she couldn't close the gate? Or what if she tried to use it herself, to bring back someone she loved? To bring back their mother...?

For a second Robert wanted to run back along the smashed corridors and up the small skeleton staircase to the Rare Books Room and warn his sister, to tell her to be strong, or maybe even take over.

But he paused.

Robert had sensed from very young that his sister was special. Rachel had some inner quality, a contact with the mysteries of life that lay hidden beneath the certainties of science and road maps. It meant she sometimes got lost in the real world, of course, because her brain was somewhere else. She was, he thought, a bit of a poet, touched by magic. And for that he loved her and trusted her more than anyone. And his job now was to guard Rachel from danger. That danger was President Charles Malstain and his troops. He must do his job and leave the rest to her.

Robert returned to his sentry post by the gap in the boarded windows.

He peeped through. There was Jackdaw Square. It was silent now in the late afternoon, the light fading in the grey sky. His father loved to read there after work and feed the birds. That was before Malstain. Now there were empty benches, just the odd lonely walker hurrying home before the evening curfew, a few crows and jackdaws pecking hopefully at the ground. All was quiet and lifeless and grey, as the whole of Brava was now, every single day. A dead fountain, dead trees, cold grey lamp posts guarding a cold grey city.

But something shifted. The birds suddenly stood alert. Their heads raised.

Robert watched.

Then the birds scattered, as one.

And Robert Klein knew that meant only one thing. The birds were afraid. They had sensed something in the growing gloom. And what they had sensed meant mortal danger to him and his genius sister.

37

The Gate

What if I was a key?
I'd enter the lock of the gate that divides us
I turn myself neatly to the left
I sense the metal give
I hear the wood creaking
And feel the cold as the gate swings open
Now I can see into the Hinterland
There you are
Why don't you welcome me in?

Rachel was reading the forty-second dream. The room was quiet. The bright colours of Benjamin Meyer's illustrations dazzled her. Gold leaf for the bark of the trees. Verdigris for the grass, and saffron and crimson for the flowers. A lapis lazuli sky. But Rachel kept her eyes fixed on the words. One mistake or hesitation could ruin everything. And she did not have time to do this twice.

She reached the end of the dream and turned to the forty-third.

For who is to say that life is not a dream
And when we think we sleep we wake?

Rachel was feeling her body start to grow heavy. Her pulse slowed as she read each poem. The floor seemed to grow a little distant from her. The walls disappeared, the chaos of the ransacked room receded and faded from view.

She felt herself in a kind of nothingness. She was floating. The words of the Book were there, but not the Book, and not the cabinet, not the velvet nor the oak, nor the floor that the cabinet stood on. Rachel thought that this should feel frightening, to be so far away from real things, from the Rare Books Room, from the library, from Robert. But she didn't feel scared. She felt free. She felt what it might feel like to have all one's worries taken away, all one's worldly cares.

She read on. Rachel reached the forty-ninth dream.

Oh these minutes together
You and I and the white lilies
There is a knocking at the gate
But we will not listen!

Rachel paused. Her eyelids felt like iron shutters, desperate to fall heavy and close. But she knew she had one more dream to read.

She turned to the fiftieth dream, now safely sealed in the Book as if it had never been away.

> Now we have come this far
> Let us vow
> To live for ever in this garden
> Say the words
> "Forever More"
> And nothing
> Not even death, my love
> Can stand between us
> We will live
> Eternal in this land of dreams

Rachel was about to say the last two lines when she stopped. She heard birdsong and smelled a strong aroma of something sweet – was it honey or maybe lavender?

She felt something warm beneath her feet. Soft. She looked down. Green grass, sun-kissed. A small pathway. Ahead of her was a wooden trellis decked with climbing plants. Around her on all sides were stone walls. Above her the blue sky. The sun shining but not casting shadows. No wind. The birds chattered in the bushes. The air was thick with lavender and rose. The gate was open.

"The walled garden," she murmured. "I'm in it."

Rachel adjusted her eyes and saw something in the corner of the grass by a white rose bush.

Not something. Someone.

A figure dressed in dark grey, the odd hole in her dress. Bare feet. A simple white blouse. A pot of something in her hand.

The figure turned.

"Mother?"

Judith Klein smiled at her daughter. "Rachel. You came. How did you do this?"

"I don't know, Mother. It's long to explain."

Judith smiled, walked across the grass. Her feet made no imprint. Her dress did not move in the breeze.

"Are you a ghost, Mother? Or can you hold me?"

Judith approached. "I can do everything except hold you," she said, smiling. "For that you need to say the last words of the fiftieth dream. Then I can live again and hold you like I always did. I can hold Robert. And your father. It will be like none of this ever happened."

Rachel nodded, unsure what to say, desperate for her mother's touch. "We haven't found Father."

"You will." Her mother smiled again. "Oh, Rachel, I've missed you so much."

Judith looked beautiful. Her face, which Rachel had last seen so pale and tired, was fresh and full of colour. She walked with a grace across the cut grass. The birds seemed to follow her, and the scent of the flowers clung to her simple dress.

Rachel knew she didn't have long. Robert was alone guarding her and if soldiers came, he couldn't hold them off for ever.

"Mother, I have to tell you something."

"Yes of course, my dear. Let's sit down."

They sat on a small stone bench by pink and purple rose bushes. Judith held the small pot in her hand and Rachel saw it contained rose petals. The scent was intoxicating. Rachel felt she might faint. She struggled to stay awake, remembered her mission and turned to her mother.

"Mother, if I say the last two lines, then I can keep the gate open for ever. And we can hold each other again."

"I know, my dear. And I promise you that I will tell no one. It will be our secret."

"But, Mother, there's a problem. If I keep the gate open, someone else may also use it. Someone bad."

Judith's face changed. A cloud entered the sky. A shadow crossed. The garden seemed to grow cool.

"Who?"

"Charles Malstain."

Judith's brow darkened. Rachel's eyes reached into her mother's.

"Malstain is dying, Mother. But he knows the secret of the Book. He wants to live for ever. To move through the gate at his choosing. Unless I destroy the Book, he will be free to do so."

"How did he find out?" Her mother spoke with a hollow sadness.

"A young man. One of the Meyer family."

"Walter." Judith nodded. "Your father said he was a troubled soul."

Rachel felt suddenly unfathomably sad. She wanted to hug her mother but could not. Her muscles would not obey her. Judith's face became very still as she sat beside her only daughter. A quiet grimace of pain seemed to pass through her. A slight cough came from her lungs.

"Mother?"

"I'm quite all right, Rachel my dear."

She smiled but it was not without effort. She spoke softly. "So what are you going to do?"

"I don't know." Rachel was trying not to cry.

"You do know. You know the right thing." Judith tried to smile.

"But I want to hold you! And I want you to hold me."

"I know. And I want that too. More than anything. But not if it means that. I do not want to live if it means living under him for ever."

Rachel let the tears come now. They trickled down her cheeks. She did not even bring a hand to stop them.

"Mum, I miss you so much. I miss your music and your orange muffins and your smile…"

"I miss you too."

The garden was cold now. The clouds were building in the sky. The wind was building. There was a strange distant sound – was it a battering? A hammering? Voices in the wind?

Her mother heard them too. She turned in fear.

"Rachel, you are right. You are in danger, I sense it. You don't have long. You must close the gate now. He is coming. He is coming fast and he will take the Book."

"But I don't want to! I want to stay here with you!"

"But you must! For your country! For Robert and for your father! Hurry!"

Rachel looked into her mother's eyes. And in that moment something magical happened. Though they were not touching, Rachel felt her mother's hand on her face. She felt her arms around her.

"Can you feel it too?" Judith said.

"Yes."

"I am holding you. And I can feel you holding me."

"Mother! I love you!"

"I love you, Rachel. Now go!"

Rachel stood. The noise from outside the garden was growing, like men were trying to smash through the brick with hammers.

She turned to her mother, who was already heading to the gate leading back to the Hinterland.

"Once I am through," her mother said, "close it. Lock it. For ever."

"I don't know how!"

"You will find the words. You always did."

Her mother passed through the gate, closing it behind her.

Rachel looked down. She saw she had another key in her hand. It was blood red. Where had it come from?

She ran to the gate that her mother had just gone through.

She put the red key in the lock. It fitted perfectly.

And Rachel said the words she knew she must say.

> Now we have come this far
> Let us vow
> To leave for ever in this garden
> Say the word
> "Nevermore"
> And nothing
> Not even death, my love
> Can stand between us
> Say the word
> Nevermore

"Nevermore!" cried Rachel and turned the key.

And as she turned the key, the breeze gusted, the clouds turned to ink, a hard rain battered the grass, the walls of the garden were whipped by a great wind, the plants uprooted, the walls fell around her, and the garden erupted into the air and was hurled into the abyss.

Rachel fell through space and landed on the hard oak floor of the Rare Books Room as Johannes Slick and his troopers stormed in, dragging Robert Klein with them.

"I held them off as long as I could!" Robert shouted. His face was bleeding. Johannes was pale with rage.

"Mr President!!" he screamed.

A soldier barged into the room and behind him staggered Charles Malstain. He leaned heavily on his black cane. His face was white as a mask. His breath was short and shallow. He stared at Rachel in rage.

"Where is the Book? I don't have long! Read it! READ IT!"

But Johannes Slick was staring in astonishment at the small oak cabinet which housed The Book of Stolen Dreams.

And Robert was staring too.

Charles Malstain followed their gaze. His hand went to his heart. A horrible strangled cry rose in his chest and stayed there. He fought for breath. Then he lost the fight and collapsed like a broken bookcase to the ground.

Rachel turned to look. Every muscle in her body ached. She had never felt so tired. But her tear-stained face was smiling.

Because where The Book of Stolen Dreams had been, there was now nothing but a small pile of ash.

And a blood-red key.

38

An Apology

Dearest and most fond reader. Earlier in this modest volume I may have given you a misleading impression. I may have suggested that if you were reading this book you should do so secretly, under the covers, in case of treacherous eavesdroppers or Malstain informants.

Forgive me my deception. I did it for a reason. There was a time when it would have been true and I wanted you to feel the fear, to understand what it was like in those dark and deadly days. When to read a book was to become an enemy of the state.

But that time is over, my friend! Now you can feel free to read this book wherever and whenever you like! Read it on a summer's evening in the park, on the tram at midnight, shout it from the rooftops! I myself am reading it aloud at nine in the morning while sipping a glass of rhubarb lemonade and wearing my most colourful pyjamas. Yes, my friend. The time of fear and sadness is over!

And why?

Because, as my daily newspaper tells me, everything has changed…

39

THE BRAVAN DAILY NEWS REPORTS!

APRIL 21ST

HORROR ATTACK! – PRESIDENT MALSTAIN IN INTENSIVE CARE!

Our great and noble President, Charles Malstain, was rushed to Brava Central Hospital last night after he was violently attacked by two children while making a presidential visit to the North Brava Public Lending Library. Few ordinary mortals would have survived the brutality of the attack but our great President is no ordinary mortal! He is in intensive care and his health is described as "good but uncertain". Meanwhile the two highly disturbed children – Robert and Rachel Klein – are being held in the palace under suspicion of his attempted murder.

The government tonight issued this warning. Keep your children under lock and key! You have no idea what is going on in their minds!

Long live President Malstain! Long live Krasnia!

PRESIDENT MALSTAIN IS DEAD!

The whole of Krasnia was plunged into shock and grief today. Our great and wonderful President Charles Malstain is dead.

Despite his enormous courage and strength, the President failed to recover from the crazed attack of Tuesday last and succumbed to his wounds. The entire country of Krasnia will enter three hundred days of mourning, said Head of Secrecy and Communications Johannes Slick. Curfew will be extended to twenty-three hours a day. Children will not be allowed out at all.

Meanwhile deranged child-assassins Robert and Rachel Klein will be formally charged with the President's murder later today. They will be found guilty and executed by firing squad at dawn. They are twelve and nearly fourteen years old.

MAY 1ST

JOHANNES SLICK ARRESTED!
EXECUTION CANCELLED!
CHILDREN FREED!

Krasnia celebrates! Johannes Slick has been arrested! Early yesterday morning Slick was surprised by his own soldiers as he shaved prior to the execution of Robert and Rachel Klein. The army has taken him to his own prison under the palace where he is being closely guarded.

An army spokesman announced the immediate cancellation of the children's execution and of the national curfew. The period of mourning will be reduced to one day! He said, "Krasnia is entering a new era. God save Krasnia!"

Meanwhile Robert and Rachel Klein, who were falsely accused of Malstain's assassination, have been freed and were met by cheering crowds as they left the palace.

Well done, you brave children!

Bravo, Krasnia!

POLITICAL PRISONERS RELEASED FROM THE MALSTAIN DUNGEONS!

News just in! The interrogation blocks beneath ex-president Malstain's palace were liberated today!

The dungeons were stormed at dawn and chief torturer Rufus O'Hare was killed after a battle with over thirty soldiers.

Inside the cells were found hundreds of political prisoners including writers, campaigners, composers and journalists. Among them was the leader of the Krasnian Resistance Front, Constanza Glimpf, who though frail and in pain, was led out of the prison to a huge ovation! Outside the palace she ordered a mango cocktail and said this was the greatest day of her life.

"Krasnia is free!" she declared as crowds gathered outside the palace to cheer her on. She paid tribute to the heroic fighters who had died resisting Malstain, including her own beloved husband Theodore Glimpf. "Let

Theodore be remembered this day. It belongs to him!"

Also found in the dungeons was a thief and musician called Josef Centurion. It is not clear what role Centurion played in the events leading to Malstain's fall. Centurion was released into the open air where he refused to talk to reporters but was seen falling into the arms of a woman of similar age, who was accompanied by a young child. "Oh, Lotte!" the man cried, before taking the boy in his arms and kissing him repeatedly for over twenty minutes.

MAY 8TH

THE SEARCH IS ON!

The search is on for other prisons throughout the country! It is thought thousands of ordinary citizens have been sent to labour camps for saying the wrong thing or failing to salute the presidential cavalcade. We must find these fallen heroes!

Late news just in! Two more prisoners discovered under the President's palace! Young artist Solomon Rose was found early this morning. He is thin and tired but in good health!

And Walter Meyer, the son of Lucius Meyer, has also been found – deep in the darkest wing of Malstain's dungeons. Sources suggest Walter Meyer may have fallen from favour with the ex-President, with whom many thought he was close. Meyer is gravely ill and has been taken to hospital. There are fears that he may not recover.

MAY 10TH

KRF MEMBERS RELEASED IN PORT CLEMENT!

The government of Port Clement announced today it is releasing without charge the four young resistance fighters who were arrested for the attempted assassination of Charles Malstain at the Hotel Excelsior last month.

Marie Lim, Laszlo Mann, Rudi Zweig and Stanley Musil were released from Port

Clement penitentiary at 10 a.m. A huge crowd greeted them, waving scarves and singing the original Krasnian National Anthem, which President Malstain had banned because it did not mention his name. The four young revolutionaries were carried head-high by the crowd through the city, before being taken by police escort to Port Clement airfield for an immediate return to Brava.

Here's to the Krasnian Resistance Front! They are heroes all!

MAY 11TH

HEROES RETURN TO BRAVA

Brava welcomed back its young resistance heroes today! Thousands gathered at the airfield on the edge of the city and roared approval as the members of the KRF disembarked the airship *Pegasus* and reached home. Laszlo Mann bent down and kissed the soil of his home country, while Rudi Zweig cried out, "Victory for Krasnia!"

History of Art student Marie Lim was seen greeting a young man whom she kissed on the lips with tears on her face. This man is rumoured to be her boyfriend Stefan Hesse, who was imprisoned by Malstain for three years. Marie also hugged a thirteen-year-old boy with freckles, who gripped on to her very tightly and turned bright red. Rumours that this boy was resistance hero and attempted assassin Robert Klein are as yet unconfirmed.

Meanwhile at Brava Central Hospital, Walter Meyer shows no signs of improvement. Twelve-year-old Rachel Klein is said to have visited him today in hospital and to have held his hand. It is unclear how they know each other.

And in other news, soldiers continue to find prison camps hidden away right across the country. All prisoners are being released and attempts are being made to reunite them with their families without delay.

MAY 20TH

ELECTIONS TO BE HELD!

It was announced today that elections will be held across Krasnia to vote in a new government. These will be the first ever elections in the history of the country. Constanza Glimpf said that this was a great day for her beloved land. "Gone are the emperors," she said. "Gone are the evil tyrants! Now is the time for the people to speak!"

JUNE 19TH

GLIMPF VOTED PRESIDENT

Constanza Glimpf was today voted the new President of Krasnia! She immediately said she would work with all areas of society to create a new and better country. Those who worked for President Malstain will be forced to admit their crimes and to express their deep remorse but, except for those at the highest levels, they will not be punished with imprisonment. "We have seen enough pain and suffering," said President Glimpf. "Now we must admit the past and move into the future."

Marie Lim will serve as her Minister for Schools, a remarkable rise for a young woman who was threatened with a life sentence for attempted murder just a few weeks ago! Marie declared that under her leadership, "Learning in school will be fun again and no one will be punished for being curious or asking questions!" Marie also said she still intends to finish her university degree.

<hr />

JUNE 30TH

MEYER OUT OF HOSPITAL!

Walter Meyer has left hospital. He spoke for the first time today about his role in events leading to the fall of ex-President Malstain. He admits his guilt in helping Malstain cement his power and says that he regrets everything he did.

It now appears that Walter tried at the end to change his ways and fight against the President, who then imprisoned and tortured him. Rachel and Robert Klein have supported this version of events and urged the government to be lenient. "Walter learned the error of his ways and helped us escape from the palace," said twelve-year-old Rachel. "He should be allowed a second chance for, without him, Krasnia would still be under the terror of Charles Malstain."

Hurrah for Rachel! Hurrah for Walter! Hurrah for Krasnia!

JULY 9TH

BRAVA OPENS ITS BORDERS!

President Constanza Glimpf announced today a complete opening of Krasnia's borders! Krasnian citizens will be free to travel when and where they want! Cafes will open, bookshops and libraries will be restored, money will be given for new parks, fountains, ice cream stores and schools. One park in Brava will be named The Theodore Glimpf Park in memory of the fallen bookseller.

Renowned illustration workshop Meyer and Sons has reopened for business in the centre of the city. Walter Meyer, the son of the much-loved Lucius, said he was sharing the business with his friend Solomon Rose. "Solomon is the single greatest illustrator in all Krasnia. We are lucky to have him," he commented.

When asked, Solomon said they are not looking for new staff. "We have some very experienced artists upstairs in our workshop," said Solomon with a smile. And Walter seemed to be smiling too.

AUGUST 4TH

MORE PRISONS FOUND IN THE EAST!

More prison camps were today found in the mountains in the very East of the country. It is believed Malstain sent his most hated political prisoners to these camps, leaving them to die a cold and lonely death. The conditions were described as "simply inhuman". No letters were allowed and only one meal a day was served as the prisoners worked in Malstain's stone quarries and mines. Trains are bringing the prisoners back to their homes as soon as they are healthy enough to travel.

Sadly not all prisoners survived the ordeal. As families wait with bated breath, not all will receive the happy news they crave.

40
Brava Central Station,
Platform 7

Robert and Rachel breathed in the cool morning air. Rachel wrinkled her nose. She held something tight in her hand.

Every morning for two months they had come to the same spot at Brava Central train station. Every morning they had watched the night trains arrive from the East, carrying the released prisoners. The men and women getting off the trains were pale and emaciated, but their faces shone with the anticipation of seeing their wives and husbands, lovers and children.

Robert and Rachel watched day after day as families kissed and hugged and shared stories. Tears flowed all around them. But the person they were waiting for did not come.

Now it was the last day of the transit.

Stratana was a mining area deep in the eastern mountains. It was miles from the nearest town, and the railway was normally only used for transporting coal. The army had recently found three prison camps there, kept secret from everyone except Malstain and Johannes Slick. They were run by Slick's secret police. The men and women in these camps had given up all hope of ever being found. They worked the mines, they slept, they were beaten, they buried the dead. That was all.

Then one morning they woke to find the guards had disappeared. The prisoners were left entirely alone in the middle of the mountains. They had no idea that Malstain had died and that this was why the guards had all fled. Slowly, the prisoners started to walk along the railway line.

When the army found them they were close to death. The prisoners were taken to hospital. They had taken longer than any other prisoners to recover, but now they were coming home to reunite with their loved ones.

The morning was quiet. Robert was staring at the station arrivals sign. It read: *Train from Stratana delayed. No further information at this time.* Rachel looked across the empty station concourse. Small expectant groups were dotted around. There had once been huge crowds at the station every day, but these were long gone. Reunited families were now eating breakfast together in happy apartments across the city, with warm coffee and pastries and fresh eggs and orange juice.

Rachel pulled her coat close to her. It was the same coat she had worn on all her travels. It had seen her through all sorts of danger and drama. It had become her lucky coat. Now it needed to be lucky one more time.

Brother and sister didn't speak. They didn't even glance at each other. They'd learned over the weeks that it was easier to stay calm without looking the other in the eye. Rachel in particular had no interest in showing her feelings. She was focused entirely on remaining strong.

How strange the last months had been, she thought. They had been praised and cheered by politicians, slapped on the back by soldiers, and kissed by adoring old ladies. Everyone knew that Rachel and Robert Klein had been part of the Krasnian Resistance Front. They were heroes! Constanza Glimpf had given them a medal. But all the time they both had only one thing on their mind. All they really wanted was to be alone and to wait for the return of the man for whom they had done all of this.

The sign flicked up. *Train due.* A voice came on the tannoy. *"Train arriving from Stratana, the delayed 0650. Platform seven. Arrival in nine minutes."*

Slowly the crowd of expectant families shuffled towards Platform 7. The station guards let them on to the platform without a question. Rachel and Robert hung back. They had done this so many times, for so many days.

Rachel almost believed that hoping too much would have the opposite effect.

The platform stretched out towards the countryside beyond the factories of the city. The sky was overcast, the air cool and damp. Summer was over and the Krasnian autumn coming in. This was normally Rachel's favourite season. She used to love the rain and the brown leaves and the muffled quiet of it all. But today she found it only sad and threatening.

Rachel thought about her mother and the last time she saw her, in the walled garden. She thought about the Book and what it did, and she wondered, if the Book had not been destroyed and the gate not closed, would she use it again? Or was it better to let things be? Still, she had been so happy to see her mother one more time. She had told Robert about it, and every night he wanted to hear about the meeting all over again, in case Rachel had missed out a small detail.

The station clock showed six minutes to go. Time was like a glacier. Rachel felt her stomach tighten; she thought she might be sick. She looked around to distract herself.

Other families had found the odd spot to sit and wait. One mother and daughter sat on a broken bench. The child was anxiously playing with her hair. A young man was crouching, biting his nails right down to the moons. A short dark-haired woman at the end of the platform was praying quietly. An old woman stood silent and still, looking into thin air. She had a basket in her hand with flowers in it.

A dozen or so pigeons rested on overhead cables as if they knew the importance of the coming event. A local train trundled into the station and disgorged a few local working people on to the platform. Then it trundled out again. The silence returned.

Rachel could bear it no more. She looked at Robert. Her brother was looking down the platform into nothingness.

"Robert…"

"What?"

"If he doesn't…" She trailed off.

"Doesn't what?"

"You know. If he doesn't…if he isn't…we still have… each…"

He turned. His eyes were empty and Rachel had never seen Robert look so sad. "Don't say it, Rachel. I know it's true. But don't say it."

She nodded. She felt the little key in her hand. The blood-red key was the one thing she had insisted on keeping. The one little connection to the walled garden, to her mother. They had agreed with Constanza Glimpf that no one should know about The Book of Stolen Dreams. No one should know the true horror of what Charles Malstain had planned, nor how close he came to achieving it. But Rachel had kept the key.

This was to be her gift for him. If he came.

The pigeons lifted their heads. Robert lifted his. Rachel listened. And heard a sound. A gentle whistle, and a humming under her feet, like a low drumming.

The young man stopped biting his nails and stood from his haunches. The praying woman held her hat. The mother and daughter on the broken bench stood. The old woman with the basket did not move.

"Look," said Robert.

There was a plume of smoke above the distant fields. It was winding its way, as if uncertain of where to go. Then it seemed to make its decision and started to approach. Rachel clutched her coat and tried to calm her breath.

The little train, like the toy train Robert so wanted but they could never afford, appeared around the corner from behind the grey factories.

Rachel felt a sudden urge to run the other way, away from the train, into the city. Better never to know, better to have a hope, better to live with the possibility.

"Robert, I can't."

"It's all right." Robert's eyes did not stray for one second from the train.

"But I can't bear it…"

"Rachel. Stay with me. I need you."

She looked at him. His eyes remained on the train.

The voice came on the tannoy. "*The train arriving at Platform 7 is the special train from Stratana. Please keep back and allow the passengers to disembark safely. Please leave the platform once you have found the person you are here to meet."*

There was the sudden squeal of brakes; steam rose in jets and engulfed the platform; smoke billowed up into the open sky.

The waiting groups all rose and, despite the tannoy's instructions, approached the train. Guards whistled and voices urged them to "Stay back! Stay back!"

The train stopped.

For a moment it seemed that no one would get off, but then a second whistle came. A door opened. And a young woman got off.

She looked around blearily, as if the light dazzled her after hours inside the train.

Then a male voice cried out, "Lucy!"

She turned and she almost fainted. The man with the bitten nails sprinted towards her; he grabbed her as she fell. A father from another family rushed to help; they gave her water. The woman came round from her faint and looked into the young man's eyes.

"Max…"

He held her. He kissed her cheeks; she fell on to his shoulder. Guards came and helped them, and slowly the couple walked from the platform.

Then a door in the middle of the train opened and a man stepped out. He was slim and dressed in a dark suit and had a grey cap.

Rachel felt her heart go double speed.

Robert gulped.

Then they heard a voice.

"Adnan?"

It was the woman who had been praying. She dropped her bag and ran towards the figure. He held out his arms wide, and she threw herself into them; he turned her in mid-air, and held her and kissed her.

She kept crying out, "They told me you were dead. They told me you were dead!" The man put her gently down on the ground and they kissed. Then they too left the platform.

Rachel breathed. She saw Robert's freckled face had lost some of its colour.

Now a few more doors were opening. Men and women, all of them alone, were getting off the train; some bounded out with energy, others stepped down with care. There was a flurry of names and conversation and tears. Rachel and Robert had seen it many times before.

Then the rhythm of doors and cries, embraces and kisses, slowed. The final few families hugged and walked from the platform. The mother and daughter on the broken bench looked downcast until a door right next to them opened and a man leaped out, saying he was sorry, he had fallen asleep, he was so tired, but nothing mattered, he was back! The man was buried in loving kisses. Then they left the platform too, eager to get home.

Now only the old woman and the children remained.

The old woman stayed very still, her eyes fixed on the train.

But no door opened.

"Rachel, let's go." Robert was turning away.

Rachel kept looking at the old woman. The woman had not moved. She was like a statue paid for by the railway company.

"Rachel, come on."

"No, wait."

"Rachel! I can't do this any more."

But Rachel did not move. The old woman did not move. Both their eyes were on the train.

The sound of a door broke the silence.

Robert turned back.

A door in the second-to-last carriage opened slowly.

A man stepped out. He was silhouetted against the pale sky. He too had a grey suit and a cap. But in his hand was a small book.

Rachel felt her breath catch in her throat and her blood tingle in her fingers.

For a second she couldn't move.

Robert didn't move either. The man in the cap stayed very still. The world stopped.

Then the old woman turned and slowly approached them. "I am happy for you," she said. And she smiled. She left the platform, still carrying the basket of flowers in her hand.

"Dad!" Robert cried, and in seconds he was running. Rachel wanted to run with him, but her legs wouldn't obey her. She walked so slowly, as if through glue. She saw Robert hurl himself at the dark silhouette. She saw the silhouette grab Robert like he was a doll, grab and hold him tight to his chest; they became one figure for a moment against the sky.

Rachel approached and looked at her father. Felix Klein let go of Robert and turned to his only daughter. His clothes were ragged, his face as thin as paper. But the eyes were there. They were the same.

For a moment neither spoke. Then Felix took off his cap and smiled.

"You did it, Rachel. You saved me," he said.

"Oh, Dad."

And Rachel fell into her father's arms.

THE END

For Bessie, Claudie, Vivie and Ramona

And in memory of Robert and Ruth Elkan,
who made journeys of their own

To discover the power
of the BLOOD-RED KEY
and the terrible truth of the
MEYERS' SECRET,
Rachel and Robert will return
to THE HINTERLAND.

READ ON
FOR AN EXCLUSIVE EXTENDED
SNEAK PEEK...

What are the Meyers hiding?

Rachel walked the streets of Brava, thinking.

When Constanza Glimpf, new President of Krasnia, had invited the Klein family for tea and medals at the Palace, Constanza (as she insisted they still call her, not Madame President or anything fancy) said she had something important to discuss.

"Mr Klein, when people ask you about your role in the fall of Charles Malstain, I must ask you and your children one thing. You must tell no one about the Book of Stolen Dreams."

A pause filled the palace hall. Felix nodded. Rachel did the same. Robert stopped cramming his mouth with the cake that Constanza had so kindly provided.

"It is simply too dangerous," said the President. "Human beings cannot be trusted to know of such magic."

Rachel knew Constanza was right. Even telling people such a book existed would cause chaos and confusion. So the Kleins had said nothing to anyone about the extraordinary book that lay at the heart of it all. Not to friends, not to neighbours, not even to Laetitia, who had become Rachel's most special friend of all.

But one worry haunted Rachel.

What about the blood-red key?

She had never mentioned it to Constanza, nor to anyone. She had not shown it to her father, and Robert had forgotten all about it. But then a boy had approached her in the park, holding a blood-red key of his own. He had spoken of having a duty to protect the Hinterland and implied that her key was very important indeed. And that normal people could not be trusted with it.

And now there was a break-in at the library. Something in Rachel's stomach told her that it all connected. And that none of it was good.

Rachel needed to talk to someone.

She took a left into a small courtyard, turned right through a cemetery, crossed the square and entered Paradise Alley.

Rachel slipped down the dark, narrow passageway to the slim, slate-grey house. It was no longer boarded up, its windows were clean and bright, the door had a new coat of paint, a cheery blue. She breathed, looked at the sign. It was also new, painted in a gorgeous gold.

MEYER AND ROSE. ILLUSTRATING THE STRANGE AND THE FANCIFUL COME IN, WE ARE OPEN!

Rachel pushed the door open and entered.

In the hallway she paused, looked at the same old pictures of the painters, the same mahogany side table.

She heard murmurings.

"Is that her? I swear it is!"

"It is me!" she called out.

"Come up! Come up!" issued a chorus of high voices.

Rachel couldn't help smiling. They were like a bunch of sparrows, chirruping and chatting. She climbed the stair to the first floor, then the second. And there at the top of the stair, arms out wide for a big ghostly hug, stood Benjamin Meyer.

"It IS her! Our saviour!" he called out and embraced her warmly. "Rachel, my dear, what a pleasure!"

"But she's cold! Make her tea! Give her crumpets," cried out various other aged Meyers, and Benjamin's tiny wife Rosica rushed to an old copper kettle and placed it on the stove.

Rachel felt better already. How much she loved coming here! How strange that in the bright new Krasnia she was happiest in a dusty attic amongst a bunch of dead people. She had to smile at herself.

Now Rosica was giving her tea, and a spectacularly buttered crumpet. The old woman looked at her, eyes gleaming.

"What is it, my dear? Tell us what is on your mind!" she asked.

"Yes, tell us everything!" the ghosts parroted. "No secrets here!"

""It's probably nothing," she began, "but there's been a

break-in at the library." And as she said this, almost immediately Rachel sensed a tension in the room. The temperature got just a little chillier.

"Oh yes?" Benjamin smiled as if it might be nothing. Rosica's nose twitched and her eyes narrowed very slightly.

"Yes. The rare books room. They took nothing but it just seems strange. As Mrs Schroedinger said, the library is open now so the person could have just come in normal hours. The whole point of a library is that anyone can read anything."

She sensed the room become unusually silent. The thirty or so painter-ghosts looked at her, as if unsure who should speak next.

"Well, I'm sure there's a perfectly innocent explanation." Benjamin suddenly exclaimed with a smile. But he glanced at his wife. Rosica nodded but seemed to butter the second crumpet she was making for Rachel with a little more speed than usual.

Rachel paused. Then gathered her strength:

"There's something I haven't told anyone. Not Constanza. Not Solomon. Not my father. Not even you. I don't know if it's relevant to the break-in, but I think maybe I should tell you now."

The ghosts turned to look at her. "What is it, my dear? Tell us! For someone so young to have secrets!"

Rachel looked at a sea of expectant eyes; she took a breath. It was time to come clean and tell the Meyers about the blood-red key and the boy on the bench.

"You remember when I closed the gate to the Hinterland? For ever?"

"Yes! Yes! Of course we remember! Splendid girl! Hero of Krasnia!"

"Well the Book was burned to ashes. But something else remained."

She opened her mouth to say what that something was. When suddenly there was a slam of the front door downstairs.

"What was that?" Rachel asked.

"Nothing, dear. Go on. Go on!" The ghosts smiled but the smiles were forced, uneasy. Rachel could hear loud steps in the hallway below.

"Could it be Walter or Solomon returning?" she asked. I'd like to tell them too."

"Oh, they won't be back for days!" Rosica cried and the ghosts all muttered in echo: "Yes, not for days! Business matters!"

"As for the front door, it must have been the wind!" cried Benjamin, and the sparrows echoed: "A passing breeze! A mere nothing! A gentle gust! Nothing to worry about! Nothing at all! Go on! Go on!"

But at that moment Rachel heard feet on the stairs. Then a man's voice, gruff and angry.

"She wouldn't even see me! Sent me a message saying she was busy! A family crisis and President Constanza